THE OUTCOME OF SIN

Margret A. Trieber

THE OUTCOME OF SIN

A DOUBLE DRAGON PAPERBACK

© Copyright 2020
Margret A. Treiber

The right of Margret A. Treiber to be identified as author of this work has been asserted in accordance with the Copyright, Designs and Patents Act 1988

All Rights Reserved

No reproduction, copy or transmission of the publication may be made without written permission. No paragraph of this publication may be reproduced, copied or transmitted save with the written permission of the publisher, or in accordance with the provisions of the Copyright Act 1956 (as amended).

Any person who does any unauthorised act in relation to this publication may be liable to criminal prosecution and civil claims for damages.

ISBN 978-1-78695-360-5

Double Dragon
is an imprint of
Fiction4All

Published 2020
Fiction4All
www.fiction4all.com

Dedication

This book is dedicated to Marie-Jessique Gonzalez, who is the best science advisor ever.

I couldn't have done it without you.

Thank you to Sara Pufahl for selflessly doing my first edits without asking for anything in return.

I also want to dedicate this to my family and friends who put up with my dreams of becoming a published writer even when I wasn't doing anything about it.

Chapter One

"Pain is the outcome of sin."
Buddha (563-483 BC)

Mass media took a break from its usual upbeat, sucralose, pop fluff to commemorate the anniversary of the modern world's most horrific cataclysm. World Day approached, commemorating the day the human race was bitch slapped by the universe. With its pending arrival, the amount of memorial footage increased exponentially.

Never forget, the headlines read. *Be forever vigilant*, *Help human progress*, and *Let's all work together*. The slogans assaulted the senses with its unending diatribe of meaningless catch phrases, all geared to one purpose: to make humanity forget how utterly fucked we were. Images of explosions and death filled my monitor. Memories of the skies and Chechnya assaulted my senses as if I was still there. Nothing ruins your day more than the colorful fusion of nuclear and meteor death raining from the sky. I would never forget watching, as the sky was ravaged by an enraged cosmos. I took a breath and reached for my coffee; it did nothing to ease my discomfort.

I scoffed and pushed the mug aside in disgust. I opened my drawer and pulled out my only savior, a bottle of Scotch. I cracked it and took a long gulp. The warm sensation down the back of my throat offered a comfort unmatched by any kind of coffee.

No therapist, no medication, no meditation could cure what ailed me. There is no cure for seeing too much, besides dying.

I felt the shaking in my hands dissipate as the painful memories faded. I leaned back in my chair and enjoyed the moment of detachment. I took another pull from the bottle and took pleasure in the familiar numbness it started to induce.

Gazing back up at the news on the screen, I flexed my right hand. Pain shot through my fingers like karmic revenge. Hit enough people, and years later you feel their agony. Decades of inflicting pain and misery had taken its toll on my entire body. My hands not only hurt, but shook from stress and overuse. My muscles were tired and strained. My joints were used up; my knees lost their bounce. Despite the time I put into staying fit, my past lifestyle far exceeded any preventative measures I could have taken. Age had caught up to me with a vengeance, leaving me little more than a sad drunk old woman.

The city sprawled outside the window. It was early winter, but that made little difference here in the desert. People tried to bring winter from their various hometowns. The streets were adorned with holiday decorations of a variety of kinds. Mechanical snowmen waved their arms, reindeer glowed and multicolored lights flashed. In the background the abandoned, unfinished decay of the Spaceport loomed, casting its shadow of hopelessness over all in its vicinity.

The empty tarmacs lay desolate. The unfinished control towers jutted out from the desert. This was Spacetown U.S.A., the future of manned space exploration. This was the big scientific and economic gamble. First private aerospace moved in, then supporting businesses like telecom, IT, banking, and so on and finally the day-to-day businesses followed. There were cleaning services, restaurants, hardware stores, everything a real town needed. Everything minus one, Spacetown lost its purpose. Soon after the initial economic boom, progress on the Spaceport screeched to a halt, due to the catastrophe that changed everything. Now, the town went on without its initial reason for existence.

The sky glowed with its otherworldly aura. I never had a chance to see the Aurora Borealis before the asteroids, but I was told this was how it looked. It was foreboding and a reminder of how screwed up life had become. This time of year depressed me even more. It wasn't only about being alone on the holidays in this soulless town, I no longer cared about that.

The part which truly sickened me was the way people tried to pretend that everything was normal, that this existence was fine and we were okay. But every Christmas season, underemployed scientists still hustled in strip malls and discount chains trying desperately to make just a few more bucks to buy their impoverished children just one toy. This town was unique; it was the only place in the world where the poorest class was the most educated. Manual laborers made more per hour than a physicist. There were so many, too. Because of the electromagnetic field the Earth's new dedicated asteroid belt generated, intercontinental travel was nearly unheard of. There was no GPS, or satellite-based communications, limiting air travel to small hops. The price of travel was too great for all but the wealthiest; even in the good times, no scientist I ever knew had much in the way of disposable income. The best and the brightest from nations around the globe were trapped, no jobs to go to, unable to return to their native lands. This place ate up wise men and spit them out broken, hungry and useless.

I reached for the bottle to take another swig when I was interrupted by a knock on my door. "Yo," I replied. The door opened a crack.

"It's me." Marissa, my second-in-command, poked her head in. She wore a simple brown suit. Her black hair pulled back with a matching headband. She was always understated, never overbearing. I trusted her implicitly. My plan was to retire soon and she would run the company. She had one of the kindest hearts of anyone I ever met. When I interviewed her, I hired her on the spot. All of my employees were good, sensitive, caring souls. Most had a nature that would not allow them to work anywhere else. I created a safe zone for them, a place where they could make a difference and not be victimized because they held no malice in their hearts. Their jobs were to help people through various charities. They were really good at it.

"Well come in."

"How are you doing?" she asked.

"Okay. Could be better, could be worse. How was Dallas?"

Marissa smiled nervously and sat across the desk from me. "Not bad. It almost looks like it used to before, you know. How was your Christmas?"

"Uneventful. I spent most of it trying to avoid World Day specials. How did yours go?"

"Oh yeah, you don't do Christmas anymore. I forgot. My holiday was wonderful. And I brought you a present."

"You didn't have to. But thank you."

Marissa put something on my desk, and watched me anxiously. It was a medicine bottle. I knew what it was. It was 'Renox', renoxontine hydrochloride, the new miracle drug of the era. It was officially described as an aggressive affinity drug that targets NMDA receptors and other motor neurons. It started as an experimental drug to cure Alzheimer's. It only worked in a fraction of a percent of its test subjects, but when it did work, it completely reversed the damage and returned the mind of the patient back to its youthful state. Researchers tried it on other neurological disorders. They tried it on Parkinson's and cerebral palsy patients. Like the previous trials it worked on a fraction of a percent of the patients. Despite the limited success, people scrambled to get it for themselves, their friends and their families. It seemed like man had discovered a magical brain repair pill.

I stared down at the bottle. "Please tell me you didn't bring me crack for Christmas."

"Becca, it will cure your depression," Marissa said, as she fidgeted with her sweater. "We all chipped in. It's the real deal. I snuck it into the state for you." The FDA tried to stop the drug's release in the U.S., partially due to the fear of the drug's unknowns, but also to protect favored drug manufacturers from a multibillion dollar loss from curing very lucrative diseases. It didn't matter though. Like Marissa, people found ways of getting it. They demanded the drug and they were willing to pay. So soon European, South American and Asian manufacturers had come up with dozens of variants; each seemed to work on different aspects of brain function and chemistry. It cost thousands per dose, due to the cost of travel, but the drug was obtainable.

"Tired of watching the old bitch suffer, huh?" I continued to stare at the bottle; it beckoned with the promise of happiness, which I was completely undeserving of. I told my staff that my moodiness and apparent misery was caused by depression. What I didn't tell them was my self-loathing and despair was a symptom of something much worse, not the ailment itself.

"Why suffer needlessly?" she asked.

"It's illegal." I fidgeted with the memory stick I wore as a pendant around my neck; a reminder of why I deserved to suffer. "I don't want to end up a zombie or something. Is this your way of securing a promotion?"

"This is serious. You're always good to us. Even when we're abusive about being late or lazy, you always understand. We all want you to be happy."

"How did you get it? I mean, are you sure it's real and not rat poison or something?"

"Yeah, it's as safe as you can get with that stuff. I have a cousin who works in biotech. He has contacts and he owed me a favor."

"I appreciate it. Shit. How the hell did you fit that into a business trip?" I couldn't even imagine her dealing with black market biotech, but that and a business trip? "It must have been a major pain in the ass."

"Not really. I just had to go to a few clandestine meetings. It was pretty exciting. Besides, I was in no danger; they only care about the money. So are you going take it or what?"

"Maybe. Maybe, when I get home." I didn't want to tell her how much this scared me. I had been afraid of taking medication prescribed to me, now I was holding stuff that could do some potentially serious damage.

"Just follow the directions on the bottle. They told me taking it all at once is not a good idea. You need to space it over a few days at least. The weekend may be best, so in case you have any side effects they'll pass before you have to deal with people."

"What kind of side effects?" I knew there had to be a catch. There were rumors of serious side effects to the stuff. Everybody had an anecdotal story of the person who took the drug and never slept again, or that one who went completely insane. There were also stories of people becoming ten years younger and tales of others suddenly gaining some random skill. The drug was a source of new and spookier urban legends.

The real, documented, potential side effects of the drug seemed very grave, permanent brain damage being one of them. Healthy people generally didn't have any desire to take it. There was just no justifiable reason to do it.

"Some people experience drowsiness when they first take the medication, but it passes in a few days. It's nothing."

"Yeah." I sighed. "I'll probably sleep for a week."

She started out of my office and smiled, looking slightly frustrated with my refusal of aid. "You'll be fine, really. Take the drug."

I shrugged.

"Promise me that you will take the drug soon, before it expires."

"Okay."

"Promise." She knew I would not break a promise.

"Okay, I promise to take the drug before it expires."

"Good. Now you have to do it." She smiled and walked out of my office.

I stuck the bottle in my purse and got up to get some fresh coffee, with the hope that fresh, hot coffee would lubricate what was already turning out to be an abrasive day. I made it to the kitchen and almost out of nowhere, Marissa appeared.

"Why didn't you ask me to get you coffee?" she asked.

"Because I'm a big girl and can pour hot liquids unsupervised."

"Just because you can do something, doesn't mean you should. I know it hurts you to walk, so let me help you."

"It hurts if I sit and do nothing. I'm used to the pain." I didn't mean to sound irritated, but I did. "I'm not a cripple, and I am not ready for the nursing home yet."

"Sorry, you're right." Marissa must have realized what I was feeling.

"Damn straight, I'm right." I poured my coffee and took a sip. It was horrible. "Who makes this crap anyway?"

"It's the coffee service, they changed the coffee to the domestic stuff two weeks ago. No matter how you make it, it tastes like crap."

"Well, switch services," I commanded. I was the boss after all.

"The staff will be happy. Can we do something a little more pricey? You know they charge an arm and a leg to ship the good stuff here."

"Yeah, pay for the boat ride; anything to make up for this crap. Why didn't anyone say anything to me before?"

"I didn't want them to bother you with it. You have enough to worry about."

I studied her for a moment; she was wasted talent. It was time to tap that talent. "Tell you what. You have just been promoted. You are now chief operating officer. You have the power to make all final decisions in the day-to-day operations of this office. That includes purchases, staffing, and whatever else falls under operations."

Marissa looked stunned.

"It's the same thing you already do, except you won't need my signature anymore. And you get a cool title."

"Are you sure?" she asked. "This is so sudden."

"Screw it, you deserve it. And this will keep you busy enough to end your days of being my babysitter."

"Won't happen. I won't stop helping you."

I rolled my eyes. "It's like being in kindergarten. When is nap time anyway?"

"You're still the boss. It's whenever you want."

"Hmm." I poured out the offensive coffee and started back to my desk. "In that case, I'm giving myself the day off. I'm going to have some real coffee somewhere. Command is yours." I saluted her and made my way to my office to gather my belongings. I'd take my nap at home.

Chapter Two

"Through zeal, knowledge is gotten; through lack of zeal, knowledge is lost."
Buddha

The ground was soggy and warm, but the air was cold. My breath was visible as I exhaled with each step, silently creeping from room to room. It was dark. In the distance, I could hear screaming, crying and approaching sirens. My job was not complete yet. I had one thing left to do before my departure. I stepped through the hall into another room; the roof was missing. The sky above was riddled with explosions. My target sat, unmoving, waiting. I advanced, but movement was increasingly difficult. My legs were sinking into the floor, deeper with each step. Something grabbed at my knee. I looked down to find an expanse of severed limbs. Legs drenched in blood twisted and convulsed around me. Arms reached up and clutched at me. They started pulling me down, I couldn't move; I couldn't escape.

I awoke and immediately vomited. I kept a trash can by the bed for just such an occasion. I also kept a bottle of blended whiskey in my end table drawer, and took the opportunity to put it to use. But even the smoky-flavored elixir could not alleviate the discomfort. This, by far, was not the first time such a thing had happened. It was just one of the most vivid occasions. I shivered from the cold sweat that enveloped my body. I wrapped myself in a blanket, but it wasn't helping.

I got up and made myself look somewhat human. It was still early, but not obscenely so. I decided to go into work, and see if I could find anything useful to do.

When I arrived, I was surprised to see Marissa sitting at her desk typing away at her PC. She was dedicated, but I never knew her to be a morning person.

"Morning," I said. "Here a little early, I see."

Marissa turned her attention from her monitor toward me. "We didn't raise enough money for the Science Foundation."

"What happened?"

"They closed the accelerator. Some important projects got canned."

"I'm sorry." Marissa had fought hard to raise money for this one. Her late father had been a physics professor, forced into early retirement due to lack of work.

"So am I." Marissa stood up and stretched. "I made some of the new coffee. Want some?"

"Sure."

Marissa left her office and came back with two steaming pleasant-smelling cups. She handed one to me. I took a sip. It tasted much better than the stuff from the previous week. "Mmmm. So what are they going to do now?"

"Nothing," Marissa lamented. "I'm trying to reallocate the donations to another science-based charity, but most of the new projects looking for funding are being shut down before I can start a dialogue. It's very frustrating."

"It's also strange. I almost thought things were getting better. What happened to the World Day Science Initiative? Weren't we supposed to make bold new advancements to better humanity?" I felt my stomach turn. "It makes me sick. The world is just going to decay. Shit, I can remember when there was hope."

"I'm glad I wasn't around then. I don't know any better. My father used to break down and cry whenever we'd talk about the days before the disaster."

"Yeah." The knot in my stomach tightened as I remembered that day. "A lot of things died." I knew I should have been one of them.

"Do you think we will ever make it out of this?"

I shrugged. "I don't know, nothing makes sense."

"No," Marissa agreed. "It makes no sense at all. Nobody seems to care either. I've tried to contact six different foundations, and four different universities. All are halting physics research. It's like everyone gave up."

"Can you try medical research?"

"I'm going that route now. But I already see a similar trend emerging."

"Just do your best. Don't let it stress you out."

"It's not me that I'm worried about."

"Who then, me?"

"The world. Somebody's killing science."

"That sounds a little melodramatic. The world is already fucked; why would anyone bother?"

"Just because it sounds crazy, doesn't mean it isn't true."

She did have a point. I was getting a bad feeling about this. What did it mean?

"How's the coffee?" Marissa broke the silence.

"Pretty decent." I welcomed the change of topic. "You did good."

"Well, at least I got something right."

Chapter Three

"Our body is precious. It is our vehicle for awakening. Treat it with care."
Buddha

The following week was pain and chaos at the office. Even Marissa, the one person I could count on to be cheerful, was on edge. We were having no luck finding even one organization still in the business of promoting the advancement of science of any kind. We all felt demoralized.

By Friday night, I was exhausted. I felt no desire to go outside, or talk to anyone. Instead, I just cracked open a bottle of good Scotch, put on some music and went online to get some entertainment. Online media was not very forgiving that day. The nations were all at odds again over a severed undersea communications line. It took three nations a week to repair it, and communications were slow globally as a result. It also delayed completion of a new line because time and money had to be diverged to fund the repair. Several nations were beefing up security around the cables.

In other news, a national baseball hero hit five home runs in one game, and six more in the following. Officials were going to test for performance-enhancing drugs. They closed down another medical research facility due to government budget cuts. The last of the communications satellites was falling out of orbit. Plans were to leave it as a monument, but it was coming down despite our wishes. The president was declaring war on some place for doing something he warned them not to do. The baby tiger in the zoo died because somebody snuck in and poisoned him.

I looked at the window and watched the moon slowly creep across the sky. My soul did flip-flops every time I saw that. I remembered the moon, the way it was supposed to be; the lone beacon of the night, shining peacefully over the world. I closed my eyes and saw it, calmly soothing the residents of Earth, journeying across the sky in no hurry; its movements barely noticeable to the naked eye. Now, in comparison, it hurried along at three times the speed, as if trying to catch up in some cosmic race. It left me anxious, and uneasy. The sky had become so brutal. The world underneath was its casualty.

A wave of overwhelming despair struck my heart. I, like the rest of my generation, had become aliens to our own world. Those of us over fifty regaled the youth with tales of strange and exotic places. Australia was like Atlantis in the eyes of a twelve-year-old. "Impossible," they'd say when they heard that North and South America used to be practically connected.

I downed the rest of the bottle and reached behind the couch for my emergency stash. Some nights it took a little more to drown out the memories. It was failing though. Within another hour, I was incoherent, depressed and ready for death. I hooked my memory stick into my PC and gazed at the images of the old world I had never appreciated and all that suffered by my hand.

The television on the wall continued to commemorate World Day with increased fervor. First-hand accounts from an ever-aging population were decreasing with each passing year, as we died off. Soon all that would be left of the old world would be some video evidence and books which would skew the truth more and more as the decades passed. My day had passed. My world was gone. The universe dropped its final hint that it was ready for me to get the fuck out. I was also prepared to leave the bullshit behind. I cursed my existence and dragged myself to my bedroom, tequila bottle in hand.

On the way, I grabbed an old expired bottle of tranquilizers and poured the contents down my throat. I got to the bedroom and reached for the bottle of Renox on the dresser. I downed all the pills, washing them down with the familiar burn of Jose Cuervo. I counted on the fact that this time I would successfully fry my brain. I looked forward to the end. I managed to write a note before I collapsed onto the floor at the foot of my bed. It read:

Do not fucking resuscitate.

***

I woke up face-down on the carpet. The half of the bottle of tequila I spilt had long since evaporated. My brain wasn't fried, but I had a god-awful hangover. I peeled my right cheek off the carpet. Bits of fuzz still stuck to my face. Everything ached and burned. It wasn't like my regular aches and pains, though. It was a dull burning, like the feeling after an intense workout. It felt like every muscle fiber in my body had been overworked. It was a good thing the tranquilizers were still floating around in my system. I would have been screwed if I had to feel this and my regular pain.

"Shit!" I muttered, frustrated by my weakness and lack of strength to curse properly. I was even further demoralized by my botched suicide attempt. I had a knack for failure when it came to physical self-destruction. Somehow, my body refused to stop going.

My cell phone was beeping, indicating both low batteries and waiting messages. I plugged it in and checked the caller ID. Marissa called 3 times. I looked at the date on the phone. It was Tuesday; I had been out for three days.

The cell had a good signal today, so I used it instead of dragging myself to the landline. I called into the office, before they sent out a search party.

"Becca!" Marissa answered her phone. "Where have you been?"

"Listen, I took the stupid drugs and it knocked me the hell out."

"Why didn't you tell me beforehand, so I didn't think you were in trouble somewhere?" The throbbing in my head increased with the volume of her voice.

"If I was in trouble, I would have made the news."

"It's not funny," Marissa complained. "I was really worried."

"I wasn't trying to be funny. But I am sorry I scared you."

"Are you okay?"

"Yeah, I just feel wiped and hungover."

"Mmm-hmm."

"Yeah, that too."

"Get some rest."

"I will. I should be able to make it in tomorrow."

"Okay, just let me know."

"I will. I promise to keep in touch."

"You better."

"Yeah." I hung up and fell back into my bed. I slept for the rest of the day and the entire night.

Chapter Four

"As an irrigator guides water to his fields, as an archer aims an arrow, as a carpenter carves wood, the wise shape their lives."
Buddha

By the weekend, I had to face the reality that the drugs Marissa gave me were sugar pills. Not only hadn't they failed to kill me, but I felt just as miserable as before, only vaguely numb. I still felt the lingering effects from the tranquilizer portion of the pharmaceutical cocktail floating around in my system. At least I was feeling no pain. The only thing I got out of the whole ordeal was three days of unconsciousness and two missed days of work. I could have done that without any Renox.

I threw together some appropriate office attire, without even bothering to comb my hair or check myself in the mirror. I just threw my hair up in a tie, put on some shades and went into the office. Because of the lack of physical pain, I was able to get my work done in almost no time. I waited for the aching to resume, but nothing happened. I tried to sit calmly and enjoy the moment, but as time progressed, I became far too wound up. My stomach alerted me to the fact I was also starving. I bounded to the lunch room to grab a snack. My knees didn't complain once. Something was off.

I got to the lunch room and pulled out my meal. Gloria from HR sat at the table across from me, mouth agape, watching me inhale my food.

"Ms. Sanderson."

"I told you to call me Becca." I hated office formality.

"Becca." Gloria stared at me like I was growing another head. "You…"

"I what?"

"Your roots."

"What?"

"Your hair. The roots. They're not gray. That's the weirdest hairstyle I ever saw."

I stood up and dashed over to the ladies' room. I looked into the mirror. My murky gray hair was being replaced by a medium golden-brown color I hadn't seen in years. It wasn't just my hair, it was my face. The small lines and wrinkles were gone. And all my pain had faded. I felt like I was walking around in the body of a twenty-year-old again. The face that stared back at me in the mirror was that of me forty or fifty years ago.

"Holy crap!" I lifted my shirt and checked out my abs. I was still a little out of shape, but much firmer than I had been. I pulled my shirt higher, and was pleased to find the ravages of gravity had been reversed in other areas too. I gazed into the mirror in awe.

"Becca!" Marissa burst into the bathroom. "I have news!" She stopped when she saw my standing before the mirror. "Wow! What happened to you?"

"The Renox, some tranquilizers and a fifth of tequila."

"You…"

"It had the opposite of the intended effect."

"Thank God." Marissa stepped closer and examined my hair. "That is freaky looking."

"Thanks."

"No, I mean, it, wow, amazing."

"Yeah."

"So what are you going to do now?"

"Do? Good question." I pondered it for a moment and only one thing came to mind. "I'm going to the gym. Screw this. I'm firming this body up."

"Be careful. You don't know what shape you're really in."

"I feel it, Marissa. My knees." I bounced in place, testing the flexibility in my joints. "They're like new." I flexed my hands. "My hands, my arms. I'm not stiff. They don't hurt. No, I'm fucking going to the gym and getting my body back."

Marissa smiled.

"What?"

"You were trouble, weren't you?"

"What? You mean when I was young?"

"Yeah."

"You never looked me up online, did you?"

"No, I never browsed the old databases. Why?"

I grinned. "Yes, I was big trouble when I was young." And worse as I got older. I decided not to ruin the moment with bad memories. "So you said you had news."

"Yeah, I found a place to donate the money. It's new, and we have no idea how reliable they really are."

"Go on."

"The foundation is called The Adams Zachary Foundation. It was formed in response to the other facilities closing. They're building their own labs and offices in a bunch of geographical locations. Their charter is to keep science alive. So at least the funds will go to the right cause."

"That's good."

"Yes it is." Marissa smiled. "Good things are happening today."

I smirked wickedly. "Maybe not so good for the world. But good for me."

"Becca, go enjoy it while you can."

"No shit. I'm outta here." With that I was out the door, looking for a good place to work out.

Chapter Five

"*Ego, this gigantic devil, has caused troubles for many lifetimes. Remember this great enemy. Exterminate it quickly.*"
Buddha

It took me less than an hour to find a gym. There were many to choose from, but I settled on a place simply named "Pete's Gym". There wasn't very much information about the place available, but what I could find was encouraging. It was a smaller place, but it had not only the standard weight lifting equipment, but it also housed an area dedicated to the fighting arts. I was dying to kick the crap out of a heavy bag. It was all I could think about.

On the way to the gym, I swung by my house and changed into some sweats and a t-shirt. The place was on the second floor of a two-story building in a strip mall. It didn't look like much from the outside. I appreciated the fact it was inconspicuous. That meant less posers and more access to the equipment for me. I entered the place ready for business. I was long overdue for a good workout, and I could barely contain myself. A few men were chatting in a group on the other side of the reception area. As I stepped in, I was immediately leered at. They leered at me. This would take some getting used to.

"Hey, honey." The man behind the front desk molested me with his eyes. "What can I do for you?"

"Not what you're thinking. I want to get a membership."

"For you or your boyfriend?"

"Excuse me?"

"Well this is not the kind of gym a lot of girls go to. You may want to go to the ladies' gym down the street."

"What century is this? No don't answer that. You're gay, right?"

A hush fell over the reception area. The group of guys, who had been content to ogle me from a distance, was now actively interested in this conversation.

"What?!?"

I grinned. I still had the knack for starting trouble. "Well, you seem to have a problem with women being here. I could only speculate it's because you don't like women."

"That would make you some kind of dyke? Because you don't like men."

"I like men just fine. Especially when I'm kicking their asses." I should have censored that comment.

Receptionist guy laughed. "Are you challenging me?"

"Well, if that's what you want. But it's been some years for me, so I am rusty. I'll need to warm up."

"Oh, y-" Receptionist guy turned his attention to the gym offices. There was a ruckus coming from the area.

"Ray!" The gruff voice of an old man echoed through the area.

Receptionist guy, also known as Ray, practically stood at attention. "Yes, sir."

"Are you pissing off customers? Sorry, he's new; last guy just took a job somewhere as a mathematician or something. You..." Pete Kaminski limped over and stopped in front of me. This time I was the one who was stunned.

"Slaughter?" He took a step back, leaning on his good leg.

"Crap." This was a confrontation I had long avoided.

"My God, it is you."

"Okay, first, I'm sorry. I should never have done that to your leg."

I was unable to read Pete. He had a good poker face, which was one of the things that made him a great fighter.

"You ruined my fucking career."

"Yeah, and my own. I was wrong."

"You were wrong? You're a fucking psycho asshole."

"Okay, I deserve that. I'm really sorry. I submit to whatever retribution you want to dish out."

"Shit, I can't fight you," he said. "You shattered my goddamned leg. And I sure the hell am not going to let you break my students."

"I'm not the same anymore. I haven't even worked out in years."

"And I'm supposed to, what, feel sorry for you? Maybe you want me to run you a benefit. Aw, she's sorry and she hasn't worked out in years. Fucking look at you. You're walking around like you're twenty again. I'm a wreck."

"If I could trade, believe me I would."

"Bullshit."

"No, really. I am sorry for what I did. I can't make up for it. Whatever you want, just name it."

Pete glared down at me for a moment and sighed. "So how did you, you know, get young?"

"I think it was the combination of Renox and tequila I took last week."

"Tequila, still at it." He shook his head. "Didn't know Renox cured psychosis. I heard it had some weird side effects. Does it feel as good as you look?"

I smiled. His backhanded compliment caught me off-guard. "No, it doesn't cure psychosis. Listen, I know that I of all people did not deserve it."

Pete shook his head again. "I don't know what you deserve. You fell off the face of the planet, what forty years ago?"

"Yeah, something like that."

"Well, maybe you did something in those years to earn a fresh start."

"I can't think of anything, but screw it. I won't do anything that fucked up again."

"Better not, not in my gym. I might risk it and sic my boys on you." Pete held up his hand before I could make any kind of quip. "Do you need a trainer to get back into shape?"

"Just to tone me up. I'm not going back into anything. I just want the exercise,"

"Okay, I'll give you Ray. He talks a lot of shit, like someone else I know."

"Uh, sir?" Ray chimed in. "Are we charging her?"

"Fuck yeah, full price," Pete replied. "Bitch still owes me a fucking leg."

Chapter Six

"What you are is what you have been, and what you will be is what you do now."
Buddha

Work grew nearly impossible for me to deal with. It wasn't an inability to do the actual work. My efficiency increased dramatically, so I could get more work done, much faster than usual. I hadn't realized how much age slows down the thought process.

My body generated boundless quantities of potential energy. Unable to continue staring at the computer another millisecond, I got up and wandered the office. I ended up in the lunch room again. I snacked on some vegetables and started browsing through the various books and magazines strewn across the coffee table. Most of them were outdated and held no interest for me; that was until I found Don's stack of unfinished logic problem books.

I started with the top book on the pile. It was full of cryptograph and Sudoku puzzles, logic questions, a few crosswords, and a couple of word finds. I completed the book and continued through the stack. Before I knew it, I had completed seven books, and it had only been an hour. It suddenly dawned on me, that even when I was young, I was never this sharp.

Back at my desk, I got online. I solved puzzle after puzzle. I remembered everything I read. I was starting to pick up things I never had any chance of understanding before. Finally I took a few online IQ tests. The results were all the same. I was turning into some kind of supergenius.

Feeling belligerent, bored and a little mischievous, I started hitting some of the hacker sites. I cracked open a beer and went in search of trouble. I started reading up on the hackers' exploits. In doing so, I accidentally stumbled on a group discussing their techniques. I was about to start screwing with them, when I got sucked into their discussion.

They discussed methods of infiltration into various types of networks and systems, and even on my third six-pack, I found it fascinating. I started following their conversation like an instruction manual, and it was not only making sense, I was accessing a lot of systems I would never have been able to access before.

I was never much into computers, or any intellectual pursuit for that matter. It just seemed too much work for too little pay off. I was about the physical action, not theory. But something unforeseen happened. After only a brief crash course into hacking, I was starting to get the idea of how it worked. This was a bit of a shock.

I spent the night reading up on network security, and became familiar with the jargon and concepts. By the morning, I was sobering up, and able to lock down my home network. I set myself up through some proxy servers and made my connection untraceable. This hacking business was like a giant puzzle to me and all the pieces were falling into place.

The next morning, I let myself sober up a little, and started hitting some of the sites from the previous evening, when I was convinced I still retained the knowledge, I started drinking and hacking again.

I called out of work on Monday, having Marissa take care of things for the week. I spent that time learning. By the time the week had passed, I was almost qualified to call myself a hacker.

Chapter Seven

"Your work is to discover your world and then with all your heart give yourself to it."
Buddha

I sat in the office and pretended to work. Most of the day I read and played games; I almost felt guilt, almost. I could have just left early but today was Marissa's birthday. I had to stay for cake. It was a moral imperative.

The staff had outdone themselves with the decorations. I was amazed at how they managed to turn an office into a catering hall with a handful of streamers and balloons, but the place looked positively festive.

We all sang *Happy Birthday* in its traditional out-of-key style. Marissa even managed to blow out all of the candles. To her and my delight, it was an ice-cream cake. After just minutes, the entire staff was happily munching down on the cool confection and engaging in idle conversation.

"I took Johnny to see Blue Shift," Edna, our bookkeeper told Marissa.

Marissa smiled. "Was he as impressive in person as he is on TV?"

"He *is* a superhero," Edna said. "Not many of those around."

"At least not yet," Marissa added. "Even I almost considered taking Renox to see if I could get superpowers."

Edna and Marisa laughed.

"You're leaving out one thing," I interjected. "Just because a person has superpowers, doesn't mean they automatically become a hero. I'm sure there are other people out there with powers we just haven't heard about."

"Like you," Marissa teased me.

"Funny," I replied. "No, I just became smarter and younger, but it is true that I am not a hero."

"Maybe you should join one of the new teams," Marissa taunted. "You could be Smart Girl."

"Yeah, sure." I hadn't seen Marissa this irreverent in a long time. It was refreshing. "And you can be Pain-in-the-Ass Lass."

The three of us burst into laughter. Although the staff didn't know the real me, they knew enough to understand that the mere concept of me becoming a hero was laughable. I was too sardonic and bitter to do anything that altruistic.

"I hear Gloria sleeps with a picture of Captain Mighty under her pillow," Edna said.

"Isn't it Mr. Mighty?" Marissa asked.

"Mr. Mighty, Captain Mighty. It's all the same." Edna shrugged. "If her husband finds out, there'll be trouble."

"You can't divorce someone for having a crush on a superhero," I said.

"You can if it's an obsession," Edna rebutted. "And trust me, it's an obsession."

"Sad." I shook my head, but I was still smiling. This was highly amusing to me. Here were people with abilities which exceeded any previous expectations of what human beings could do, and all we could do was turn them into celebrities to gossip about. "At least she isn't obsessing over some supervillain. That really could be grounds for divorce."

We laughed again. Once more, Edna jump-started the conversation. "I know this guy who took Renox and never slept again. He went psycho and turned into a serial killer. But he didn't get any powers."

"That's cheerful birthday conversation," I said. "Besides, it's all urban legend. We know the stuff is dangerous, but no one has proven any of these stories. I heard some guy's brain exploded when he took Renox. That doesn't mean it's true."

"Well," Marissa countered. "They also said there was no proof it caused superpowers either, and look at Blue Shift and his team."

I shrugged. She did have a point. The only certainty about Renox was that it was extremely dangerous and unpredictable. It killed as many people as it helped, and most of the time it just did nothing at all. "Well, let's hope nobody spiked the birthday cake with it, or we'll get no work done at all. Anyone want seconds?"

Marissa shook her head no, but Edna joined me in overindulgence. The day continued on that note. We ate cake and gossiped. No work got done, but that was okay with me.

Chapter Eight

"Let yourself be open and life will be easier. A spoon of salt in a glass of water makes the water undrinkable. A spoon of salt in a lake is almost unnoticed."
Buddha

Have that, you! I wrote across the screen during the Crap-mart commercial. Under my newly acquired battle cry, a picture of a smiley face donning a bullet hole in its forehead appeared on the TV screen. I forgot what Crap-mart did to piss me off in the first place, but I felt a warm sense of satisfaction knowing every television viewer in Spacetown and its outlying viewing area would see my handiwork.

I didn't really have to go to the office anymore, but I still did from time to time. Marissa liked having me there as a lifeline. She was fully capable of running the place, and it wouldn't be long until I named her CEO and I went back to being young again.

I felt alive for the first time since I was in my twenties. I was still drinking, which was not the wisest of decisions, but I was happy. The austere attitudes that accompanied me throughout my previous existence were slowly being replaced with a hopefulness well overdue. I wasn't sure if it was the booze or the fact my brain had gotten younger, but I felt very juvenile and free. Sometimes, I even forgot what a monster I really was.

I did my daily check of my bank accounts; they were all full. I had no compunction against stealing from bastards. I found the most despicable people I could and sucked away a small, barely detectable amount of cash from them. When they finally noticed, I would let it rest for a while, and then find another target. The one constant in the world was there would always be a steady supply of rich bastards.

Most of the money I funneled to worthy causes, the rest kept me in computer equipment and toys. I left my legitimate money and old overseas accounts alone. I still had to be careful. All my 'fun' accounts were not traceable to me, and I bought most of my toys at computer shows with cash so nobody would wonder about my spending habits. I already lived in a small house. I continued to keep it looking modest. I disguised most of my good hardware in old cases and carried the portable stuff wherever I could. I had a decent personal area network going, and I had automated a number of my security attacks. I was having the time of my life.

At first, I had carefully secured myself so I was anonymous. People caught brief glimpses of my handiwork while in progress, but I never got online and bragged or took credit for anything. I was like a ghost that flowed through all electronic media. I was nameless, formless, but definitely there. Sometimes I was that 'thing'. Other times I was 'that hacker dude'. But I was never called by name; I was never more than a passing phenomenon.

At this point, I was getting much bolder in my chosen targets. I ignored countries and corporations, going straight for the bad guys. I went for dictators, drug lords, and self-declared supervillains. It rocked. I messed up a lot of bad people's days, and it paid for itself.

Today I was preparing for a raid on a new victim. He was a dumbass going by the name of 'Deprave'. He had risen out of nowhere, taking leadership of the supervillainous underworld and proclaiming the entire world as his dominion. Tonight, I was going to take down his sorry delusional ass.

I got my virtual weapons in order. I locked myself inside the house with a few bottles of tequila and prepared for battle. This network was a tough little nut to crack. It was very well armored and put up a fight, but as I predicted, by the end of my first bottle, I found a way in.

I browsed through the network and mapped it out in my head. Simultaneously, I was leaving hidden shortcuts into it. He might find a few, but not all. This would guarantee easy access at my whim. I was planning to go straight for the mainframe, but something told me that this guy would anticipate that. Instead I went for his PC. It was filled with plans and diagrams detailing weapons, attack plans, force fields, and other nifty toys. Despite his obvious superior intellect and grasp of science, most of his plans were flawed in some way. He made a lot of careless errors in addition and decimal points. I decided to make notes detailing his failures. I felt like a teacher grading her second grade students' essays. I made my notes in red, graded each project and put little stars on the plans that had some degree of merit. After I finished trashing his personal files, I went for his surveillance system. I had to see the bozo who gave himself such a corny superhandle.

I scanned his house. It was more like a fortress. This guy even had a cheesy supervillain lair. This just kept getting better and better. I hit all of the cameras, but couldn't see anyone. So I decided to go for the mainframe.

It was a nice machine. It was powerful, fast and had lots of storage space. I checked the running processes to see what it was up to. I loved my hunches. They almost never let me down. There was indeed a strange process running on this machine. It wasn't initiated from this system, so I didn't kill it off. I popped open another bottle of tequila and investigated further.

On closer inspection, it revealed itself to be a chat session of some kind. So, I just cut in.

...idea of his plans. I caught the tail end of someone's sentence.

I can't find anything in here, another person replied.

Look harder, it has to be in there, the first person apparently responded.

Mr. Poser man doesn't keep his files here. That's why you can't find them, I cut in.

Come again? one of them typed.

Are you a good witch or a bad witch? I asked.

Imp, is that you?

Not me, Imp apparently replied.

I couldn't help but snicker at the choice of name.

Who is that then? asked not-Imp.

This is the Computer speaking. Knock off all that evil.

Well, that isn't Deprave, one of the people stated.

How do you know that? the other asked.

Because Deprave has no sense of humor. I assumed this had to be Imp.

And his choice of décor is also unoriginal and lacking any flare, I added.

Okay, who the hell is this? demanded not-Imp.

It is I, the Computer. Are you with the IRS? I was having too much fun.

We are here on serious business, you little hacker brat. Get off of this network and let the grown-ups get to work. Not-Imp was getting angry.

The grown-ups are failing miserably. I am the superior being. Tell me what you are looking for, and I will get it for you.

Okay, Computer, one of the two typed. *If you're so bad, tell me where his files on the plasma launcher are.*

You don't need those files. It's pointless, I answered.

Why is that? Another inquiry came from the Imp/not-Imp team.

Because his calculations were all wrong and it wouldn't have worked anyway. The plans were really flawed.

Okay, can I see them anyway?

Sure! I cheerfully replied, and initiated a file transfer. Meanwhile, I made a point to download all of his files.

The chat remained quiet for a few moments.

Imp?

Yeah, Imp responded.

These are really the files. Not-Imp admitted. *And it looks like the Computer graded them and added notes.*

I had forgotten about that. *Yes, his plans are flawed. He is sloppy. He needs to learn from his mistakes.*

Athena? Imp typed.

Yes, Imp. Thanks for giving out my name, Athena responded.

Sorry, but does this mean I can quit now and you can hire this guy?

I don't know, Athena replied. *Hey, Computer, looking for some superhero work? Imp here wants to go back to college.*

I don't need work, I answered. *The Computer works alone.*

Well if you change your mind, get in touch with me. If you are that good, you'll find me. Athena dropped off the line.

Later, Computer, Imp added and then also dropped off.

Computer, hmmm. A new entity entered the arena.

Yes, I responded. *Is this the dork with the bad name and worse decorating sense?*

You amuse me.

I amuse myself. I opened the cams until I found him in his poserific laboratory. He was nothing like I expected. Besides the over-the-top supervillain costume, he looked like he should have been out playing video games and skateboarding with his friends. He had the face of an angry teenager. He was Asian, with intense green eyes. His hair was down to his shoulders, but not really styled in any particular way. He appeared almost disarming, but on the other hand, his youthful appearance was bringing out my inner fourteen-year-old.

Apparently so. Why are you here?

I threw on the audio one way. I could hear him, but he couldn't hear me. *You don't have to type. I can hear you. I can see you too. Nice costume, not.*

I pissed him off good. "Why are you here?" he repeated dryly.

Ah, the age-old life question. Why are any of us here? The Buddha says that our purpose is to find refuge within our own hearts. He said, 'Make yourself a refuge unto yourself.' Christianity suggests that we are here to indulge God's pleasure. According to Revelations 4:11, 'Thou art worthy, O Lord, to receive glory and honor and power: for thou hast created all things, and for thy pleasure they are and were created.' The Hindus say the universe is limitless, beginningless, beyond being and nonbeing. Our own internal perceptions superimpose illusions that create form.

"What?" Deprave didn't seem to appreciate my well thought-out answer.

Okay. Let's try again. I decided to take another route with my explanation. *I'm fucking drunk and bored and I'm here to screw with you. That's just what I do for fun.*

"Who are you?"

Wow, for a self-proclaimed supergenius you are awfully one-dimensional. I was going for full-blown rage.

"Listen, you little fucker. I will destroy you."

Blah, blah, blah, blah, blah. You're just not scary. You look like you were never even in a fight. I couldn't stop laughing. *Go ahead, destroy me. What are you going to do? Unplug me? You don't even know what system I reside in. You cannot destroy the Computer.*

I could almost see the smoke coming out of his ears. "Okay, Computer. I'll play your game," Deprave agreed. "But know this. You have made an enemy today. I will track you down. And you will pay for your insolence."

Okie dookie, Mr. Man.

"Are you twelve?" Deprave was obviously taken off-guard by my drunken, cavalier and juvenile behavior. "Don't you realize who you are messing with? I have the world's resources at my disposal. I can destroy you with just a word."

Yeah, me too. Want me to order you a pizza?

Deprave just stood there looking angry and befuddled. Then he must have found what I did to his personal files. "What?!? Computer, did you do this?"

Yes. I gave you a 'D'. I would have failed you, but you made such an effort and I didn't want to completely discourage you.

"There is nothing wrong with my plasma weapon!"

It sucks. You have addition errors throughout the thing. Decimal points are in the wrong places, and you completely disregard the laws of physics. Don't you double-check your math?

"No. I don't need to. My basic math skills are…"

...lacking. At least use a calculator. Come on. Look at the power requirements alone. I was now looking at the document myself. I didn't realize I knew this stuff. *Look, if you put the decimal point in the right spot, you'll see that you need the energy equivalent to half of our sun just to operate the thing. I am not even going into the ramifications it will have on the planet's gravity. Look just admit it, your plans are piss-poor. What do you use that supercomputer for, porn?*

Deprave stood there slack-jawed. I had put him in his place, and good.

I'm getting bored. I'm gonna go do something more challenging, like play some video games or something. You have a good night.

"Wait..." Deprave started, but I closed the sessions and went out for a bite to eat. I considered screwing with him again really soon.

Chapter Nine

"Let go the past, let go the future, and let go what is in between, transcending the things of time. With your mind free in every direction, you will not return to birth and aging."
Buddha

Though I had regained my youth, I soon realized I should not lose track of who I was. As time passed, I was more inclined to do reckless and foolhardy things, especially with all my drinking. I had to find a way to maintain perspective, before I made the same mistakes as the first time.

I started visiting the local nursing home. The staff and patients thought I was just a kind soul visiting to cheer up the old folks. None had any clue that my motives were a bit more self-serving.

Today, I sat in a small den with a lady named Lila. She was, by far, one of the people I liked to spend time with the most. If she had been a few years younger, we would be raising serious hell together. On the outside, she looked like a sweet little old lady in a wheelchair. Now frail, white-haired and wheelchair bound, she gave no indication of the terror she used to be. She looked like someone's angelic grandmother, but she wasn't entirely what she appeared to be. The thing I liked most about her was that she didn't care what anyone thought. She, like me, had gotten into a huge amount of trouble in her youth. Unlike me, she had been a sex worker. She put herself through college by working in a brothel in Nevada; once she graduated school with her teaching degree, she realized she preferred prostitution to teaching. She bore no shame about it. She would regale me with tales of her crazy experiences during her time in the world of prostitution.

She liked me because I would openly defy the nurses on her behalf, and I would sneak in marijuana for her when nobody was looking. There was nothing funnier than an old lady stoner.

"Want to wheel me out to the woods so I can get my buzz on?" Lila asked. Her voice still had a sultry quality to it, despite her advanced age.

"Can't now, the Gestapo is watching." I rolled my eyes.

Lila smiled and patted my knee. "You'd make a good ornery old lady."

"I'd rather be a dirty old lady like you." I laughed.

"Oh, I remember my sex drive. It drove off when I stopped being able to hold my vibrator."

"It's not fair, you know. You learn everything, you're ready to put it to good use, and then just like that, your body gives the fuck up."

Lila eyed me with curiosity. "Shit, Becca, sometimes I could swear you were older than me."

"Nah." The truth was she had five years on me. "Maybe I'm just fatalistic."

"I think you're hiding something, sweetie, but that's okay, because I know you will tell me when you're ready."

"Ah, patience. That's something I still need to learn."

"Why do you come here?"

I shrugged. "I like it here. I almost feel at peace, and when I'm here, I'm not drunk in front of a computer."

"Drinking is bad for you, you should smoke pot instead."

"Liver or lungs... Let's see...both are bad. So screw it. I make a great lush and at least having alcohol in my house is legal."

"You don't strike me as someone who cares about legality. What is it that brings you here?"

"Your company. You make me laugh."

"Hmm. So I'm entertainment, that's familiar."

"Oh please. It was a compliment. Seeing you is like a breath of fresh air."

"Ah, fresh air huh?" Lila laughed. "You're piling it on deep."

"Oh, come on. Stop being like that. My life is bleak enough. Your stories cheer me up, and you give me hope. Now stop bitching and tell me a happy memory."

Lila rolled her eyes at me. "You are really working it." She sighed. "I remember a beautiful day in May. I was in the front yard of my house. The temperature was perfect. I must have been five, maybe six years old. There was a gentle breeze; the sky was a perfect bright blue. The sun warmed my face, but it wasn't overbearing. Everything was exploding with color. I could hear the bees buzzing from flower to flower. I remember my mother coming outside. She was young and beautiful. I told her that this was the most beautiful day I ever saw. I was at peace."

"Ah, I remember those days. No asteroid belt, your cell phone worked all the time, and there was satellite radio."

"Busted." Lila pointed her finger at me in accusation.

"Doh! I can't believe you set me up like that." I threw my head back and sank into my seat. I noticed I was letting my guard down for the first time in decades. It was good to be able to trust a little.

"So, you took Renox?" Lila asked.

"Yeah."

"And?"

"I'm months from my seventieth birthday. I feel alienated, and I'm acting like a kid again, even though I know better. I guess I come here so I can be with my own kind and get some perspective."

"Seventy. Hmm." Lila cocked her head and looked at me. "You don't look a day over twenty-five, and you act like you're twelve."

"It's really confusing. Sometimes I feel very lost. My mind tells me one thing, and my body leads me in other directions. I guess physical age really does affect behavior. Imagine that."

"So young people can't help acting retarded."

"Guess not. Kind of takes the wind out of sitting on the front porch yelling at the kids to get the hell off of your lawn and stop acting like 'tards. They just can't help it."

"Promise me just one thing."

"What is that?"

"Promise me that you will find yourself a sweet young thing, have your way with him and report back to me." Lila smirked evilly. "Promise."

"You know I could just get the drug for you, if you want."

Lila shook her head. "Already tried it. I risked brain damage for youth. It didn't do a damned thing. So I am stuck living vicariously through your sex life."

"Vicariously, huh? Okay, I'll try. My history with men has been dangerous."

"Oh, oh." Lila poked me. "Do tell."

"Oh no. I'll tell you about some of the madness, if you promise not to tell anyone."

"I promise! But first, you need to take me out to smoke a bowl."

I looked around. "Okay, the coast seems clear, let's go."

I wheeled out to our hiding place in a small undeveloped area of the grounds. It was a lovely spring day. It was early May and everything was alive. The nursing home was on the outskirts of the city. It was close enough to access everything, but far enough that the pollution and noise didn't quite make it out this far. The bushes and palm trees hid us from the eyes of onlookers, the birds sang their cheerful melodies, and the trees rustled in a gentle breeze. From this perspective, the sky looked normal; the trees blocked out the offensive bits of the debris-polluted heavens. I rolled Lila a joint, and handed it to her. She lit it and took a toke.

"You should have some. It's good for you." She coughed and I openly laughed at her.

"Yeah right, I have enough vices, thank you."

"So what did you do in your misspent youth?" Lila asked.

"The opposite of what you did."

"You slept with women?" Lila giggled.

I smacked her lightly on the leg. "No. I used to hurt people."

"Oooh, do tell."

"There's nothing to tell. I was a pro fighter. I had a career in Supreme Fighting for a while. I was the first women put in the cage against guys. I usually won too."

"You beat up men for a living."

"Yup, and then they came running to you for comfort. I prepped 'em for you."

"Wait. You weren't, nah…"

"What?" I grinned sheepishly, as I watched the gears turning in her head.

"You were 'Slaughter' Sanderson." Lila shook her head. "Damn, girl."

"You followed Supreme Fighting?"

"I serviced men. Of course I followed it. Didn't they throw you out of the league for being too violent?"

"No. They asked me to step down because nobody would get in the ring with me anymore, because I was too good."

"You broke bones."

"Yeah, that." Lila was absolutely correct. I just hated to admit how extreme I was in those days. I liked to blame others for my eventual descent into darkness, but I had already been well on my way down that road.

"Yeah that? Didn't you cripple some guy?"

"I just gave him a limp, and we recently made up, I think."

"Just a limp, huh?" Lila shook her head. "Remind me never to get on your bad side."

"Oh, please. You are deriving too much amusement from this." I hadn't heard any of these accusations in a while.

"Hey, I wasn't the one who crimpled a guy and got busted for using the death touch in the ring."

"Dim Mak is not really the death touch and they never proved that anyway."

"How do you prove something like that?" Lila asked

"Um, you can't. Okay, maybe I used my knowledge for my own personal gain, at others' expense. But I fixed the alleged Dim Mak victim after he stopped talking so much shit. Besides, I don't do that crap anymore."

"Yeah, well that was over thirty years ago. Where does the time go?"

"I don't know, but I am glad to have as many years between me and that crap as possible. I can't believe you remember all that. Damn. That will teach me to keep my fucking mouth shut."

"So what happened after?"

"What do you mean? After what, the sky falling?"

"No! You quit before you were thirty. You had to do something between then and now."

"Nothing, I was retired," I lied. "I had a lot of money to sit on my ass."

"Bullshit. I know your type, restless and dangerous. Something changed you into who you are now. Let me guess, you were really bad and then you found God."

"Oh? I'm being analyzed. You have the answers, please continue."

"No, you tell me."

"Listen, I got my money and I quit. Or would you rather believe I was some kind of highly paid assassin, who had to retire due to aging reflexes and too many aches and pains." I grinned. "Or maybe I was a soulless demon that wandered the world in search of blood. And then I found God."

"Wow. I vote for the first choice."

"You're mistaken."

"Am I? It's okay, I'm not telling anyone. Besides I'm old, nobody believes the stories of an old lady."

"You're telling me. But I was joking about the assassin thing."

"Liar." Lila took another hit of the joint.

"No, you're just high."

"Come on. Stop being so uptight."

"Damn it. You are so bad."

"Yeah, yeah. Roll me another one, Slaughter." I did and watched Lila get baked.

Chapter Ten

"Little by little a person becomes evil, as a water pot is filled by drops of water...

"Little by little a person becomes good, as a water pot is filled by drops of water."
Buddha

A few weeks later I was bored again. I had very few targets that were of any challenge. Supervillains seemed to be my only worthwhile form of entertainment, so I figured why not hook up with the people who have all their names and numbers? I decided to check out what the deal was with Athena. It took a little digging, but I found out she was part of a team named 'Team Power'. The name was laughable, but so was their enemy. They had set up their headquarters at a coffee shop Athena owned and operated. Although she did all the work, she was not the team leader.

Blue Shift was the leader. He was a large muscle-bound guy who shot blue energy bolts from his hands. One shot knocked you out, two exploded your heart. He could take out buildings with his energy bolts. He didn't seem able to control the intensity, so he had to be careful who and what he shot. He made a lot of public appearances and seemed to be more interested in his public image than he did about leading the team.

These people intrigued me, so I decided to check them out.

Team Power was the first ever superhero team. While they primarily operated in the local metropolitan area, they were an international sensation. The government provided some of the funding for the group. Travel, for example, was provided by government-issued transportation. Which branch of the government provided the funding was unclear.

I arrived at Athena's coffee shop. It was a small place in the middle of a small city block. During the morning and afternoon rush hour, the place would get fairly busy. But I was there after the evening rush and things were starting to wind down. I set myself up in a booth toward the back. The place was well kept. The smell of various coffee blends filled the area with hearty, earthy warmth and an occasional whiff of pastry would drift through the air.

There was a small crowd there of normal people, chatting, drinking coffee, doing regular coffee shop stuff. I sent Athena a text message warning of my impending arrival and watched. The first of the team to arrive was Mr. Mighty. He paced around the place checking everyone out. I sat there typing away at my laptop, but he took no notice of me. Finally he took a seat at the counter and watched the door.

Athena came out from the back. She walked up to Mighty. She said something to him and he made some gestures. She walked away from him and looked around; he followed behind her still talking.

"...the guy's not here," Mighty whined.

"Did you think maybe to look for a woman? Look." She gestured at me. I smiled and waved. She smacked Mighty in the head.

"Ow," he complained.

"Hi," she said as she took a seat across from me. Mighty just stood at the edge of the table looking awkward.

"Hi."

"So, what was the grade?" She of course was referring to the grade I gave Deprave's plans.

"I gave it a 'D'. I should have failed it though. He needs to learn how to add."

Athena looked me in the eye and grinned from ear to ear. "Our science advisor agreed with your comments. I am very glad to meet you, Computer. Finally, someone competent and with a few brain cells." She was setting off all my alarms. Her presence smelled familiar.

"I never made any promises. I'm just considering the idea. My life is comfortable. I'm not sure I want to be a public figure or anything." I considered that instead of saving me, this might be the path to further damnation.

"I understand," Athena conceded. "But realize that you can stay behind the scenes if you want. You don't have to be on the front lines. I own this place and we use it at night as headquarters. During the day we keep it low-key, no costumes, no overt planning. You know the drill. You can stay here all night, eat doughnuts and drink coffee to your heart's content. Nobody will bother you."

"I appreciate the doughnut offer, but I stick to a strict diet and exercise plan. Maybe coffee would work though. Got any booze?"

Athena laughed. "Eat right, exercise and drink. That's some combination."

"Yeah, well we all do what we need to get by. What about Blue Shift, isn't he the one who does the hiring?"

Mighty and Athena gave each other a look of concern. "Mighty, can you go do a security sweep?" Athena didn't disguise her intent to get rid of him.

"Yeah, I'll keep it clear." Mighty didn't seem to be put off at all by his dismissal.

"Yeah, about him."

"Oh God, don't tell me that he's a complete ass. He is, isn't he?"

"Yeah, and then some. He's a bully, a chauvinist, a bigot, foul-mouthed and a show-off. A lot of what I do is damage control behind him. But I will deal with him."

"Why even bother? Why not ditch him and have your own team?"

"Because, we can't let him run around unchecked. We just let him do his publicity thing, engage in a few low-level operations and we take care of the rest behind his back. He thinks he's the man, and we maintain the public good."

"Okay, but why do you want me?"

"You know why. Nobody else can do that computer stuff you do. And besides, Deprave has declared war on you personally. He keeps sending messages through us. You may as well join up so you can get your pile of death threats. They're taking up too much space already."

"No way!"

"Way." Athena laughed. "Please, save my sanity. It doesn't have to be full-time. I just need a clear head with common sense beyond the twelve-year-old level to help me out."

"Okay, why the hell not? But I do have the sense of humor of an adolescent, and I don't always have the clearest head. You may not be getting any kind of improvement here."

"Just demonstrate some intelligence and show up at our monthly meetings and we'll be fine." Mighty walked up and handed Athena a box. She put it on the table in front of me. It was all the threats from Deprave. "Have a nice read." Athena laughed as she walked away and greeted Acid as she walked in the door.

It took a couple of hours to get through all the notes. They all had the same theme. *I would suffer. It would be painful. The end was near.* They were all so repetitive. Between threats, I got to chat with the other members of the team. I met everyone with the exception of Mind Master and Blue Shift, which as I was told was a good thing. I got the feeling I belonged. Even though Athena seemed off, who was I to judge? Maybe like me, she was once lost and trying to find her way. Maybe we would both walk the path of virtue this time.

Chapter Eleven

"Just as the bee takes the nectar and leaves without damaging the color or scent of the flowers, so should the sage act in a village."
Buddha

Friday night was 'screw with a villain' night, but I just wasn't feeling it yet. The fifth of liquor I downed wasn't even doing it. The night before I had just scrambled the entire network of some bozo named Manta, throwing spyware on every computer in the place, and bringing all of them to a crawl. Deprave was still fuming about my weeklong, impromptu search and replace spree. I went through all of his documents and replaced random words with the words 'potato', 'turnip' and 'squash'. I threw in a few numbers and colors just to make it that much harder to repair. I called it my 'veggie attack'. It really screwed up a bunch of his calculations. I half expected him to put a hit on me for that one. I was still looking over my shoulder when I was outdoors. But at least I taught him a valuable lesson about making backups.

So, instead of launching an attack right away, I decided to do some light reading. I hit a few school research sites to see if there were any advances in anything interesting. I noticed something funky. There was some unspecified research being conducted at a small, remote university in Italy. That fact was not all that interesting. What was weird was the way references to some of the staff seemed to be deliberately expunged from any of the project's documents. The project was named 'Zeus' and besides only one brief mention, the project leader Antonio Bianchi was completely absent from any documents linked to it at all. What started really working on my head was the fact there was no abstract anywhere related to Zeus. Nothing indicated what it was trying to accomplish. For all I knew, they were building a lightning gun. There was no way to tell. What deepened the mystery even further was that most of the links related to Zeus' website were dead.

The website was the front-end to a network just begging to be hacked. The fact there was so much information obscured from the public, made it that much more enticing to me.

It turned out to be one of the hardest systems I ever tried to get into, but by midnight I had all of Zeus' files and was safely back out of their network. I started reading the files. First I read through the biographies of some of the researchers. Besides Bianchi, they were all fresh-faced students, all in the project solely for their love of science. Bianchi hand-picked each of them. It was an international group. Some of the team members came as exchange students from other universities. It was a great honor to be chosen to even have a small part in this project. Even the administrative staff had been carefully screened out of a pool of eager undergraduates. This was a high prestige project.

Bianchi was a brilliant man. He had taught particle physics at many of the best universities. His work was never given the credit it really deserved, mostly due to politics. He wasn't part of the popular science crowd. This didn't seem to dissuade him at all. He still did some remarkable work.

The information on the project itself was a muddled mess of incomplete tests and formulas. It took hours to make any sense of it. But at four twenty a.m., a time I will never forget, I found the answer.

I sat there frozen at my computer. "How?" I muttered out loud. The calculations were correct, the tests supported it, but it couldn't be.

I needed some confirmation, a reality check. I had nobody to bounce this off of. I struggled for a couple of hours, racking my brain trying to come up with someone I could talk to. Eventually, I found myself desperate enough to do the unthinkable. I had to contact the only other mind who could comprehend this. I crashed into Deprave's network, intentionally setting off all his alarms.

WAKE UP! I typed across all of his monitors. I flipped on the cameras and found him stumbling to the lab looking bleary-eyed and aggravated.

"I was sleeping," he complained.

Stop bitching. I don't know what time zone you're in, I typed.

"What is it, Computer? Come to grade more of my projects? Want to leave some more recipes for me?" He was still angry.

No. I'm having a crisis of science and I really need a sanity check.

Deprave raised an eyebrow and sat in his chair. "Speak."

Okay. I know I shouldn't be talking to you about this, but nobody else is smart enough to get it.

I'm not trying to be snobby or anything, but people don't se-

"Get to the point. It's the middle of the night." Deprave yawned.

Okay, just promise not to use this for anything bad.

"You know I can't do that. I'm a supervillain. It's what I do."

No seriously, you're not really evil. Besides, I know the whole villain thing is your way, but this is important. I don't know you, but you are the only person I can talk to. I know it's weird, but all my instincts tell me that I can trust you with this. Promise me that you will take this seriously. The implications are boggling.

"Okay, Computer, calm down. I promise to try not to be tempted into using your information for evil. That's all I can give you."

Dammit! Can you just give me a little more?

"You know, technically speaking, my word should mean nothing, since I am a villain."

Don't give me that. I know you have some kind of code.

"Okay, I give you my word that I will not use what you are about to tell me for evil, but any information I gain as a result of this knowledge is fair game."

Okay, I guess that will have to do. Something inside assured me this was the right thing to do. *They made a Space Tether.*

Deprave sat up in his chair. "What about a Space Tether?"

I found it.

"You built a Space Tether?" Deprave asked in apparent awe.

No, not me! I don't even have a lab. I found a project that was shut down, but they did it. I have the papers. It works. They harnessed the energy from the asteroid belt, nearly unlimited energy.

"No shit? I was wondering about that."

About what? I asked.

"Oh nothing." Deprave waved his hand in dismissal. "I wondered why they hadn't built a tether yet. I knew there had been projects, but they never amounted to anything."

Do you know what this means? They could harness this power to clean up the mess. We could clear up the sky so we can resume space exploration. We could put up new satellites, get communications back to the way they were. Hell, we could get satellite TV and radio back!

Deprave shook his head in apparent disagreement. "They could also screw it up like they did in the first place. If they demolish one of those asteroids in the wrong Lagrange Point, they will darken the entire sky with debris. Life on this planet would cease to exist. Do you really trust the morons in power to do it right?"

No. He had a point. Nobody could agree on how to deal with the original asteroid problem to begin with. If countries bickered about how to deal with the problem of several huge asteroids careening toward the planet, they would never agree on how to fix the problem now. *The last thing we need is the Russians sending up another nuke or something. Or the Antarcticans building a giant robot.*

"What is it with you people and stereotyping Asians with giant robots?"

Sorry, bad joke. I didn't mean ALL Asians though. I grinned from behind my electronic cloak. I was glad he at least got the reference, since most people wouldn't have. I missed Japanese culture. It was never the same since Japan sank and they populated Antarctica with Australians. *You know the Russians were probably right.*

"They were completely correct. I went over the old data. The asteroids would have hit us dead-on. The Coalition was wrong. The Russians saved the planet. If people had put their political biases aside, we may not have been the recipients of this unwanted asteroid belt."

The memory of my Chechnyan failure briefly drifted through my thoughts. It was followed by a sigh of relief. Sometimes failure was good. *I'm going to take a huge risk. I'm trusting you.*

"Okay, you said that already. With what?"

I dropped the files on his mainframe. *Please crunch the numbers and see if it's for real.*

He jumped up and went to his main console. He typed for a moment and grinned. "I'll run it. I'll tell you if it works. But if it does, you know you owe me an apology and an 'A'."

What?

Deprave laughed. "For my plasma weapon. This would solve the power problem, making it a viable weapon."

You didn't know about this when you made it. B minus.

"Hard ass."

I'm gonna go now. I want to see what other weird stuff is out there. I have this nagging feeling.

"I can't believe I'm telling you this, but be careful."

I'll watch out.

"And, Computer?"

Yeah?

"You can trust me with this. You did the right thing."

Chapter Twelve

"A family is a place where minds come in contact with one another. If these minds love one another, the home will be beautiful as a flower garden. But if these minds get out of harmony with one another, it is like a storm that plays havoc with the garden."
Buddha

I started hitting the coffee shop regularly. I slowed down my drinking a little, so I was mostly sober when I was there. I found it harder to focus without alcohol in my system, though.

The other team members were fun to hang out with, and I had to admit that there was something comforting about being around people who were different too. I was spending time with Acid learning the way of the team. She was easy to work with. Acid looked like she was sixteen years old, even though she was closer to thirty. She had a very slight build, black hair with platinum highlights, brown eyes, and a pale complexion. She usually wore black, and carried a backpack with all of her stuff in it. She was addicted to coffee, and had a sarcastic bite I really respected. She had fire powers, and she was really good at wielding them.

DJ Ghost looked on; he was a skinny, baby-faced, twenty-something. He had the power of invisibility, which he used to play frequent pranks. He was tall, with hair that seemed to change color weekly. His eyes were light brown, but he wore different-colored contacts to match his hair color. He had the personality of a rave kid, only with some responsibility. He was fun. Whenever he arrived, the mood would kick up a few notches.

Mr. Mighty was the team brick, meaning he was slow, but really strong and nigh invulnerable. Nobody had ever dropped a bus on him or anything, but he was tough and could take some serious abuse. He was a big guy, almost seven feet tall, all lean muscle, and very handsome. He had dirty blond hair, blue eyes, and the girls really dug him. He was painfully shy though, hiding from the public eye as best as he could. I really liked him; he was in the hero business for the right reasons. Of everyone there, he was the one who most wanted to help people. I never once doubted his motivations.

Athena was fast and also fairly strong. She was trained in a bunch of martial arts and battle tactics. She was also reported to have some experience with covert operations and combat strategy. She looked like an Amazon woman. She was five foot eleven inches, all muscle and absolutely drop-dead beautiful. She had perfect bronze skin, dark brown eyes, and black hair which she wore in a tight bun. She looked like she was barely twenty-one years old, yet she had an aura of strength and was the true leader, despite the lack of title. Although everyone trusted her implicitly, I could see something ominous in her eyes. I did the smart thing and kept the hell quiet.

Acid was quizzing me on the bad guys. We sipped at Athena's special brew as we studied.

"Pain?" Acid asked.

"He's a miserable bastard. We don't know much about him, but we do know he hates everybody. He lives on an island somewhere in southeast Asia with his army of minions and a few hand-picked generals, who he hates too. He claims to be the first person with powers, and therefore the ruler of the universe. He conducts human experimentation, drug trafficking, slave trading and uses a lot of toilet paper to wipe up all the bullshit."

Acid laughed, and I continued.

"His powers are unknown, but he claims to have eternal youth, tremendous telekinesis, levitation, flight, and toaster powers. He can make a mean BLT and likes to watch public television. He enjoys long walks on the beach and fine wine."

Now DJ was laughing, too.

"Come on; take this at least a little seriously," Athena said. "I know it's boring, but you need to know this stuff."

"Okay." I sighed and went back to it. "He has his fingers in everything bad. He doesn't play well with others, so he is not aligned with anyone. We don't mess with Pain. He's too big and bad. We leave him to the government."

"Good." Athena nodded.

"Okay, Gloom." Acid moved onto the next on the list.

"Gloom has the power of energy dampening. He can shut off alarms, the lights, phones, surveillance and anything else that uses power. He can't make a living alone because it's an all-or-nothing power. He can't turn on a flashlight when his powers are active because it stays out too. He solved the problem by teaming up with Conduit, now known by her real name, Alicia. She has the power of energy redirection. She can do things like stick her finger in an electric socket and direct the beam to an appliance across the room. She also can store and generate small amounts of power within her body. Now she holds the flashlight. They've been rolling in money ever since they hooked up. Apparently she lit up Gloom's life too, 'cause he married her. They also pissed off Deprave. He claims they lost their edge once the relationship started. He was the best man and they are still all aligned. He was just pissed that the He-Man Women Haters Club was disbanded."

Snickers filled the shop. Even Athena was clearly amused.

"Okay." Athena jumped in. "Tell us about Deprave."

"The man can't get enough of me." The laughter resumed. "He's a self-proclaimed supergenius. But I smack him down regularly. He has bad fashion sense and can't decorate himself out of a paper bag. He also orders a lot of porn on the Internet, and has a thing for really bad martial arts films. He's the first and final word in all whiney supervillain drama. He has no powers, besides his ability to write really bad world domination plots. Rumor is, he got his name through some act of twisted perversion. Nothing specific, but with all the porn he downloads, I say the name fits. He has a lair somewhere with a super laboratory. His experiments are mostly weapons. He has a small number of henchmen. He probably keeps the numbers down, so nobody catches him whacking off to all the porn. He named me as his adversary because I mock him so well. I think he's a masochist or something because he seems to love the abuse."

We went on like this throughout the evening. I was quizzed on most of the known bad guys.

I studied all throughout the week. There were many others. But it was a central core of characters who did the majority of the mayhem. Deadbeat had a sonic attack and could adjust the sound levels of a small area. He had a thing for music. He loved to steal rare instruments from museums. He also robbed the occasional bank, assumingly to get money for the bills. He, like most of our adversaries, never really hurt anyone. Nobody ever saw him use his power to kill or maim anyone, even though he was powerful enough to do so.

Fuzzy Logic had the power of confusion. He could walk into a room full of people and suddenly everyone would forget why they were there. He seemed to have no motive or clear-cut agenda. He would just show up sometimes, confuse a large crowd and walk off with some random object. Some claimed he was completely insane and following orders from the voices in his head. Others believed he was putting together some extradimensional device, and that he walked the line between dimensions. Whatever he was, he was not really a threat, just odd.

Ganjasaurus was exactly what his name implied. He was the king of weed. He had plant powers. He put his powers to what he considered good use. He spread his ganja throughout the world. He mostly kept to himself and his affairs, and was not considered a threat to life nor limb.

Manta was just some kind of freak who dressed up like something out of a cartoon. I gave him the fitting nickname of 'Muppet Head'. He started out as a low-level mobster wannabe. When that didn't work out, he threw on some weird polystyrene outfit, took a name and started trafficking drugs and weapons. People assumed he had some powers because of the crazy costume and bad dialogue. By the time anyone realized he was a fake, he already put himself in a position of power. It was pretty clever; however, he refused to drop the act. So he still ran around in the ridiculous outfit. Nobody told him that he was a loser to his face, because he had his boys and was well armed.

Once I was given the green light from the team to become a full-fledged member, I started getting to work. I made good use of my time there. We set up a monitoring center I would man when people went out on missions. Through me, they would be able to coordinate, and I could access whatever I might around them and report back on what to expect. We practiced a few times and it worked out incredibly well.

I started hacking into the computer and surveillance systems of many of the villains. Manta was particularly peeved, because I really let loose on his systems. I secretly forged a deal with Ganjasaurus. He was a very reasonable guy, and we saw eye-to-eye on a lot of issues. He really wasn't a villain, just on the wrong side of the law. The deal was that I would not screw with him, if he and his underlings didn't deal to children. We both came away feeling like winners in the bargain. I even gave him a few hints on how to move his money around.

I did what I could to keep the hard work to a minimum. I dropped monitors on the systems I could, and we were now more in the business of prevention as opposed to reaction. Athena was thrilled. There were still fires we had to put out, but the dopey stuff was on the decrease.

By the time Blue Shift returned from his tour, we had things down to a science. We could split the team up and coordinate strikes. We were fast, efficient and worked as a cohesive unit. Crime was down for the first time since supervillains appeared. We were getting great PR and according to the press, Blue Shift was the man. I happily stayed behind the scenes. Most people had no idea I even existed, and those who did could only speculate on who or what I was.

I was informed that my existence displeased Blue Shift. I didn't know what I did to upset him, but clearly he didn't like me and we hadn't even met. One night he came storming in acting like he was looking for a fight. I decided to be pleasant. We didn't know each other. Maybe if I was nice, he'd at least respect my effort.

"Good evening," I greeted him.

"What the hell is this?" he bellowed, apparently addressing everyone but me.

Athena popped up out of nowhere. "This is Computer. She's been very useful in our operations."

"It's nice to meet you." I offered my hand. He looked at me and snarled.

"She's taken down several plots of Manta's and Deprave's the past few weeks alone," Athena reported. "And she monitors our missions, warning us to avoid any surprises."

Blue still looked at me disdainfully. "I don't like geeks, especially ones who think they're equal to people like us."

"I don't think I'm equal." I held back the grin. "You obviously have many traits I am lacking." I was not an asshole. I was not a bully. The number of similarities we shared was truly minimal.

Athena cast a sideways glance at me, fearing that Blue would catch on to my sarcasm. Luckily he didn't.

"You can help the team, but you're not one of us. You don't go public, and you get no costume. You're lucky we let you stick around." Blue must have been feeling generous. He turned his attention to the rest of the team. "Mind and I will be leaving next week on another publicity tour. I expect you losers to keep things together until I get back. Don't screw up. Don't say stupid stuff to the press. And keep the geek out of sight. Got it?"

Everyone agreed to do what Blue commanded.

"I'm out of here," Blue announced and he started out the door.

"Wait." I jumped up to follow him. Despite my earlier sarcasm, I didn't really want to leave it ugly between us.

Athena and the others signaled me to back off, but I followed anyway.

"Blue." He was just a few steps down the street from the door. He spun around in response.

"What do you want?" he asked.

"Listen, you didn't seem too happy about me being here, so I thought we could talk about it. Maybe we can work this out." I was really trying.

"Yeah?" He took a step forward. "How so?"

"Maybe I can buy us a couple of beers and we can hang out," I suggested.

"You want to buy me a drink." He laughed.

"Yeah." I shrugged. "Maybe if we get to know each other, it'll prevent any friction between us."

"You want friction, alright. I know you want to fuck me."

"Huh?"

"I'm sorry, but I don't fuck geeks. I get too many supermodels and hot groupies to make time for a loser like you."

I wanted to smack him, but this was a peace mission. "That's not what I meant. I really want to make peace with you, that's it. I don't understand why you hate me. I never did anything to you."

"I hate you because you are a loser. Bitches with no powers are only good for one thing, and you are not hot enough for that, so you are useless to me."

"Why do you believe that?" I just couldn't believe Blue Shift was that two-dimensional. "You save people, how can you hate them?"

Blue's expression went blank for a moment as he spoke. "It is my destiny to lead the other evolved beings to protect the human race. But they in turn must satisfy my needs and desires." It was as if he was spewing forth a pre-programmed response.

"You believe that? Really." I found this pretty creepy.

"I believe..." A look of confusion crossed his face for a moment, but before he could finish his thought, a limo pulled up and honked its horn. "I believe you are a loser geek." A driver popped out, opening the door for him. He climbed inside, giving me the finger as he entered.

"Well that was special," I muttered as he drove off. I went back inside and did my best to forget about Blue. The others were back to their jovial selves. We all agreed that the less he was around, the better off we all were.

Chapter Thirteen

"Better than a thousand useless words is one word that gives peace."
Buddha

"Morning, Lila!" I sat down in the garden of the nursing home. "Hi, Mo." Mo was another patient and a stoner like Lila. He was dying of lung cancer, but refused to stop smoking.

"Hey, old lady Slaughter," Mo teased. "Did you bring me my weed?"

"I am not a drug dealer, and stop calling me that." The last thing I needed was the nurses reporting me to the cops.

Mo and Lila were amused by my discomfort.

"The one thing about being close to death is that you really don't give a fuck." Mo coughed and laughed.

"Just stop," I shushed them. "I can't believe you outed me to your boyfriend here," I scolded Lila.

The two of them kept laughing. "Speaking of boyfriends, did you do what I asked?" Lila asked.

"No." I replied. "Not yet."

"Jesus Christ," Mo exclaimed. "Go get laid, woman. Do it for us old folks."

"No." I shook my head. "You two are out of control. Next you'll ask me to videotape it too."

"If you don't do it soon, it's going to do you." Lila smiled smugly, fighting to hold in the laughter.

"That's not funny," I objected. "It doesn't even make any sense."

"Sure it does," Mo explained. "If you don't make a choice, fate will make a choice for you."

"So what?" I asked. "I better get laid or fate will do me? You two are too wrapped up in physical desires."

"Oh, now she's talking like an old lady again," Mo complained.

"Am not!" I protested. "Hunger for things is the supreme disease."

Mo shook his head in disappointment. "They wasted the gift of youth on a goddamned monk."

"Actually, she would be a nun," Lila pointed out.

"Actually," I corrected them, "you would both be pissing me off. And I'm a drunk, get it right."

Lila smiled warmly. "Becca just needs to find her place again, right?"

"Yeah, yeah." Lila was right. "Shit, I don't even know who I am anymore. I don't know if I should be smacking people around or solving world hunger."

"So what are you doing about it?" Mo got right to the point.

"I started doing stuff to help people for a change." I tried to be as vague as possible.

"What kind of stuff?" Mo asked.

"You know random things, here and there."

"Like feeding the poor random or fighting evil random?" He seemed to already know the answer.

"Yes," I replied.

"You be careful," Mo warned. "No good deed goes unpunished."

"Yeah, like bringing you drugs is going to get me thrown in jail." I laughed.

"Just give me my reefer, woman." Mo was getting impatient.

"Do it before he tries to smoke you," Lila cautioned.

"Yeah, yeah, common Mo." I wheeled Lila to our spot with Mo slowly hobbling alongside. I gave them what they wanted and then spent an hour being lectured about the virtues of human relationships. I wondered if they could be right, maybe I was just lonely.

Chapter Fourteen

"All that we are is the result of what we have thought. The mind is everything. What we think, we become."
Buddha

It was a quiet night until Fuzzy decided to run amok. He was hitting dollar stores looking for what he referred to as the 'illustrious thing'. This posed a few problems. The first was we had to get to where he was quickly, and it was nearly impossible to predict his path. He was completely random in the locations he hit. He could be in a dollar store on a particular street and ignore the one two blocks away, instead heading across town hitting another shop and later returning to the one he missed. But it wasn't even that predicable, because he wasn't hitting all of the stores and even hit some twice. The next problem was crowd control. There was very little that freaked crowds out more than all of them losing the ability to maintain coherent thought for a short period of time, and then regain it spontaneously. People were panicking and getting hurt. Our main goal had to be, not capturing Fuzzy Logic, but keeping people calm until he found his thing and went away. Blue Shift didn't agree, thus creating our third problem, controlling him.

Athena told him her plan. We'd station someone in various sectors and they would respond to crime scenes after Fuzzy left. We would calm the people down and move onto the next crime scene. It was a bad idea to confront the guy because we had absolutely no idea how he would react and what could happen.

"It's a good plan," Athena asserted.

"It's a plan for pussies," Blue objected. "I thought you dykes at least had balls."

Athena stayed calm. "We don't want any bystanders to get hurt. We need to keep things calm."

"Fuck that!" Blue replied. "I'm taking this freak down."

"That isn't wise," I interjected. "We don't know what he will do if he's cornered. You could end up affected by his confusion and get hurt yourself."

Blue turned and glared at me with complete disdain. "Was that you speaking, Cunt-puter? I thought I made it clear. Only people who have superpowers get to make decisions on this team. You just keep your loser geek mouth shut and be glad we let you stay here."

"Don't talk to her like that," Athena objected. "Take it back."

"Fuck you, dyke." Blue Shift gave us the finger and stormed out in search of Fuzzy.

"Okay." I threw my arms up in frustration. "What now?"

Athena leaned against the counter and thought. "Okay, lead him away from Fuzzy."

"No, he'll know." I pondered the problem for a second. "Got it! I'll keep him two steps behind. I'll report locations we've already been to on the open channel. I'll send encoded messages on another channel with the legit info to the rest of the team.

He'll get to the crime scenes after Fuzzy has left and hit another one already. That way there is no chance of his running into the guy."

Athena let out a sigh of relief. "Good. That's why I'm glad that you're here. You see what I am up against?"

"Oh boy." I just shook my head.

Athena took off for the field. She passed word to every one of our updated plan. It didn't take long for everyone to get into position and report in on our encoded channel. As reports came in from varying sources, I directed individual team members to the crime scenes and they managed to resume order. People were no longer getting hurt. This was clearly a victory. That was until we discovered the fault in my logic.

"Got the little freak!" Blue shouted into the com. I had forgotten that Fuzzy was hitting some stores twice. He ran right into Blue Shift, and the destruction began.

"Athena! We have trouble." I hit her private channel so I wouldn't antagonize Blue into any further violence. "Blue bumped into Fuzzy. I think he's about to shoot up the place." As predicted, alarms started going off like crazy throughout a mile radius from the store. I lost contact with the entire block, because everything computerized was down. I couldn't get through to Blue Shift. Out of desperation, I tried calling the store. To my surprise, the line rang. Then someone picked up.

"Ah, put-put the dark angel," the voice greeted me. "Don't let the pain break you. Did you see inside? Did you see? Did you see? Did you see?"

It continued on, echoing in my head until I blacked out. I regained consciousness only moments later. I reported in.

"Computer! Computer, where are you?" Athena sounded alarmed.

"I'm here. Got hit with confusion." I explained. "He got me through the phone."

"You okay?"

"Yeah, yeah," I assured her. "I was trying to get hold of Blue by calling the store and I got a special surprise." I laughed and clutch my throbbing head.

"Fuzzy's gone. He got his thing. Mighty says it was some weird doll-headed whistle thing. Who the hell knows…?"

"So we're okay then?" I asked hopefully.

"No," Athena replied dryly. "I'll explain when I get back."

The team returned, looking beaten. Mighty moped and sat next to me. He looked like he was about to cry.

"You look like your dog died," I observed. "Did something happen to Blue?"

"She was four years old." Mighty started to sob. I stopped what I was doing and rubbed his back as he cried. Athena stepped up looking irritated.

"I'm going to kill him." Fury rang through her voice. "The bastard dropped a building on a four-year-old. He couldn't just let it go." She sat on the other side of the table. "Fuzzy was done. He had the thing and was leaving. Blue just started shooting. He destroyed two buildings and a little girl."

I continued to comfort Mighty. "She was only four," he repeated.

"He saw it," Athena explained. "He got there as it happened."

"News," I suggested.

"Yeah." Athena turned on the news and the whole sorry scene splashed across the screen. Firefighters raced to put out the resulting fire from the incident. People were crying, screaming, and yelling. The mother of the four-year-old girl howled in agony as they carted off her child's lifeless body. Athena turned up the volume.

"Witnesses were unable to provide any information about what happened tonight. According to reports, the stores, all of them discount dollar stores, were attacked by Gloom, a well-known and dangerous villain. Why he attacked is unknown, but we do know that due to his vicious attack, a four-year-old lost her life. If you're just reporting in, it appears that seventeen discount stores were viciously attacked by Gloom, killing a four-year-old girl."

A picture of the girl appeared on the screen. She was a tiny dark-haired child, with huge brown eyes. Her eyes tore through me.

"Initial reports..." Athena shut the TV off.

I wasn't expecting the flashback that hit me. I jumped up and ran for the bathroom. Memories rushed through my head. Visions of blood, screams of despair, and the smell of death assaulted me in this waking nightmare.

I locked myself in a stall and felt the images tear through me. I felt the power of life and death as I killed the security forces of a ruthless dictator. I saw the fear in his eyes when he realized nobody would save him. I looked him in the eyes and laughed as I shredded him into pieces. I remembered the thrill of taking out an entire embassy full of people. Good, bad, young, old, it didn't matter. I took them all and felt elation as I did. I remembered killing soldiers and freedom fighters and drug lords and bystanders. The memories were graphic, overpowering and left me shaken.

After I vomited everything I ate, and apparently everything I would eat in the future, I composed myself and re-joined the team. I must have looked like hell.

"You okay?" Mighty asked.

"Yeah. It was just from the confusion thing," I lied. I was still trembling. Athena and I exchanged glances. For a split second, it felt like she was reading me.

"Well I wouldn't blame you if it was from this bullshit," Acid replied disdainfully. "This makes me sick too. Why is Blue saying it was Gloom?"

I still felt nauseous. "No clue. Does anything Blue does make sense? Maybe he figured nobody would believe Fuzzy Logic could do that kind of damage. He had to blame someone. Crap, my head hurts."

"Has anyone seen Mind?" DJ appeared behind me.

Athena rolled her eyes. "You know he's with his boy."

"So what do we do now?" DJ asked.

"Nothing," I said. "I'm going to do some minor damage control, but Blue made sure his ass wouldn't be held accountable."

"She's right." Athena backed me up. "The best we can do is send some flowers and support the family of that child."

Everyone agreed and spent the night consoling each other over the most fucked-up mission in team history. We all reminded ourselves that we didn't mess up. One by one, people went home, until it was just me and Athena.

"So, girl, what damage control?"

I smiled. I both loved and hated the fact that Athena had a mind like a steel trap. "I'm going to whisper in the ear of someone about sending our apologies about something."

"Is that wise?" she asked.

"Very," I replied. "We don't need a war declared on us over this bullshit. Maybe I can nip it in the bud and save us some grief."

Athena shook her head in agreement. "Okay. You do it. Just let me know how it goes. And I'm sure you know that we keep this between us."

"No problem." I got up and started to walk out, but something was still nagging at me. "Athena?"

"What?"

"I'm just curious. What happened to Blue that made him such an ass?" I figured that nobody was that bad without a catalyst.

Athena looked around nervously and dropped her voice low. "We don't talk about that."

"So he wasn't always a dickhead?" I asked.

"Well, yeah," Athena replied. "He was, but compared to now, he used to be a saint."

"So what happened?"

"Something bad." Athena motioned me to sit down next to her. I did.

"You see," she continued. "Before there really was a team, back in the beginning, the bad guys were pretty informal too. This happened before Deprave was in charge, back when Gloom was still single and his lair was a swinging bachelor pad. The only people who knew each other on our side were me, Mind and Blue. One day, Blue heard that Gloom was getting ready to start some kind of consortium of bad guys. Blue figured if we moved on them then fast, we would fracture them before they could be a cohesive group. Mind and I told him it was a bad idea because we had no idea what their numbers were and we were only three people. Blue didn't like that, so without telling us, he decided to take on the mission alone."

"Yeah, and then what?"

"Then what?" Athena just laughed. "What do you think happened? He got captured. He got into Gloom's lair and found him and the soon-to-be Deprave drinking beer and on video conference with Pain, Conduit, Dead Beat, and a few others negotiating a pact. Before Blue had a chance, Gloom's goons took him down."

"What happened next?"

"Well, this is where people's stories start to conflict." Athena dropped her voice to a low whisper. "Pain wanted Blue killed, but Deprave suggested it would be better to humiliate him and send him back as an example to their other enemies. Some people say that Blue was tortured, sodomized and force to admit his incompetence on tape; others claim they put him on a machine that regenerates body tissues and cut off various body parts, grew them back and repeated it over and over."

"Which was it?" I asked.

Athena shook her head. "None of that. I never saw the real tape, but I was there when Mind saw it and destroyed it. I saw the look on his face, and I heard some of the audio."

"Well?"

"Deprave and his buddies did make him humiliate himself on tape. They had him do crap like wear his underwear on his head; they made him dance wearing nothing but shaving cream; they made him be their dog, which included making him eat dog food and be walked on a leash. They kept him for over a week and made him do everything they could come up with to make him look like the biggest loser there is. The worst part was when they made him admit that he had no real powers. They made him call himself 'Static Boy' and admit the only thing that gives him powers is the bracers he wears to focus his static energy. They also got him to confess that he didn't take Renox for any medical condition. He took it just to get powers. All of it was filmed, and most of the ideas came from Deprave. When they finished, they duct taped the videos to Blue's naked body and dumped him off on the side of a highway. Blue was never the same after that. And that's what earned Deprave his name and status."

"That's why Blue has been gunning for Deprave all this time?" It started making some sense to me. I found it somewhat funny, but did my best to suppress my amusement.

"Wouldn't you do the same?" Athena asked.

"I don't know. I wouldn't be that much of a jerk in the first place." I almost felt sorry for Blue, but not quite. I looked at my watch and saw the time. "I don't mean to gossip and run, but I need to get home before sunrise. I don't want to melt."

Athena smiled and slapped me on the back. "Get some rest. We need you functional."

I packed up my crap, worked out and did some research.

Chapter Fifteen

"More than those who hate you, more than all your enemies, an undisciplined mind does greater harm."
Buddha

I thought about what Athena said and considered what Blue went through. I tried to conjure up some sympathy for Blue, but found it tough. That was until I found articles on Blue's early days.

According to the press, Blue Shift was a saint. He always did the right thing for the right reasons. In fact, the type of personality he was attributed with was almost identical to Mighty's. Blue saved a lot of people. He helped charities, and schools, and civic groups. There was little in the way of good that Blue hadn't done. Then he started the team.

The press still spoke of him favorably, but the good deeds slowed to a halt and suddenly he was just the PR man for Team Power. What made it even creepier was that his downslide not only coincided with the team's initial beginnings, but it also seemed to be concurrent with Blue meeting Athena. Besides Athena, all the original team members already knew each other. Athena was the wild card. Not only did she seem to be the catalyst of the problem, but she was a mystery herself. I looked all over; she simply did not exist.

There were some places I could have checked, which I guessed would have her data stashed. But those networks were well secured, and I didn't want to risk detection. I figured she would slip up and give me something to go on soon enough. She was more than just some retired government field operative. There was something much more disturbing about her. I would find out in time.

The other thing that bothered me about Athena's story was not what she said about Blue, but her casual mention of Pain being somehow involved. I wondered why Pain would be mixed up with Deprave at all. It made no sense. Pain was a loner, why would Athena tell me something so unbelievable?

I dug through all the history I could find. Athena wasn't completely off-base. Pain had at one point been in contact with the others, but it was extremely short-lived. He was originally going to be the great leader of the mighty force of evil that was forming. He had plans, dreams, and ambitions. But something happened, something without explanation. He simply gave up.

I searched the facts and could find nothing. Pain was very competent. All his plots were well thought out and very successful. What could make the man simply give up?

After a couple of brief months, he threw in the towel leaving Deprave to take the reins of leadership. Many people believed this was better for the world, because as bad as Deprave was, Pain was many times worse.

No matter how many times I went over it, it still left me wondering. Why did the bastard quit? Why?

I also did some digging into Deprave, too. For all his reputed evil-doing, I could find nothing substantial. He stole, he plotted, he postured, but I saw no evidence of wanton destruction, or murder. I tracked his money trail. It was so convoluted that I almost lost it a handful of times. I almost wet myself laughing when I discovered that most of his funds were extracted from the bank accounts of not only terrorist organizations, but of other supervillains, including Pain himself. I didn't know what his game was, but it wasn't the evil Athena purported it to be. I was having trouble understanding how he was a supervillain at all. I dug into the other villains too. Gloom and Alicia were both diehard thieves, but they never killed anyone. Fuzzy Logic was just crazy. Manta, yes, he was bad. But he was also fairly inept and easy to stop. I wondered why nobody had thrown him in prison yet. He wasn't that elusive, or even the slightest bit powerful. His army of minions was just a bunch of thugs. Any trained military unit could take them out.

The more I read, the more I realized that Athena's story was highly unlikely.

I finally went to bed late. I slept like a rock, which was rare. When I woke up in the morning, I noticed my closet door was wide open. I knew it was closed before I went to sleep. There was also evidence of someone moving around the house. Things were moved around; someone had made themselves at home while I slept.

I installed a new security system that day.

96

Chapter Sixteen

"When a wise man is advised of his errors, he will reflect on and improve his conduct. When his misconduct is pointed out, a foolish man will not only disregard the advice but rather repeat the same error."
Buddha

Guess who! My message filled the main plasma screen of the lair's laboratory.

"You." Deprave sneered. "You are on my list."

Doesn't it hurt to speak like that? I asked. *It must tear the hell out of your throat to maintain that grating voice. Do you use some kind of lozenge to help with the pain? Maybe some tequila.*

"Does it hurt to keep your brain in your ass?" he countered. "Aren't you afraid you will shit them out every time you use the toilet?"

Still pissed about me deleting all your porn? Maybe now you have enough space on your hard drive to use the supercomputer for science instead of self-gratification. I didn't really delete his files. I just moved them to another directory and hid them. I should have deleted it, there was some nasty stuff in there, but I wasn't that mean.

"I will find you and you will suffer." He pointed at the camera trying to look menacing with that baby face of his. I would never get used to supervillains who looked like they stepped out of *Teen People* magazine.

Oh okay. I'm afraid, I mocked him. *You know, you don't need porn to beat off. You could just use your imagination.*

"I'm imagining that I am strangling you right now." He was really unhappy.

I sighed, though he couldn't hear me. *Okay. Here's your porn back. But don't blame me if you grow hair on your palms. I never deleted it, I just hid it. Geez, what the hell do you need with three and a half petabytes of porn anyway? Petabytes, that's three thousand, five hundred terabytes. I mean how much do you whack off in a day anyway? By all accounts, your genitals should be rubbed raw.*

He typed on his keyboard, apparently confirming the return of his smut, and smiled. "That's what lubricant is for, Computer. I thought you knew everything."

You must have industrial-sized drums in that place. You know, you could get a real person to get off with. It's not like you are nasty looking or anything. You wouldn't even have to pay…

"Is there anything else, Computer?" Deprave cut me off abruptly. "Or are you looking for a new line of work?"

That one stung. He was a sharp one. *You wish that's why I was here.* It was a lame reply, but he did slam me down good with the last comment. *But before we get on with tonight's critique of your ill-conceived plans, I have a serious issue to not discuss.*

"Your *not* typos are pathetic and indicate your lack of intelligence," Deprave attempted to snipe.

No, I corrected him. *We are not going to discuss something. The conversation will never have happened. Understand?*

"I'm intrigued," he confessed. "Continue."

The other night something very bad happened. Somebody was negligent and acted out with a blatant disregard to public safety. Do you follow? I am going to erase what I don't say as I don't say it.

"Yes," Deprave replied.

I erased my paragraph.

"I know the event you are not speaking of."

I was glad he was at least playing along. *Okay, here is a message. I never said it. Nobody did. It will be erased as soon as you read it.*

The team is aware of what really happened. We did not partake in any of the events that led up to the tragedy, nor were we involved in the disinformation campaign. We had been trying to minimize the panic resulting from events beyond our control when a certain individual acted on his own accord. When the disinformation was announced through the press, the team was as shocked as the other parties involved must be. We are aware that we have an ongoing situation on our hands. We voluntarily accept that burden in the interest of protecting the public good. Certain elements must be closely monitored to minimize the threat. We understand if any backlash is directed our way. We still wanted to send our apologies for the outrageous accusations which resulted from that individual's actions. Will you relay our message?

"Yes, I will pass on the message to Gloom," Deprave agreed.

I cleared the screen. *Thank you. That conversation never happened. Now onto your pathetic plans for the...* I read through his plan. *...theft of the crowned jewels? Oh God, you have got to be kidding me. How completely played out. The name and the costume are bad enough, but the crowned jewels?*

Deprave sighed and threw his head back. "I left that for you last week. It was supposed to divert you from my real plan, which I may add was a complete success."

Oooh... My interest was piqued. *What you pull off?*

"I stole the moon." Deprave proudly announced.

You what? This couldn't be real.

"Why must I repeat myself? I stole the moon."

I heard what you said, but how? How did you even reach it?

Deprave grinned and turned on a monitor across the room. "Can you see that?"

I adjusted one of his security cameras to point toward the screen. *Yup.*

He hit a key and the screen displayed an animated depiction of his plan.

"I shot several hundred robots with EM proof guidance systems up. Half didn't make it, but those that did, well, they're there. They have built-in force field generators. I got them onto the moon slowly over several months, and then carefully positioned them into equidistant points from each other. Last week I flipped them on and enveloped the entire surface of the moon with a force field that only I have access to. So I, in effect, now own the moon."

Wow. I was genuinely impressed. So what are the effects of this force field on the moon's gravity? What about the asteroid field? Will it impact the moon's orbit of Earth or the Earth's orbit of the sun? How high above the surface is the field? Did you alert the space agencies so nobody tries to land and gets killed? Are you going to charge a toll and rent for anyone who wants access?

Deprave was basking in his success and my questions seemed to stroke his ego even more. "My dear Computer, I took all of that into consideration. The force field is calibrated so it does not impact the gravity of the moon nor the Earth or the asteroid belt. It is a mile above the surface. And I relayed word to the space agencies days ago. Access to the moon will cost a million dollars a day; however, I am willing to negotiate reasonable yearly leasing terms. That is if they really care. They do seem to be preoccupied with other concerns. However, I'm counting on this being a matter of pride."

I was blown away. I was glad he couldn't see my facial expression or hear my laughter. I decided not to ruin his day. *I acknowledge your success and admit to being very impressed.*

"Really?" Deprave seemed surprised by my admission.

Why should I lie? It was a well-conceived plan, carefully executed and successful. Nobody got hurt, nobody suffered any loss, and maybe you will piss off the nations of the world enough that they will want to populate the moon just to spite you. It's possible that you will actually inspire them to get off their asses and do something to get beyond this asteroid prison; hence the potential for advancing science, and bettering mankind. And I am glad you are using your computer for something more than porno. I applaud you.

"Thank you." His tone was genuine. "That means a great deal to me."

No problem, but I gotta go. I had a long day. I already pissed off Manta today. He thought he was building a rail gun, but it looked more like a tinker toy with a few pieces missing. I think he's miffed 'cause I exploded it.

"Well have a good night." Deprave waved goodnight.

Oh, yeah. I almost forgot. I found your cell number. I hope you don't mind if I text you when I'm bored.

I disconnected before he could respond. Just for emphasis, I text messaged *Night, night* to his cell. I set up the text messaging engine to relay any responses to my phone. He wouldn't be able to initiate a text conversation with me, but he would be able to reply if he wanted. I knew it was silly, but I liked having the ability to screw with him at will. Tonight he would stew about the cell phone for a while. It wasn't enough to ruin his moment of glory, but it would remind him that I could slap him down.

I finished my bedtime ritual of setting my devices to charge, and getting myself showered and ready to crash. I crawled under the sheets and drifted off to sleep.

I awoke in the middle of the night. The power had gone off and everything was completely dark and still. I went to the kitchen to get a glass of juice, but I found myself unable to get out of my bedroom door. Each time I walked out, I was back inside where I started.

I figured that I must be dreaming, so I started to climb back into bed. Out of the corner of my eye, I caught a light. It was coming from my desk, light leaked out from my closed laptop. I sat at my desk, and opened the computer. Multicolored light filled the room, blinding me. I felt gust of wind and the light faded. Now, I was standing on the moon.

In the back of my mind, I knew this couldn't be. I was only wearing a white bathrobe and slippers, yet I was breathing. I saw the Earth serenely floating in space; its beautiful blue-green glow sparkled against the blackness of space.

I looked down and saw a set of footprints leading from my position. I followed them until I reached a desk and chair with a solitary computer station on it. Behind it, the perfect view of the Earth remained. I sat at the chair and looked at the screen. It was blank save a single word: *Doomsday*.

I tried to erase the word by backspacing on the keyboard, but it wouldn't disappear. Before me, the Earth stopped spinning and simply disintegrated. I reached out toward it screaming.

From behind me, a voice whispered in my ear. It took a moment to recognize the voice and the words. "Time to wake up," Deprave said.

I awoke still screaming. This time I wasn't vomiting, which was an improvement. As I caught my breath and reached for the bottle, I noticed the message indicator flashing on my phone.

Deprave replied to my earlier message. *Sleep well, Computer. The Space Tether does exist.*

I went back to sleep, sober.

The next day I found my white silk gi folded on top of my dresser. I ran and reran diagnostics on the alarm system. Just to be sure, I replaced all the sensors. Things were getting too weird.

Chapter Seventeen

"Our life is shaped by our mind; we become what we think. Suffering follows an evil thought as the wheels of a cart follow the oxen that draws it.

"Our life is shaped by our mind; we become what we think. Joy follows a pure thought like a shadow that never leaves."
Buddha

The fallout from Blue Shift's disaster was minimal. Life went on for him like nothing had ever happened. He continued to tour and espouse upon his great deeds and his campaign to do good. In every interview he made a point to admonish Gloom for his evil murderous rampage and the life of that poor little girl. I wished Gloom would just take him out. I had no guilt about feeling that way either.

With Blue on tour, things ran smoothly. We regained that groove we had, and it was even better. When he was around, Mind Master would even participate in our operations. He would avoid me in person, claiming I was unholy. I never disputed his accusations which made him even more uncomfortable. It was fine, because on missions, he would coordinate with me without any issues. I soon realized Mind was only an asshole when Blue was around. There was hope for Mind after all. He really demonstrated teamwork and cooperation. He was a genuine asset to the team.

The team was forming a cohesive bond too. Mind was still technically Blue's boy and DJ and Acid still kept their emotional distances, but we had something stronger now than existed when I first joined the team. I spent a lot of my off time with Athena and Mighty. I still didn't trust Athena, but there was something comforting about being near her. That alone made my suspicions of her worsen. However, I did find myself getting out more. The three of us would see movies, hit an occasional club, and do the things normal people do. We didn't talk business when we were out, and we never pushed each other to divulge any personal information. We just enjoyed each other's company and made the best of the time we shared.

My main function still remained coordination of the troops and monitoring Deprave. I did get a rash of crap over the moon incident. He managed to hold onto the moon and nobody could do anything about it. But as I predicted, there now was a mad dash of the world's nations to see who could get to the moon first and neutralize Deprave's force field. Every so often when Athena would remember, she would admonish me about how we lost the moon and it was my fault.

Otherwise, life was good. My drinking was almost under control. I stuck to my diet and exercise regimen and felt better than I had in years. Some days I almost believed the Renox had cured me, and nearly forgot my past. I was sure this was due to my feeling of belonging to the group and this newfound purpose in my life. That was fine with me; as long as I didn't have to suffer anymore flashbacks, or blackouts, I didn't care if it was all in my head or coming from a pill.

It was another Friday night, which was my favorite time to trash a certain supervillain's mainframe. I did most of my Deprave attacks at night from my house. That way, I could relax, and enjoy the challenge.

I logged in easily, as usual. It looked like it was going to be a light night. Deprave had done almost no new work this week and what he had was extremely sloppy. First I found some plans for some corny looking laser weapon. *Looks like a six-year-old designed this,* I typed in red font across the top of the document, and then graded it with an 'F'.

The next plan was for some Death Star wannabe space platform of doom that lobbed flaming plasma at unsuspecting nations. It was completely independent of any reality I knew of. There was no accounting for the asteroid belt, or power concerns. It was like he didn't even try to use any logic. My only comment was, *Way to go, Darth Dumbass.* I was starting to get concerned that he had another plan in the moon-stealing range and this was all just a diversion.

The next candidate was some half-assed plans to nuke the remaining bits of southeast Asia. Just the idea of him launching a nuclear strike at all seemed out of character, and why southeast Asia of all places? There really wasn't much of Asia left. Just as I got halfway through the first paragraph, Deprave detected my intrusion. I opened the lab cam to see him standing at his control console. He looked off. Something was askew.

Have that, you! My trademarked battle cry appeared across the largest of Deprave's plasma screens. *You have failed. Your plans are lame and retarded, like yourself.*

Deprave definitely wasn't looking quite right. In fact, there was an uncharacteristic pause. Instead of firing back with the usually witty repartee, he just stared at the ground and moped. "Take it back," he demanded.

Your failure is blaringly obvious. I will not take it back. Bwa-ha-ha. I also laughed out loud, even though he couldn't hear me. I didn't even stop to consider why he was acting so strange. *I mock your superior intellect.* As far as I saw it, there was always room for a Star Trek quote.

"Take it back, you fucking asshole!" he screamed and threw a beaker at the screen.

Whoa. Are you trashed or something? I'm supposed to be the only drunk here. On closer inspection, he was unshaven and disheveled. He was practically stumbling around. *Calm yourself, man. Did you get a hold of a bad batch of crack or something? You should know better than to buy that cheap street shit.* I really thought I was being funny. I meant to lighten the mood. I failed.

He screamed and started trashing the laboratory. "You piece of shit! I'll fucking kill you."

Huh... I couldn't think of anything else to type in. It didn't matter, because before I realized what exactly was happening, the cameras went dead and my link was broken. He had taken the whole lair completely off the grid. "What the fuck just happened?" I wondered.

This was not good. I opened the messaging client and texted his cell. *Okay, what was that?*

After waiting ten minutes, I knew I was not going to get a response.

I stared blankly at the screen for the next half an hour. I had no idea what just happened. What happened today that was different? After a while, I surfed the net, but found myself getting bored. Bored was bad. Bored and feeling rejected was even worse. I felt so ridiculous feeling rejected by my sworn enemy. The whole enemy thing should have been a clue that I should not invest any feelings into it. The more I tried to convince myself to feel otherwise, the more I just kept feeling crappier and crappier. I grabbed my stuff and went down to the coffee shop.

I grabbed a booth and set up my personal area network. I had some coffee, and then I found the flask in my jacket. I poured whatever it was into my coffee and chugged it. I grabbed another coffee and repeated the process. It was time to say good-bye to sobriety again.

I checked my normal access points, but Deprave was completely down. He had no outside links at all. I thought briefly about hacking him wirelessly, maybe through his satellite TV, but it felt like too much effort. I just wanted to go back home and crawl into bed. I laid my head down on the table and felt failure and defeat wash over me with its cold chill.

"What the hell is wrong with you?" I looked up to see Athena towering over me. "Since when do you drink on duty?" She pointed at the flask which I was failing to conceal.

I shrugged. "It doesn't matter anyway."

"Wow, you sound great." Athena sat down across from me. "What happened, boyfriend trouble?"

"Nothing," I lied.

"Mmm-hmm." Athena rolled her eyes.

"No really." What was I going to say? "I think my arch nemesis just dumped me." I realized how ludicrous that had to sound.

"Oh geez." Athena laughed and then realized what I said. "Wait, what happened?"

I threw my head back in frustration. "I dunno. I was mocking him like normal and he freaked out. I think I really pissed him off."

"You're supposed to piss him off. He's your sworn enemy. That's what we do. We stop them from hurting anyone, stealing anything or doing anything else illegal. There's not supposed to be any emotional drama involved in this." Athena looked concerned. She leaned in close. "Exactly what kind of relationship do you have with this guy?"

"I dunno. It's like a friendly chess game." I began to wonder if it wasn't more than that. "He thinks up plots and I poke holes in them before he can even use them. We have our witty banter through my remote connections. Most of his inventions never even make it out of his lab, and the ones that do usually explode in unpopulated areas. It's been fun up till now. But today he freaked out."

"Fun." Athena leaned back into her seat looking disgusted. "That's some of the strangest shit I have ever heard. You need to get it together, especially before he finds out. Blue is still sore that you get to fight the big bad guy, when in his opinion, you have no real powers."

"He's not going to find out crap. You forget, I am below the radar. Mostly." I caught myself pouting but found myself unable to stop. "God, I can't believe I feel like this."

"He's not your boyfriend. Get over it. Go out and have fun. Stop moping over a loser you are trying to put in jail. It's bad enough you let him steal the moon."

"He snuck the moon by me. Not my fault." I still was replaying the whole thing in my head. "I just don't get it, that's all."

"Maybe he's just on the rag," Athena suggested. "He'll get over it, and you get a few days off of crime fighting. Then you catch the bastard and put him in jail and stop playing this weird mind game."

"I just don't think it's going to be the same anymore anyway."

"Good. You'll get over it." Athena got out of the booth. "I gotta go out on patrol. I'll call you if I need anything. Stop with the drinking. It's unbecoming of you."

Athena zipped out her jacket and headed out. I ran diagnostics on the network and browsed the web while I waited.

I checked my email. Spam.

I checked my buddy lists. There was nobody I felt like chatting with.

I still wasn't in the mood for online gaming.

Then an alarm went off. I contacted Athena. "We have a situation."

"What do you have?" She asked.

"It looks like Fuzzy Logic is back in town. Should I contact the group?"

"No, I got this one," she replied. "Just keep the channels clear and make sure nobody surprises me." The comm went silent.

I tracked down where he was. It was a lamp factory of all things. I decided to get into the security system to see what he was up to. My first attempt to gain access didn't work. Neither did the second. The third try did it, but I was still ill at ease. A lamp factory should not be this hard to gain access to.

I panned the security cameras until I spotted him. He spun around and looked directly into the camera. I felt my brain blow a gasket when I saw his face; it was Bianchi, the creator of the Space Tether.

"Dark angel of God," he said. "It's almost finished." He reached up and touched the side of the camera.

I couldn't respond. I had no way of communicating. There were so many questions I wanted to ask. Somehow he seemed to be aware that not only was I there, but what I wanted to know.

"Don't make my mistake," he implored. "Don't look into God's eye and wave a stick." He turned in response to something he saw. "The Devil!" He ducked out of view and I heard him shouting. There was silence for a while, until I was able to find him on another security camera.

"There you are, Angel," he whispered as he approached the camera. "The road to hell is paved with good intentions. The way to madness is through a hole in your pockets." The sound of gunshots echoed through the air. He ducked out of sight again. Was Athena shooting at him?

I tried to raise Athena to no avail. I was unable to find Bianchi anymore either. Just when I thought I caught a glimpse of something, the cameras went dead. Then a loud explosion echoed through the night.

"Computer," Athena called, coughing.

"Here," I replied.

"Fuzzy blew up the factory on 8th," she reported.

"Are you okay?"

"Yeah," she replied. "Just bruised."

"Did he get away?"

"Unfortunately." She coughed again. "We'll get him next time."

Something told me that we weren't going to hear from him any time soon. Somehow he had passed on his message. I just had to figure out what it meant.

Chapter Eighteen

"There is no fire like passion, there is no shark like hatred, there is no snare like folly, there is no torrent like greed."
Buddha

After the evening's fun, I wanted to lock myself in my house. I wanted to stay home for the whole weekend, and intoxicate myself into another reality. But I found myself with a renewed reserve of willpower. I went into work despite myself, to get my mind off the psychodrama and the interpersonal bullshit. I remembered why I used to avoid emotional connections. They were bad for me.

I tried to do some useful work, but it seemed that Marissa was more efficient than I had ever been. I looked for something to keep me busy. Before I could get on to the second level of the web game 'Kill the Politician', Marissa called.

"You may want to see this," she said with excitement in her voice.

"What is *this*?" I asked.

"The report from the Adams Zachary foundation."

"Okay…"

"They started a project to address the problem of space travel and the asteroid belt."

"Really?" I was glad to hear somebody was finally doing something.

"Yeah, they're hiring scientists like mad. I hear they pay well too."

"How much of our staff are we losing?"

"None yet," Marissa said. "Most of our staff is more of the social sciences type anyway."

"Well I guess that's good news all around. So I guess there's nothing for me to do here. You have it under control."

"Go do something fun. Take some time off."

"Okay." I didn't have the heart to tell her that I had nothing better to do. I was feeling obsolete and unneeded. But she did have it under control. "I'm out of here."

I grabbed my jacket and bag and headed back home.

***

The news pages were, as always, full of anything but useful information. I scrolled through meaningless gossip and fluff, gleaning nothing but a headache. I hit the video feeds and watched some horrible but riveting daytime TV. A random talk show was on the topic, 'My friend cheated to be beautiful.' The audience was berating this woman on stage.

"You're only pretty, because you took Renox," a woman from the audience spoke into a mic, cheered on by the rest of the crowd. "You cheated."

"No," the woman pleaded. "I took the medicine because I was sick."

The audience continued to boo the woman to the point that they were too loud for her to speak over. Finally the hostess of the show quieted the crowd, and addressed her guest, "Please, Stephanie, tell the audience why you took the drug?"

Tears rolled down the woman's face as she spoke. The embarrassment and humiliation she was feeling could not be concealed. "I-I was severely autistic."

The crowd fell silent. The hostess continued, "Stephanie, I know this must be painful for you, but can you tell the audience what it was like to go from being severely developmentally disabled to the beautiful intelligent young woman you are today?"

Stephanie started to speak, but I couldn't take it. I shut off the TV, feeling a pang of guilt inside. I realized how badly I had stepped over the line. Everyone took Renox for a reason. Everyone had been defective and held that memory inside. I called Deprave a retard, and that must have really struck a nerve. Bad guy or not, nobody deserved to feel that way.

I opened the messaging engine again and typed furiously. I put it on the line, knowing it was not the brightest idea in the world.

I'm sorry. I think I know why I pissed you off. Here's one of my secrets that nobody else knows, not even my team. I took the drug to cure my severe mental illness. It didn't work, so I am still broken. That means you're one up on me, because whatever was wrong with you is fixed.

I hit send and waited.

Ten minutes later, my alarm went off alerting me that he was back online.

A new document appeared among his latest directory of diabolical plans. It was labeled 'Sinister plot number 572'. The contents simply read:

Last week was the anniversary.

I hit the cams and found him alone in his room. I opened a window on the plasma. *I am really sorry. I wasn't thinking,* I typed.

"I know," he said. "So you're really still damaged?"

Yeah, I responded. *I'm psycho, and I spent all weekend in bed feeling miserable.*

Deprave arched an eyebrow. "I have that profound of an effect on your life?"

Bite me. I felt naked. I wanted to tell him what really knocked me off track, but it didn't feel safe.

"It's okay," Deprave assured me. "I broke the lab when you called me a retard. It's going to take weeks to fix."

Were you really that bad?

Deprave shook his head. "Worse. I was…" His voice cracked. "I am still ashamed of what I was."

You shouldn't be. Whatever you were before, you are awesome now. I was a little over the line encouraging a supervillain like that, but I only said what I felt. I realized at that point, I truly liked him. I found him intriguing, and I enjoyed our interactions. The fact I felt anything positive was odd to begin with, but to feel a real connection with another person was downright frightening. Athena was right, I was not thinking clearly.

Deprave's demeanor seemed to lighten the moment I made the comment. He looked directly into the camera. "Computer. Now that I know for sure that you are a real person and not an AI or some asshole, can I ask you a question?"

Go for it. I wondered if I would regret this.

"Are you male or female?" He grinned.

Are you straight or gay? I felt satisfied in my slightly witty and somewhat noncommittal response.

He was still grinning. My response appeared to have amused him. "My default is straight, but I have been known to make exceptions."

Well then it makes no difference. I was starting to feel much better. I wondered what was in my head that I felt compelled to talk to this guy. I couldn't wrap my head around the fact that his happiness directly impacted mine. Maybe I did need to see a shrink.

"I want to know who to imagine I'm bending over and fucking while I beat off." The grin still hadn't left his face.

I wasn't sure how to take the last remark. Was it an insult or was he flirting? I wondered if all of these interactions were actually something else. Was I actually having feelings about this guy? I thought I was about to blow a gasket. Yet I just kept typing. *You have it backwards. You'd be the one bent over your control console.*

"So you are male," he replied smugly.

I never said that. They do sell attachments.

He paused. Maybe he had blown a gasket. It would only be fair. Sadly, I wasn't that fortunate. "Yes that they do. In either case, I bet it would feel really good."

I was feeling somewhat disturbed, and strangely aroused. It had been an extremely long time since I even considered my sexuality, and now I was struggling to keep it in check. I was convinced that the drugs had destroyed the tiny remnants of sanity I had previously possessed. *Of course it would. I am superior in all things.*

In that moment everything changed, my universe took a one-eighty. Before I could blink, comment or disconnect, Deprave started getting undressed, and I found myself unable to look away.

"Talk dirty to me, Computer." He pulled off his shirt and kicked off his shoes.

Wow. I typed. I was still unable to turn away. I was affixed to the screen. *You're seriously hot.* My wit was gone, shot completely out the window. I knew I was about to do something extremely stupid.

Deprave pulled off his socks and started opening his fly. "Is that all you've got? I thought you were superior in all things." Off went his pants and all he was left wearing was a smile and an erection.

I tried to look away. I really did. I reached for the off switch, but could not find the will to push it. This was compelling, like looking at a train wreck, only good. He was so goddamned perfect. All of his parts flowed smoothly into each other like someone sculpted the perfect human form and brought it to life. There were no scars, no flaws. Everything was in precise proportion. He had to work out, a lot. *I was wrong. You have the superior body. God, I bet you taste good.* My mind filled with lecherous thoughts. My breathing was heavy, and I was feeling warm. The last time I felt anything like this was… I cringed, but instead of getting ill, I let myself go. *Show me your ass.* My fingers were typing all my wicked dirty thoughts.

He spun around; his head crooked facing the screen. "What do you think? Do you need me to pull my ass cheeks apart?"

No that's just fine, I replied. *I'm just enjoying the view.* My heart pounded. This was bad, very bad, but I didn't care.

"Let me give you something better to look at." He spun around and sat on the bed and started to stroke himself. "I'm imagining you bending me over the lab console. Tell me what you would do to me!"

I was sweating and shaking. *I'd talk dirty to you as I rammed your ass.* I surprised myself with the violent imagery, but it made me feel even hotter.

"Mmm, talk dirty to me," he continued.

I'd do better than that. I let my twisted supergenius intellect take over. *I would change the internal energy of your closed thermodynamic system.*

"Oh God!" he moaned. "Keep talking."

That's right. I'll make your body heat equal to the sum of the amount of heat energy supplied to the system and the work done on it.

"Oh yeah, Computer, make me scream, tell me the rules."

Our total entropy of our thermodynamic system will increase over time, approaching a maximum value.

"*Oh God!* I'm about to explode!"

I almost had no response for that. Almost. *Let me feel your diathermic system.*

"Oh, tap my thermal potential…" He let out a moan, and fell back onto the bed. "Oh God yes." Then he screamed something in what sounded like Thai and ejaculated.

I watched in complete shock. Did I do that? I wasn't even there. *I never saw anything that hot in my entire life.*

"Get a cam," he demanded. "I want to see you."

I can't. Nobody knows what I look like.

"Damn it. I will have you."

That's when my finger hit the off button. I slammed my laptop closed, symbolically shutting him out. I couldn't give him a cam, but I couldn't stop thinking about what I just saw.

My panic was interrupted by the phone. It was Mighty. "Yeah," I answered.

"Um...Computer?"

"Yeah what?" I knew I was being bitchy, but I had other things on my mind.

"I kinda need a favor," he stuttered.

"Oh geez. Out with it already." I was just not in the mood.

"I need a date for Gloom and Alicia's anniversary party next month, and nobody else wants to go."

"A supervillain party? Why the hell are you going?"

"One of us has to go," he explained. "We got an invite. Blue Shift told me I had to do it, but I don't want to go alone."

"Of course he doesn't want to go. Gloom would fillet him. But he wants us to go to the party full of supervillains who want to kill us. Lovely. Who's going to be there?"

"All of 'em," he replied.

"All of them," I repeated. "All of them like Muppet Head, and all the other small-time freaks?"

"All of 'em, like all of 'em. The heavy hitters too. Listen, I understand if you don't..."

"All of them?" I interrupted. "Even their illustrious leader?"

"Well yeah, Deprave was supposedly the best man at the wedding. You don't have to..."

"I am so in."

Chapter Nineteen

"Wherever we go, wherever we remain, the results of our actions follow us."
Buddha

The following week was uneventful. Work was nothing more than the final formalities of passing on the reins of responsibility. Villain activity was fairly low. I avoided the lair's network, figuring I shouldn't fan the fires, so to speak. By now Deprave was most likely regretting his actions as much as I was, and he probably didn't need a reminder. He seemed to be lying low also. In fact, by the time Friday evening rolled around, it seemed like absolutely nothing was going on and everybody was bored.

I walked into the coffee shop to find Mr. Mighty and DJ Ghost playing cards. Athena and Acid were in the corner having a heated discussion, no doubt about field tactics or Acid's lack of fighting style. I pulled up a chair next to Mighty and glanced at his hand.

"Don't sit next to me. She might hit me by mistake." He tried to push me away. "You really should leave before it gets bad."

"Why? Are Blue Bastard and Mind back already?"

"No," Mighty replied. "I'm pretty sure Athena is going to kill you."

"Hmm, any idea why?" This was unexpected.

"Something about a package or something. She read the note and she's fuming now."

"A package." My mind couldn't make any connections. "What package?"

"I dunno; she said it has something to do with your boyfriend. I didn't think you had one." Mighty shrugged. "Ask her. But she may kill you first."

Before it all registered, Athena was storming over, looking like she was going to kick the living crap out of me. "What the hell is this?" She held a small, plain, brown box. "I thought you had some sense."

"Um." I looked at the box cluelessly. "That's a box."

"I know it's a box, but why is the world going to be destroyed if you don't open it and follow the instructions to the letter?"

"Huh?" I still wasn't making the connection. "I think I need some clarification here. What's in the box?"

"I don't know." Athena's voice was full of frustration and anger. "But it came with a note. Would you like to hear it?"

"No?" I replied, truly concerned it would be really bad. "If it pissed you off, it's gonna piss me off too."

Ignoring me, Athena whipped out the note and started to read. "Team Stupid, I have hacked into the launch computers of several nations' nuclear arsenals. Give this package to Computer and tell him/her to follow the directions exactly or I will systematically start launching nuclear weapons." Athena held the letter out for me to see. "It's signed.

See. By your enemy or boyfriend or whatever he is."

"Oh please." I pulled out my PDA and started to load my portable Deprave lair infiltration software. "I'll put an end to this nonsense." The software loaded, but could not connect. "Uh…wait…" I tried again. It was still inaccessible. "I think I need to hack him again for real. He must still be peeved." The whole group was staring at me now. "What? Open the box. Here…" I grabbed the box from Athena and tore it open. I stared in complete shock at its contents.

Athena looked down at it and exploded. "What the hell is with the cam?" I looked and saw another note inside. I reached to grab it, but with my distraction added to Athena's reflexes, she had the note before I was even close.

"Computer," she started reading out loud. "You know what to do with this. Text message me when you have this set up or the world goes boom. I will feel the Earth shake one way or another." Athena slammed the note to the table in complete rage. "What kind of sick thing do you have going?"

"Er…" I just stared blankly. I knew no answer would work.

I could hear DJ and Mighty laughing behind me.

"It's not funny!" Athena scolded them. "This is serious business." She turned her attention back to me. "What is this all about?"

"Nothing," I lied. "Deprave figured out that I'm not an AI and is obsessed with what I look like. You'd think he'd have better things to obsess about.

Guess he's just mad 'cause I fooled him for so long." I waited to see if my story would work.

She looked at me and the rest of the group. "Ladies' room, now."

"Great." I dragged myself to the ladies' room, dreading the upcoming inquisition.

We got inside and she locked the door behind me. She leaned up on a sink, and looked away from me. "You know I can tell when people are bullshitting me. It's not a power but a skill from my previous career."

"Ooooh, spooky! What did you used to do?" Deflect. I had to deflect.

Athena shook her head. "Won't work, you can't side-track me. You're good, but I was trained for interrogation. So spit it out."

"Spit what out?" I was completed hosed.

Athena grabbed me by the neck and threw me against the tile wall. It hurt. I considered breaking free, but knew it would just make things worse. "The truth, damn you. If I have to trust you with my life out there, I need to know where your loyalties are. Do you understand?"

Loyalties. That was a loaded question, one I had struggled with before. "Yeah." I couldn't really speak. I could barely breathe. It wasn't her choke hold messing me up, it was the memories.

Athena released her grip on my neck and I sank to the floor. "Well?" She looked down at me expectantly.

"My loyalties are with the team," I replied.

"And…" She wasn't going to let it go.

"I fucked up," I confessed.

"How?"

"I kind of saw something I shouldn't have." I looked down at my hand and it was shaking.

"The whole story, please, before I have to hurt you again." Athena's tone was less harsh, but I knew not to push it.

"I-I..." I had no idea how to explain it. "Dammit..." Remorse. No confusion, I was feeling something I couldn't identify. Something about Deprave and his twisted perversions had an impact on me that I just couldn't shake. I laughed remembering how it used to be. If only Athena knew how bad it could have been. My heart was pounding, and both of my hands were trembling. I needed a drink.

"Oh God." Athena pulled me up off the floor. "What did he do to you?"

"I didn't mean to do it. Really, it just happened." I snapped back to the moment. I wasn't able to conceal the emotional distress, but that didn't matter. I'd let her have the truth she wanted.

"What the hell happened?" Athena was losing her patience again.

"It started as just typical bullshit grandstanding. Then he asked me if I was a guy or a girl and I wouldn't tell him, but he didn't care. Shit. I didn't know he was flirting with me until it was too late."

Athena's mouth hit the floor. "Too late, how?"

"The man's built like a god. I know I'm weak, but I just couldn't look away. I..."

"I am trying to understand." She paced around the bathroom. "I really am, but I can't believe what you are trying not to tell me."

"I tried to stop it, I swear, but he was...and I..." I was about to get hit. "I think I had netsex with him."

Athena let out an inhuman scream. "Netsex?!"

I was sure everyone in a five-hundred-mile radius heard her. I would never be able to show my face again in public.

"I swear I was just being my regular wiseass self and it just kind of escalated. I don't know how it happened." That was a partial lie. The truth was that behind all of my darkest choices, stood a man. The previous one had been a real winner. Deprave was a saint in comparison. I had a weakness for really bad men.

"You are grounded," she announced. "I want you in for a psych review and off-duty until you get this sick obsession out of your head. Fix it. Do you understand?"

"Yeah," I acknowledged.

"Yeah what?" she snapped.

"Yeah, I understand. I will fix it."

"Good." She pointed at the door. "I want you out of here and I don't want to see your face until you have worked it out. I'm expecting a call from a doctor, telling me that you have been evaluated and cleared for duty. I can recommend one."

My life was sucking more by the minute. I wasn't going to go see any doctor. Doctor/patient confidentiality only went so far. "No, I'll take care of it."

I left the bathroom, grabbed the box and my stuff, and got out of the coffee shop as fast and with as little eye contact as I could. I heard snickers as I walked out the door. I didn't care. It wasn't Athena and the team that bothered me about this. It was all me. The trip home was a blur. I got in the door, threw all my crap on the sofa, and hit the bottle. I got into my hacked IM program and texted Deprave.

You ass. I just got suspended from the team.

There was almost no delay in the response. *Did you set up the cam?*

No. There is no way that is going to happen. I wasn't bending on this one. I switched on the link to his lab. He was there as usual.

"So should I push the button?"

Go for it. I'd rather be nuked than deal with this stress. I should have been nuked a long time ago anyway.

There was a long pause.

"Because I will," he added.

I'm not going to let you bully me into this.

"I swear to God!" he shouted. "Plug in that cam or I'm destroying the planet."

If you do that, you'll never see me naked. The alcohol started working its magic, the stress started to wash away.

He paused again. "Okay I won't destroy the world. Will you still be my dirty little Computer?"

What? Things were back to weird.

"Meet me in my room and talk dirty to me."

I think we need to set some boundaries, I replied.

"You weren't thinking of boundaries last week."

I was weak.

"So, you do want me." He wasn't letting go.

Stop, just stop. I can't let you control me like this. I could feel myself losing control of the situation again.

"I'm not controlling you. I didn't force you to participate in anything. You could have disconnected at any time. I think you know that and it bothers you."

Yes, it bothers me. I did want him, but I had to exercise restraint. *I already got into trouble because of this.*

"Trouble?" He laughed. "Trouble with who? Athena?"

She was pissed, I replied. *I thought she was going to kill me.*

This obviously amused Deprave. "She's afraid of you getting too close to me. Excellent. She really thinks you'll go rogue."

Go rogue. I couldn't believe he used those words. I felt myself go pale. I took a long gulp from the bottle. *Whatever. I told her that I was not a bad guy.*

"No, you are definitely one of the good guys. Maybe a little misguided." He grinned. "I'm going to my room. I'm taking off my shirt. Come on, forget all that bullshit and be my dirty little Computer for a little while."

This time I did the smart thing and disconnected. I started feeling bad for Deprave. He had no idea who he was messing with. But I had no intentions of being played for a sucker again. So, I drank myself to sleep. I was still bitter, confused and frustrated, but at least I was numb. I just hoped it would be better tomorrow.

Chapter Twenty

"The fool who thinks he is wise is just a fool. The fool who knows he is a fool is wise indeed."
Buddha

The next day I wasn't feeling any more in control than before. I was hung over, and still frustrated. I went to the coffee shop, despite Athena's warning. Acid was there downing coffee and reading the comics. "Athena says you're reinstated."

"Okay, why?" This was becoming way too much of a mind fuck. I grabbed half of a cup of coffee and filled the other half with the contents of my flask.

Acid watched me, but didn't comment. "Well you did stop Deprave from exploding the world and made him tell the truth in that note."

"Okay. Do you have the note?" I took a long sip of my coffee mix.

"No, she does, but he did what you said and apologized for making you say all that stuff and admitted defeat due to your superior skills, blah, blah, blah. You know how he just goes on and on."

"Uh, yeah." I remembered the universe was still punishing me. "I need a vacation."

"Nah," Acid replied. "You just need some non-alcoholic coffee."

"Yeah, everything's coffee with you." I finished my cup and went straight for the flask. I was almost out.

"Everything's alcohol with you," Acid countered.

I shrugged. "Yeah, well fuck it."

"Are you really going to the party with Mr. Mighty?" Acid asked.

"I said I'd go. Why, do you want to go?"

"Oh, Hell no. I don't need any girlie villain drama in my life." Acid refilled her coffee. "You can have it."

"Joy. I have to find something to wear. I don't own a costume, remember."

"Just throw together some spandex and call it a costume. Nobody remembers anything the next day anyway. I hear they all just get plastered and black out at these things."

"That doesn't make me feel any better." Where the hell was I going to find a costume? I would just have to go the little black dress route.

"You're probably the best person to go to this thing. Nobody knows who you are so you can just lay low and keep an eye on Mighty."

"True," I agreed, knowing I was actually the worst person to send now. "Maybe it will even be fun; I can sabotage some evil plots and blame Blue for it."

Acid laughed and smacked me on the back. "That's our Computer, a smartass till the end."

Chapter Twenty-one

"Like a beautiful flower that is colorful but has no fragrance, even well spoken words bear no fruit in one who does not put them into practice."
Buddha

I slumped down in the chair and pouted. Lila poured me some tea.

"You look upset," she stated the obvious.

"I'm, er..." I didn't have an answer for her.

She handed me a mug of green tea, and let me sit in silence. I sipped at my tea, trying to make sense of things in my head.

"I almost did what you asked." I felt my eyes well up with tears, but I didn't know why.

"What?" Lila asked, then she smiled and handed me a tissue. "Ah, what stopped you?"

"Distance." I wiped my eyes. "I kinda had netsex."

"That's a horrible substitution for the real thing." She sounded disappointed.

"Well it's very complicated."

"It shouldn't be," Lila advised. "He's a man; you're a woman. You're the one making it complicated. We are talking about a man, aren't we?"

I sighed and felt the tears starting again. I went for forty-five years without a single tear, and it felt like I was bawling my eyes out on a daily basis now. "He looks like a boy. I feel dirty even thinking about it. Even if he hadn't taken the drugs and looked normal, I'm still at least twice his age. And he's bad."

This got Lila's attention. "A bad boy. Oh, Becca, how can you resist?"

"Come on, I don't need to walk this path of destruction again. I'm being serious."

"I know," Lila acknowledged. "That's most of your problem. You are so carefree on the outside with the trivial shit, but you lock down your feelings like they are a bad thing. And don't start quoting Buddha at me, because it's a cop out."

"It is not," I disagreed.

"Yes it is," Lila scolded me. "You are so frightened by the possibility of losing control that you have to drink to take a shit. You're destroying any chances of happiness."

"I don't even know what I'm feeling." Besides, I didn't deserve to be happy.

"I know that too." Lila patted my hand. "But you're not actually a computer, you're a person. You need to let yourself live."

"How? I never…" I wiped my eyes again.

"What? You of all people should know old people can see through all the guises people try to throw out there. I pinned you a while ago, especially since you carry that arsenal of technology wherever you go. Which one is he?" she asked.

"I'm not telling. Are you nuts?"

"Let's see." Lila sipped her tea. "Who would be the most interesting?" Lila smirked. "I think I know."

"No you don't." I tried to steer the conversation to something else. "I'm going to a party."

Lila looked at me with the goofy smirk still on her face. "You're afraid to say it out loud. Come on, admit to it."

"No." I put down my tea and stood up. "I'm out of here."

I stormed out of the den and toward the exit. A few nurses' aides were gathered chatting by the desk at the entrance. They were dressed in blue medical scrub-like outfits and were just too well made-up and accessorized for my liking.

"She really enjoys your visits," one cheerfully announced as I approached. The other three aides were still talking among themselves.

I shrugged. "She's cool." I wasn't sure what else to say.

"I think it's cute." The aide smiled. I was surprised her make-up didn't crack when she moved her face.

"You know, she's a grown woman. She's not a child or pet or toy to be cute for your amusement."

The aide looked at me blankly; the others stopped talking and turned their attention to us.

"Her body just gave out because of age," I continued. "When she was young, she would have made you bitches look like fucking hags."

The one aide who started the conversation was put off by my attitude. "Don't talk to me like that."

"You're lucky I don't backhand you into next week." I was a heartbeat away from smacking her.

"Slaughter!" Lila wheeled herself over from the other room. "Don't you break my nurses."

I turned my back to the nurses' aides. "They were talking shit," I said in my defense.

"They're like twenty-five years old. They don't have any sense yet," Lila reminded me. "Why are you sinking to that level? Is your brain malfunctioning or something?"

"That one was out of line." I pointed at the aide I wanted to hit.

"They can get out of line once in a while." Lila rolled closer, I felt bad that she had to go through all that physical effort. "They take care of old people for a living. What were you doing at that age?"

"This is bullshit," I complained.

"You are too tense. Instead of getting violent, maybe you should focus your energy on something else," Lila suggested.

"Like what, fucking? It always comes down to that with you."

"And you're less one-dimensional?" Lila asked. "With you, it's always drinking and breaking bones. Beating people up is a sad substitute for intimacy. You need to get laid more desperately than anyone I have ever known. How many years has it been, Slaughter? Or are we counting decades now?"

The aides stood frozen and silent. They looked like mannequins in a medical supply store. The remained still, as if they were placed in realistic poses to display nursing products.

I couldn't respond to Lila. No witty retort came to mind, and I was certainly not going to give her an honest answer to the question. I felt humiliated, angry, and disappointed in myself. The only thing I could do to maintain any self-respect and dignity was just leave.

This was the first time I walked out on Lila, never mind storming off angry. I glanced behind me as I walked out. She shook her head in disappointment. I heard one of the aides quietly ask another, "Wasn't she that crazy cage fighter from like fifty years ago?"

I hit the liquor store on my way home.

Chapter Twenty-two

"Everything changes, nothing remains without change."
Buddha

The night of the party arrived quicker than I expected. Luckily, I had just enough time to get an outfit together.

I met Mighty at the coffee shop and we headed over to the party in a limo. The party was on the top floor of a very exclusive hotel. It was a place that even I would have trouble getting a room in. The people who stayed here were all celebrities of some sort and security was top notch. Even the elevators were impressively decorated. I made a mental note to try to comp myself a room there one of these days.

As the elevator door opened, techno music met our ears with its booming and thumping. A maître d' greeted us at the door.

"May I have your names?" Before Mighty answered, I elbowed him in reminder not to divulge my identity.

"Mr. Mighty and guest," Mighty replied.

"Does the guest have a name?" the maître d' inquired.

"No," I replied. "She doesn't."

The maître d' didn't show any sign of surprise with my response. "Very well. Please go on in." He waved us inside.

"Mr. Mighty and guest," he announced over the music. Heads turned and people watched us as we walked in. I saw Muppet Head out of the corner of my eye and was really relived I remained anonymous.

The place was packed with poserific characters of all types. It seemed like the villainous crowd really lived up to their fashion reputation.

"I think that I'm way underdressed," I stated the obvious as I saw a woman in a red satin and sequin gown and cape walk by. She looked like she stepped off of the set of Flash Gordon. I could almost hear Queen playing in the background.

"No," Mighty replied. "You look amazing. I should have told you that before we got here." He smiled but he seemed distracted.

I looked around at the guests again. I saw Gloom and Alicia on the other side of the room trying to look sexy together. Actually, they didn't really have to try very hard. They were pulling it off fairly well. Gloom was a tall muscular man with chocolate-colored skin and a booming deep voice. He kept his head shaved and wore the evil supervillain goatee. Alicia was petite, willowy, with golden skin and eyes, and light brown hair. They made a perfect couple.

The techno music pumped hard as the crowd danced, drank and participated in chemical vices without any shame. "Is that guy snorting coke off of that chick's shoe?" I shook my head. "What's this party celebrating again?" I knew the answer to the question; I just felt the need to ask again to make a point and to mess with Mighty.

"Anniversary. Gloom and Alicia. And yes, people are snorting drugs off of everything here. I thought you didn't mind that sort of thing."

I shrugged. "I'm not into hard drugs. I keep telling you people that I'm just a drunk."

Mighty shook his head in disappointment. "You should do something about that…"

"Oh crap, is that your girlfriend over there?" I interrupted.

"She's not my girlfriend," Mighty corrected me. "We never dated. She can only be my girlfriend if we dated."

"So why don't you ask her out, dumbass? You always talk about how wonderful she is." I did not want to live through an entire night of Mighty moping.

"She wouldn't, she's so…" Mighty just watched Freesia as she greeted everyone and cheerfully flittered about. Her levity was part of her persona. She was some kind of empath and shrink. She worked alone, helping the mentally ill. I met her once at a mood disorder workshop while I was incognito. She seemed extremely uncomfortable with me, and the feeling was mutual.

"Okay, Mr. Mighty. You mean you can bend steel, deflect bullets, and defend freedom, but you can't talk to a girl?" I mocked him openly. He needed the nudge.

"I never deflected bullets. Beside, when was the last time you went on a date? Not including supervillain netsex."

"Ouch." I never expected the quip from Mighty. "That hurt, you've been practicing your witty banter again." I grinned. "Just go talk to the girl."

"What about you?" Mighty looked around. "Will you be okay here?"

"You mean without any combat powers? At a party? Oh my God, I may die from the killer punch!"

"Your sarcasm is getting old."

"Old like me. Besides, it's all I got. Deal with it." I nudged him off toward Freesia's direction. "Go. Maybe I'll go find Ganjasaurus and smoke some blunts."

"Yeah sure." Mighty just smiled nervously and walked off. This was a good thing. He needed to grow up a little, and as far as I was concerned, that meant going out with a real live girl. He was wound way too tight, possibly even more tightly than me. Despite what Lila said, I did not need to loosen up tonight. Armed with age and wisdom, I decided to enjoy the hospitality. Instead of hitting the bar straight off, I was good and hit the hors d'oeuvres. This was an excellent decision on my part. The food was delicious, and there was plenty of champagne being served anyway.

Still, I had that nagging urge to go seek forbidden fruit. I wanted to find Deprave and see if he really was all that in person. Lila's words were also still echoing in my head. Had it really been decades? Maybe it was time to end this dry spell. Filthy thoughts of nasty acts flashed through my foul mind.

As I became increasingly acquainted with the food, I couldn't help but feel like I was being observed. I looked around, but saw nobody looking in my direction. I couldn't shake the feeling, however.

I chugged a champagne flute, realizing it wasn't a very smart thing to do after the fact. "Go ahead, you lush," I scolded myself. "Get drunk in the hornets' nest." I was losing my edge. I had to seriously control myself. I lived my entire life under the assumption that everyone was a potential foe. I was prepared for my inevitable death all my life, but tonight I was being sloppy. I should have been vigilant. I should have been observant and avoided distraction. Instead, I grabbed another glass; that made it four, no five. At least I wasn't armed and chugging hard liquor.

I spotted Mighty out of the corner of my eye actually doing what I instructed him to. It even looked like I would need to catch a cab home tonight. I was glad for him, but now I lost my safety net. I had to work the party alone. I took a deep breath and attempted to gather my senses together. I was definitely intoxicated already, but not dangerously so. Luckily, I was still in control of my actions. I figured I just needed a little air, get my ass together and then mingle appropriately. I felt no need to drink myself into oblivion and I refused to piss anyone off tonight. I just had to keep myself in line and not start any trouble.

I got to the balcony. It was a beautiful night, and a decent view. There was a slight chill in the air, but not too uncomfortable. I looked up at the moon and couldn't help but snicker. The moon was my constant companion; both of us careened through existence barely in control. I focused on the beat of the music inside and on my breathing and soon I felt my mind clearing.

"Good evening," a deep gravelly voice said from behind me. It could not be mistaken for anyone else. Like nails on a chalkboard, it sent a chill up my spine. I managed to suppress the shiver.

"Off-duty," I muttered to myself. I turned around and faced my arch nemesis.

"What was that?" he asked.

"Nothing. Enjoying the party?"

"Which one are you?" In the true villainous self-serving spirit, he completely disregarded anything I had to say.

"Me?" I decided to play dumb. "I'm nobody."

"No." He scanned me without even trying to hide it. "You're somebody. You feel familiar and you do have a presence. Besides, you are here and only somebodies are here."

"I'm certainly nobody as important as you." I hoped I wasn't sounding too sarcastic. "I came with a friend. He thought I'd get a kick out of all this." I motioned around at the party, and then dropped my voice to a stage whisper. "I don't think he could get another date."

Deprave cracked a small smile. He was never able to resist disparaging remarks about pretty much anyone. "So then what are you off-duty from?"

Doh! He heard my slip-up. I wanted to say, *Fucking up your plans*. Instead I held it in and replied, "Wow, you catch everything." It was a neutral enough response and I really tried to stop myself, but my mouth wouldn't stay shut. "Well, almost everything."

"Oh? Coming from a nobody, that's a bold thing to say. You are very fearless." He started to pose. I prepared for the verbal diarrhoea. "What have I missed?" He seemed to actually be pondering a list in his head. "All my plans are always meticulously orchestrated. Even a nobody would know that about me. And even now as I am forced to participate in this party, my latest plan is unraveling soon to bring defeat to my enemies and victory to me."

The posturing was just pathetic. And the costume was even more ludicrous in person. I couldn't help but laugh. He'd probably try to kick my ass, but I just couldn't hold it in. "I'm sorry," I apologized even though I wasn't the slightest bit sorry.

"You have the nerve to mock me?" He maintained the façade.

"It's just that…" I got a grip on my laughter and continued. "It's just that your plans unraveled into a pile of crap hours ago. Your so-called superweapon had so many design flaws, that it took almost no work to make it disintegrate itself. Your plans sucked, big time." As the final word left my mouth, I knew violence was imminent.

"Computer…" he said, awe in his voice. He ogled me and smiled perversely. "Wow, you are definitely female."

"That's what the doctor told my mother when he smacked my new-born ass." I was surprised at my ability to keep my shit together through this twilight zone of perversion. None of his responses lately made sense in my universe. He was supposed to get angry, maybe pull a weapon out and shoot me, perhaps even have his minions beat me to a pulp or perform some other act of violence. He was not supposed to be drooling as he shamelessly stared at my cleavage. But then again, his name was Deprave, and he had been on that whole netsex kick for almost a month.

"And you are incredibly beautiful." He took a step closer.

Again, not a response I had calculated. "You look pretty hot yourself. Maybe I will bend you over that console." I could have kicked myself for saying that.

Again he stepped forward. Now he couldn't be any closer. Even through his pathetically gaudy pleather outfit, I could feel his body heat rising. He leaned in and whispered into my ear, "Yes, I'd like that."

He was calling my bluff again. The more I said, the deeper I got. Yet I just could not shut myself up. Deep within my soul, I knew I wanted him badly. I didn't care that it was sick; I felt alive. "Are you willing to be defeated? Remember, I am superior in all things."

He let out a very faint moan. He ran his hand through my hair and then stroked the back of my neck. Electricity shot through my body. I hadn't felt anything like that since, well ever. This time I realized it was me who was moaning. "I have a suite in this hotel," he advised me.

My new heroic parts, the parts that rescued cats from trees, and protected children and little old ladies, these parts screamed for me to run away. My mind was filled with scenario after scenario of bad things that could result from this. The inner hero urged me to do a strategic withdrawal and go find Mr. Mighty. The fight-or-flight alarm was ringing flight with full lights and sirens. But tonight that part of my mind stood no chance. Something else was in control, something older and considerably hungrier, something that had been denied for decades. I looked him in the eyes, hot, shaking and completely aroused. "I will wreck you."

He led me away from the party through the back hallways. Before I had a moment to regain any sense, we were in his room and out of our clothes. At this point, that inner voice that urged my escape fell silent. I knew I just had to go with it. Tomorrow I would have plenty of time to question my sanity, but now...

His body felt incredible. He was in impressive shape for an evil supergenius. Hell, it was impressive for a normal person. It was just freakin' impressive. He pulled me close and kissed me. I practically shoved my tongue down his throat. He didn't seem to object. He just groaned and clutched me tighter.

"It's been a while since I've, you know..." There I was confiding about my sexual inadequacies with a madman.

"Me too," he admitted as he tossed me onto the bed. "We'll make up for that tonight." He was on me.

"God, I want you," I gasped as he entered me. He didn't say anything else; neither of us was able to speak. I was really glad we were in a suite, because I was not quiet, and neither was he. I didn't care, though. I didn't care if our asses were flashed on the evening news as the main story. I didn't care if my teammates knew. I didn't care if my identity was blown and I could no longer walk the streets in peace. I just wanted him to keep fucking me. I could feel the ecstasy building, hotter, faster...

Alas, as he said, it had been a long time for him. His body tensed up, he cried out, practically screaming, and then he went limp.

"Crap!" he cursed, looking down at me with an expression of both self-loathing and determination.

What could I say? "It's okay, we can do it ag-" Before I could complete the statement, he was already taking care of business. And he was taking care of it well.

I had to fight to catch my breath as he went down on me. He knew exactly where to go and what to do. "Oh yeah, suck me, bitch," I moaned. For the first time in my life, I was completely sexually uncensored. The ecstasy approached again, and this time exploded into rapture that engulfed my entire body. After I had a moment to recover, I opened my eyes to see him staring down at me.

"Wow, that was-"

'Uh-uh," he interrupted. He pulled off his used condom and flung it in the direction of the trash can. "I'm not done with you yet." He replaced the condom, mounted me and picked up where he originally left off.

"Oh yes. Give it to me." I never wanted it to end. "Don't stop."

"Oh, we'll be doing this all night," he said as he thrust harder.

And we did.

Chapter Twenty-three

"When you realize how perfect everything is you will tilt your head back and laugh at the sky."
Buddha

I woke up in a hotel room bed alone. This was the moment my superego was trying to warn me about. My right wrist was a little numb, and as I discovered, tied to the bedpost by my own stockings. I freed my arm and looked at the destruction wrought upon the room. The place was decimated. There were empty champagne bottles strewn across the floor. All the furniture was either tipped over or broken. I looked at the splintered coffee table and smiled at the memory of breaking it. My clothes were missing in action, and I couldn't remember where I put my phone and purse. On top of that, I felt like I had been gang raped by a pack of wild gorillas. I rolled over clutching my head and initiated procedures to start dragging my sorry ass out of bed. Before I could sit up, a tray appeared. It was full of food and coffee and was being wheeled over by the mostly nude body of my evil arch-nemesis boy toy.

"Maybe, I destroyed you." He sat on the edge of the bed and poured me a cup of coffee. Oddly enough, he prepared it the way I liked it, light and sweet.

"When did I tell you how I take coffee?" I pulled myself up and leaned on Deprave.

He laughed. "I made it the way I like it. I guess great minds do think alike."

I took the cup, and poured in half of a bottle of Kalua from the minibar. I sipped at it and then finished the bottle. I hadn't expected to feel hung over. "God, how much champagne did I drink? There's a party of pain in my head."

"Apparently, enough to sleep with your sworn foe." He handed me a piece of melon off the tray.

I took a bite. It was sweet and cool. "Well, you are guilty of the same faulty logic. Were you drunk too?"

"Was it really faulty logic?" he asked, apparently rhetorically. "I wasn't drunk until after you ordered room service. Before that, I only had one glass of Scotch early in the evening. I was under another influence."

"Well, it wasn't really the booze that made me do it either," I admitted. "So what do we do now?" The million-dollar question.

"We eat breakfast, and go to work," he replied as he stroked my thigh. "Maybe get some morning-after sex in before we leave."

"No, I mean…um…us." I felt pain and elation wrapped up in one weird uncomfortable emotion. "Do we…I stop…" I reached for another bottle.

Deprave shook his head and took my hand before I reached the bar. "No, you are the only mind worthy of my time. You keep me sharp. And the sex…" He smirked. "Yeah, you can destroy me any time you want."

"So you want to stay arch enemies?" This was truly bizarre. "And still sleep together?"

"Not enemies, opponents. Nemeses. We both enjoy this elaborate chess game of ours, and we take pleasure in doing each other. Besides, you still have to bend me over my control console."

I laughed. "I'm not properly equipped."

Deprave pulled me close and put his arm around me. "They make attachments."

"Yes that they do." I grinned.

"I never thought I'd meet a woman as degenerate as myself." Deprave started playing with my hair.

"You have no idea. I just hope you don't get too much grief for the room. Sorry about the coffee table."

Deprave smirked. "It's covered, but what I am wondering, is how such a sweet and lovely lady learned to body slam a grown man like that."

"I was a supreme fighter," I boasted. "And I always won."

"Bullshit," Deprave replied. "You're not that old."

"Yes I am. I was one of the first coed fighters. You just spent all night banging an old lady." I smiled.

"You are not that old," Deprave again differed.

"Okay, smartass, quick quiz. How old do I look?" I asked.

"Twenty-five or so," he answered.

"How old do you look? And don't lie."

"I don't know," he answered. "Young."

"You look like I should go to jail for even looking at you." I touched his face and smiled. "You look like a teenager. That means that you were probably pretty young when you took the drug.

Most people I know who took it look like they should be going to high school. I don't even look like I should be carded. Put it together."

"The age reversal is supposed to range anywhere from a quarter to two-thirds of a person's age," Deprave pointed out. "Even at thirty-five, you could look twenty-five."

"It's exponential, but it can only go so far. We all know it. The older you are, the more years you take off, but you're not going to look sixteen again. Not that I am complaining." I grinned.

"Okay," Deprave agreed. "Let's say you look one-third of your age, and I'll be generous. I'll put you at twenty-one. That would make you..." Deprave stopped, "...no, that can't be right."

"Yup. You twisted bastard. You're doing grandma."

Deprave got that perverse twinkle in his eye. "You have experience."

"Not as much as you might think, but enough," I replied. "At least now I have the energy to back it all up. And I got myself a completely deranged boyfriend who will try anything. I don't know if life gets much better than that."

"Boyfriend?" Deprave grinned. "I like that."

"Good." I was relieved I didn't frighten him off. "Because sometimes I think you're the only one who gets me. Well the only one who speaks coherent sentences, that is."

"Oh?" Deprave inquired. "Who's my competition who speaks incoherently?"

"Not competition. Weirdness." I pushed away and walked to the window. I should not have brought up this topic.

"What is it?" he asked.

"It's like I said, just weird." I peeked out the window; the view was incredible. "I had an exchange with Fuzzy Logic."

"He spoke to you?" Deprave got up and stood next to me.

"It was through a security camera. I didn't say anything, but he seemed to know who it was. He kept calling me angel, and…" I bit my lip nervously. I tried to quiet my mind, but it was preoccupied with too many external stimuli to be calm.

"What?" Deprave grabbed me by my shoulders and shook me. "What did he tell you?"

"It's Bianchi," I blurted out. "Fuzzy Logic is freakin' Bianchi. Do you understand? Something drove him completely over the edge."

"What did he tell you?" Deprave pleaded.

"He said not to look in God's eyes while waving a stick."

Deprave looked baffled.

I continued, "He also said the way to madness is through holes in your pockets."

Deprave looked lost in thought. "Can you tell me exactly what he said?"

"Okay. He called me an angel of God. He said it was almost finished. He said not to look in God's eyes while waving a stick, and then he said the road to hell is paved with good intentions. The way to madness is through the holes in your pockets. And I think he may have called Athena the devil."

"She is the devil." Deprave sat on the foot of the bed. "He spoke to you; he chose you."

"I'm sorry. I was just there at the time. I didn't mean to take it from you."

"No," Deprave replied. "It's not about me. Apparently you possess whatever he thinks we need to stop this."

"Stop what?"

Deprave got up, and threw me to the bed. "Stop me from going insane with horniness." He landed on the bed and kissed me.

"That was a terrible attempt at a deflection."

"I know," he replied. "Can you let me deflect this one?" He brushed the hair out of my face. "We both know this discussion is not going to lead anywhere pleasant. I don't want to ruin the day."

"Okay, fair enough. But I'm going to find out what the hell is going on at some point."

"I just want you to be blissfully ignorant as long as possible. You're about to tread on extremely dangerous territory." Before I could object, he kissed me again, and the conversation was over.

Chapter Twenty-four

"He who loves 50 people has 50 woes; he who loves no one has no woes."
Buddha

After a morning of complete abandon, we both had to get back to our real lives. We had a long decadent shower, complete with never-ending hot water. I was completely blindsided by Deprave's affection. He was not the cold-hearted bastard he was reputed to be. Either he was really good at fooling me, or he had an excellent PR campaign going.

We said our good-byes, planning to see each other very soon and very often. I grabbed a cab and made my way home. The ride was uneventful, besides my discovery that my cell phone was dead and needed recharging as much as I did. On closer inspection, I noticed my other electronics were all drained too. This was slightly unnerving, as this never happened.

I arrived home and changed into some sweats. I threw all my devices on their chargers, still curious why they were drained. Almost immediately after being put on the charger, my cell started beeping with alert after alert. Mighty had been calling and texting since six in the morning. I had forgotten about ditching him at the party. I called him back.

"Hello." Mighty sounded tired himself.

"Yo!" I greeted him. "You ran the batteries down on my phone with your constant harassment."

"Where the fuck have you been?" Mighty sounded displeased.

"Um, I was passed out," I lied. "Where did you end up?"

"I ended up talking with Freesia all night. We stayed the whole night and all this morning. You disappeared less than an hour after we got there. Where did you go?"

"I got drunk and passed out in a room." That was half true.

"Are you sure?" Mighty was obviously reaching for something.

"Why?" I asked. "What's up?"

"There were a couple of incidents with the hotel," Mighty explained. "They were both in Deprave's room."

"No shit." I had to laugh. "Do tell."

"There's nothing to tell." I could hear the exhaustion in Mighty's voice. He really was running on no sleep. "The first time they almost thought he was attacked. A bunch of them were about to storm the suite when Gloom called it off. Alicia was really peeved, too."

"Why?" This couldn't be good.

"You tell me," Mighty replied. "Gloom thought you were killing Deprave, and he wanted to know who the hell you were. He said he saw you leave with him."

"Oh shit. Did you tell him?"

"No," Mighty answered. "Do you think I'm stupid? He found out who you who were anyway later."

"Um, how?" I did not like where this was going.

"You were still passed out, in bed with Deprave, when the maid came in this morning and saw what you both did to the room. She freaked, and it got back to Gloom, whose name the room was under."

"Uh, okay, and..."

"And," Mighty continued. "Gloom let himself in to see the extent of the damage. He told me that you were both in the shower. He almost kicked in the door and beat the crap out of Deprave, but he was too amused by the irony of you being there to actually smack him." Gloom had been there while pissed off; that explained why my devices were all dead.

"It wasn't me," I was lying again. "It could have been anyone."

"Your shit was all over the room," Mighty countered. "Nobody else goes to a black tie function carrying a personal network with them. It wasn't hard for Gloom to figure out."

"Lies, I tell you."

"What the hell were you thinking?" Mighty inquired.

"I don't know. I wasn't thinking with my head," I whined. "Squeal on me and you pay."

"I'm not saying crap," Mighty asserted. "I'm not going to be the one to get smacked for not stopping you. You really fucked up."

"Yeah, that too." I sighed. It had been an excellent night.

Mighty laughed. He must not have been that angry. "Okay, I have to know."

"What? I'm afraid."

"Why did you destroy all the furniture?" Mighty laughed.

"Oh, that." I laughed too. "He was holding out on the champagne, so I body slammed him a few times."

"You are a total freak."

"Am not." I thought about it for a second and changed my mind. "Okay, maybe a little."

"So what are you going to do now?" Mighty continued his line of questioning. "Is there going to be some kind of thing between you two?"

"No, nothing is going on." I was lying for real now. "It was just a drunken, one-night stand."

Mighty laughed again. "You really need to stop drinking. So, wanna meet for coffee?"

"Yeah, you can tell me all about Freesia."

Chapter Twenty-five

"To conquer oneself is a greater task than conquering others."
Buddha

Life after the party had taken a turn toward the bizarre but happy. I was pretty sure I convinced Mighty that I had a moment of weakness and everything was back to normal. This was a good thing since I didn't need any grief. My relationship with Deprave was a strange mix of sexual perversion, intellectual challenge and something else intangible. We clicked in a way that was completely unexpected to me. Maybe I wouldn't spend this new lifetime alone.

I sat with the crew and we were teasing Mighty.

"Mighty went out with Freesia again. Did you get lucky?" Acid mocked.

"Shut up." Mighty flung a balled-up napkin at Acid. "I am a perfect gentleman."

"So you let her down," Acid teased. "Poor girl will have to wait five years for a kiss at this rate."

"I kissed her." Mighty blushed. "Besides I'm not the only one who's been seeing someone."

"Oh?" Acid asked.

"Yeah," DJ popped out from nowhere. "I followed Computer to a motel a bunch of times this week. Very scandalous."

DJ actually made me blush. Mighty raised an eyebrow at me; he didn't need to say a word. I was busted.

"Why the hell would you follow me?" I asked.

DJ shrugged. "I was bored. Don't worry; I didn't peek in any windows or anything. I only followed you to the parking lot."

"That's bad enough. Geez, what happened to privacy?"

"That's what I was saying," Mighty interjected. "It's none of anyone's business what I do on my date."

"You don't do anything on your dates," Acid replied. "You just hold hands and think wholesome thoughts."

"Screw you!" Mighty cursed.

"Oh, stop." I hated to see Mighty abused so badly. "Acid, you made him curse. We don't do that."

"Okay," Acid agreed. "Tell us about you clandestine affair."

"No," I simply responded.

Athena came out from the back just in time to end the discussion.

"Okay, people, tonight instead of gabbing, we're training." She looked like she was primed and ready to go.

"Okay, what kind of training?" DJ asked.

"Physical training." She dropped a bag full of clothing on the table.

DJ was the first to investigate. He held up a t-shirt and balked. "Li's Karate? What the hell?"

"Well we can't tell them that we're a superteam. We're supposed to be incognito. So we are a small displaced karate school. Got it?"

"Who can't we tell?" Acid asked.

"The people at the gym. They close at eleven and I have a friend who knows the owner. We'll have the place to ourselves. I think some of you are a little soft around the edges." Athena looked at Acid. "Not eating does not put you in good shape, exercise does."

"Crap," Acid whined as she picked up her stuff. I sat and watched them all return from changing and complain as they made their way out the door.

"Are you coming, Computer?" Athena asked.

"I thought this was for front line superheroes. I'm just the geek."

"Get your ass up and come on," Athena ordered.

I quickly changed, packed up my stuff and followed everyone out. Athena locked the door behind us.

"Which gym?" I asked.

"Pete's place down the block," Athena replied. "It's the best equipped place in the city."

"Um. I think I'm about to have a case of explosive diarrhoea, so I'll sit this one out…"

"…Stop with the excuses. We're *all* training."

We arrived at the gym. None of the staff was there. Pete was waiting to let us in. I ducked behind Mighty, trying not to be seen. However, Pete still caught a glimpse of me and simply shook his head. He unlocked the door and showed us in. "I will be back in two hours to lock up behind you. Will that be enough time?"

Athena looked at the group for a moment and replied, "Better make it three. Is that okay?"

"Sure," Pete agreed. "Don't hurt them," he said to her as he walked away.

"I'll be easy on them," Athena replied.

"I didn't mean you," he muttered. As he passed me, he gave me a light pat on the shoulder. I pretended not to notice. Mighty caught it though and kept glancing over at me, as if trying to make a connection.

We got inside and Athena immediately herded us over to the Smith cage. "Okay, first we're going to test your strength. So let's do some bench presses and see what you can lift."

"A bench press is not a good indicator of overall strength," I pointed out.

Athena didn't like my comment at all. "Yes, Computer, I know that, but we have to start somewhere."

"Okay." I shrugged and sat down on the floor.

She began with Mighty, starting with five hundred pounds and working up to eight hundred before she decided that testing him was futile. Next was DJ. He managed to lift one hundred and eighty pounds. Acid could bench ninety. Athena berated her about that and insisted she work out regularly.

"Okay, Computer. You're up." Athena took off all but fifty pounds.

"You can put on more. That's too low," I said.

"Just lift the fifty pounds and we'll see." Athena was not in one of her better moods.

I got into position and lifted the bar like it was nothing. "Throw on a couple more hundred," I told

Athena. She thought I was being smart and threw on another fifty.

I lifted the now one hundred pounds like it was still nothing. "Come on, let's get this over with. Put on some weight."

Mighty walked over and threw on two hundred pounds. The rest of the team stood there dumbfounded and watched as I benched three hundred pounds. "Hey, let's see if I can do fifty more." Mighty threw two more twenty-five pound plates on. I lifted it, but it took some effort. Mighty grabbed another set of ten pound plates and loaded the bar. I lifted it, but just barely.

"Not bad." Mighty helped me off the bench. "Three hundred and seventy. Work out a little, huh?"

"Yup. Gotta keep the body in top shape."

"Hmm." Athena didn't like surprises. Now she wasn't sure what I was packing. "Let's see how we do with a few hand-to-hand techniques." She brought us over to a floor training area. "I'm going to attack. You dodge and counterattack. Don't worry, I'll pull my punches, but none of you should. I want you all to give me everything you have. Computer. You're first."

"Can I just sit this one out? I asked.

She mistook my apprehension for fear. "Get up here. I said I wasn't going to hurt you."

"It's not that…"

"Come on," she interrupted. "Stop wasting time."

I stepped up. The rest of the team watched and waited for the pain to begin. "Don't be afraid," Athena instructed. "I won't hurt you."

"I know," I replied. Athena and I bowed to each other. I would have to let her win, but playing weak was getting very old. She threw a straight karate punch. I considered letting her hit me. That was the plan. Instead, pride pushed common sense aside and my fighting instincts took over. Something inside me was waking up. I parried her blow, as I stuck her with a back punch in the face. I was careful not to hit her hard, but it had to hurt her pride. She didn't flinch, but she was thrown slightly off balance. It had been a while since I sparred. The urge to show off and conquer was nearly overwhelming. I wanted to wipe the floor with her and laugh at her defeat. I could easily have destroyed her from my current position, but I reminded myself that this was just a demonstration. I stepped back, allowing her to recover. She was unable to conceal her surprise. I watched her eyes, seeing her recalculate her attack. She switched styles to American boxing. She tried to manipulate my space, by throwing short blows to my face. I let her think she had me, swinging and missing. As expected, she connected with a left hook to my face. It stung, but I was pleased to find that my training never wore off. My brain ignored the pain and my legs retaliated with a low-line Savate style kick to the knee. She maintained a deadpan expression, but leaned back, taking her weight off of the knee. Taking my kick into account, she again changed styles. She protected her head and neck with her arm and tried for a high kick to my head. I grinned, remembering the intensity and satisfaction of my Muay Thai training days. I sidestepped the kick and gave her a good knee to her rib cage. I was getting too sadistic, enjoying the fight too much. I knew I should just end it. I should have let her hit me and play humble, but it just wasn't in my nature. I loved to fight more than anything. I especially liked to inflict pain.

Athena broke off, stepping back, thinking. She was thinking too much. Wondering and plotting. She needed to let go and feel the fight, not try to understand it as it unfolded. Again, she stepped forward and took a shot at me. Now, she was being sloppy. I struck her in the leg with the same Savate kick as before; she fell to one knee. I should have pulled my kick better. My body tingled; I fought the urge to finish her. I even offered my hand to help her up. But she snarled and got up on her own. As she got up, I could see the wheels turning. She went back to a karate stance, glaring at me.

I smiled again and went into a bai jong. She paused. She should have stopped there, but like me, she had impulse issues. But her eyes showed she was frustrated, and she was unable to find a way in. I had seen this look before. She knew she had lost the fight. However, desperation does strange things to fighters. Instead of attempting a rational attack or accepting defeat, she tried for a spinning back kick. She had to know it was the worst thing she could have done. Automatically, I went to destroy her leg. Mid-action, I remembered Pete and stopped myself.

"What the hell?" I muttered, as I stepped out of the way of the kick. Athena momentarily lost balance. Now, her back was to me. I could have demolished her. Instead I stood there wondering what the hell she was thinking. Maybe this was a setup of some kind. She turned around to face me again; the deadpan expression was replaced with rage. Before she had no clue what I could do, but now she knew she was outskilled. I returned her stare, still grinning. We stood there for half a minute, while the others sat in silence. Finally, Athena had the sense to call it off.

"Sit down." She paced the mat, muttering to herself. I never saw her that pissed before. She had nobody to blame but herself. She knew it, too.

I bowed and sat. She stopped pacing and stood there for a moment recomposing herself. The rest of the team just sat quietly, afraid to even breathe too loud.

"Mighty, you're next." He stood up apprehensively. Athena maintained control, however, and Mighty was not put through any major discomfort.

She took turns with the rest of the team, showing them basic moves to make their combat skills more effective. I sat on the bench and watched. Every so often she would glance over at me, as if to remind me that she hadn't forgotten I was there.

When Pete returned, Athena was still in a foul mood. We all filed out, Athena in the back of the pack, with a slight limp from the two kicks to the knee. "She didn't kick your asses too bad?" Pete asked.

"No," Mighty replied. "Athena was gentle on us."

Pete laughed. "Athena, hmm. Nobody lost any legs or anything?" He glanced at Athena's leg, noticing the limp. "Wow, she's not usually that merciful." He glared at me. I was getting tired of the dirty looks.

I started to walk off, hoping to escape the inevitable. Athena caught up with me and put her hand on my shoulder. "Wait up, Computer."

"Damn it." I didn't mean to say it out loud, but it came out.

"Yeah." Athena walked next to me. "Out with it."

"Out with what?" I had to play dumb.

"Your training. Don't lie."

"I'm old. I used to be a pro-fighter. That's it. You probably saw me on TV." I hoped she would stop there. I knew she wouldn't, but I didn't want to deal with a mess.

"No," she replied. "I always got a vibe from you; there's something else."

"No. There's not."

She studied me for a while. "Damn, you are familiar." She smiled. "You're not going to tell me."

"I don't know what you mean. Where do you recognize me from?" If she truly recognized me from somewhere else, she had been into some hard core crap at some point. She would have to reveal too much of herself to get anything from me. Apparently she got the message.

"No, I must be mistaken. TV, huh?"

"Yup," I replied. "You may be able to find some old reruns."

She nodded, her glance never leaving my face. "I might just check it out. Have a good night, Computer."

"You too." I felt a tinge of relief as she walked off. Still, if she figured it out, my days of nonviolence would be over. All I could do was hope for the best.

Chapter Twenty-six

"If we could see the miracle of a single flower clearly, our whole life would change."
Buddha

"It happened again." I rolled up a joint, lit it and handed it to Lila. Mo was in intensive care. He probably wouldn't last much longer. We visited him earlier, and it left us somewhat drained.

"What did?" Lila took a hit off of the joint and passed it back.

"People thinking I don't know shit, and then learning the hard way." I laughed, and then smoked.

"It's nice to see you finally pick up a worthy vice." Lila took the joint from me and inhaled. She coughed and took a sip of some iced tea. "But maybe this isn't your only new vice." She nudged me with her elbow.

"I have no idea what you mean; I'm just out of booze." The marijuana was kicking in and I started to laugh for almost no reason.

"You got yourself a man?" Lila really wasn't asking. "You haven't been around much since that party."

"Oh yeah, I'm getting some." I looked at Lila and grinned. "You want details?"

"Who, what, where and when?" Lila queried. "Oh, and how?"

"Deprave, every kinky thing you can think of, many hotel rooms, weekly, sometimes daily." I giggled. "And it is all good."

Lila's face lit up. "Oh, you weren't kidding when you said bad boy, excellent job! Where's the video?"

"Oh, shut up." I hit the joint and passed it back to Lila. "You have to settle for first-hand reports."

"Well?"

"Well." Thinking about it made me feel warm inside. "He's turned on when I quote science at him. He is always ready for action, and he does the job very well. He likes his coffee the same way I do, we trade music, watch the occasional movie, play strip chess, and he screams in Thai whenever he gets off."

"Oh! He's a screamer." Lila grinned. "Screamers are good; it's like having a cheerleading squad in the bedroom."

"Yeah, apparently, I'm one too. Go team."

"Okay, I have to ask." Lila took another hit. "How does he treat you? I'm assuming he's not really all that evil."

I smiled. I was glad to accept her concern. "He is a complete poser. He's about as evil as an angry kitten. I think he really cares about me. No, I know he does."

"Good." Lila coughed. "How do you feel, inside?"

"Free, I think."

"Good. That's how you're supposed to feel when you're in love."

"Who said anything about love?"

"You don't have to say it; I can see it all over you. Remember, I'm an expert."

"You're an expert in sex, not love."

"True, but they are related."

"A lot of things are related," I said. "S&M for example. Sex and violence. What do you have to say about that?"

"Are you into that?"

I blushed slightly, uncertain why. "No. The violence I used to get off on had nothing to do with sex."

"Too bad." Lila smirked. "I misinterpreted you."

"Misinterpreted? How?"

"My specialty." Lila beamed. "I was a celebrity impersonator. Guys had fantasies about famous women, and I gave them their dream."

"You dressed up like other women and did guys."

"I was good at it. You should have seen my Gwen Stefani."

"Wait." It started to sink in. "You misinterpreted me."

"Yes."

"You dressed up like me, smacked guys around and then did them?"

"Yes. You were one of my favorites, easy costume, lots of attitude."

"This is creeping me out."

"Lighten up, Slaughter, lots of men have fantasies of strong women smacking them down and taking them. You were the perfect representation of the archetype."

"Great, now I'm an archetype. Were there, you know, a lot of requests?"

"Ah yes, Slaughter, you were very popular."

"Oh God, I think I'm going to be sick."

"Chill out, it's just sex. So how does your man like it; who's on top?"

"Don't you ever let up?"

"No, so you might as well tell me."

"We take turns. Okay?"

"Ah, you do love him."

"Stop."

"You are so tightly wound. I think he needs to pound more of the uptight out of you."

"Lila!" I turned beat red.

Lila was clearly amused. Her entire body shook with laughter. "Take me to the cafeteria, Slaughter, I got the munchies."

Chapter Twenty-seven

"There are only two mistakes one can make along the road to truth; not going all the way, and not starting."
Buddha

I stretched and rolled over on my side. It was two in the morning. I must have fallen asleep. Deprave was still awake and flipping through the hotel satellite TV offerings. I hadn't expected him to stick around that long.

He smiled at me. "I was just watching your biography." He paused to correct himself. "Well, the little they have. They focused on your fighting career. Nobody seems to know where you come from or where you went."

"Me?" I didn't address the issue of my origin. "No shit?"

"Yeah," he replied. "You were hot back then too."

I inched closer to him. "You really think I was hot when I was smacking people around?"

"Oh yeah." He slid closer to me. "You have a little sadistic streak in you. We can use that."

"Use that, huh?"

"Mmm." He kissed me and I felt the rest of the universe fade away. I pulled back and snapped myself back to reality.

"Always looking for new and better ways to fuck me. How long do I have until you get bored of me and you move on?" I wasn't sure why I said that.

Deprave sat back, with a look of concern on his face. "That came out of nowhere. Is that a serious question?"

It was a slip-up. I didn't mean to go there, but somewhere in my head, I felt like it needed to be said. "Yes, no, I mean…"

"You want to know how I feel about you." He grinned.

My breathing was becoming difficult and I had the urge to run away. I started to sweat. "No, I just wanted a timeframe."

"A timeframe? All things don't need to have an end," Deprave replied.

"All things end," I countered. "You'll get sick of my bullshit eventually."

"I see. You have intimacy and control issues," Deprave observed. "You're scared."

"Shut up!" I wasn't sure why I was getting angry. "I'm not scared of anything."

"Yeah?" he asked. "How long have you been alone?"

"I said to shut up." I jumped out of the bed.

He stood up and tried to touch me. I took a wild, sloppy swing at him. He dodged it easily, stepped in and pushed me against the wall. "No, you're not going to push me away."

"I told you to back off." I squirmed in a half-hearted attempt at escape.

"Look at me," he demanded.

I turned away, refusing to make eye contact, but no matter which direction I turned, he was in my face.

"I'm not going anywhere." He continued to press me up against the wall.

"Let me go!" I yelled.

"No. Get used to it. You have to depend on someone other than yourself now." He wasn't going to let up.

"No. It's a bad idea…"

"All the best things in the world start out as bad ideas." He smiled.

I struggled again, knowing I could escape if I really wanted to. I just didn't want to, but he was right, I was scared. "You're going to destroy me."

"No."

"You'll leave as soon as you get whatever you're after." Memories of my past few dysfunctional relationships flashed through my mind.

"No," he repeated. I let him wrap his arms around me. "No." He clutched me tight. "I don't know who did what to you before, but I am not going to ruin a good thing."

"I…" I noticed I was shaking. "I had some very bad experiences."

Deprave snickered. "We all did. My life hasn't been pain-free either. You have nothing to fear from me. I mean you no harm."

"That's what my handler said," I muttered.

Deprave arched an eyebrow. "Your what?"

"My agent." I covered my slip-up. "For fighting."

"Ah." Deprave squeezed me tighter. "Were all your past relationships working relationships?"

I rested my head on his shoulder. "All three, yes."

"In all those years, only three men," Deprave commented. "Wow. I'm not the only one who's been lonely."

Deprave's admission broke down the last bit of defense I had left. "Don't hurt me." I started trembling again. "I'll kill you."

"Never." He didn't even react to my threat. He held me until the shaking disappeared.

Chapter Twenty-eight

"If there is only empty space, with no suns nor planets in it, then space loses its substantiality."
Buddha

Another night in the coffee shop, and nothing was happening. I sat and read web comics and watched Acid drink pot after pot of coffee.

"So how many kung fu styles do you know?" Acid inquired.

"Why do you ask?"

"Because," Acid explained, "I think I counted three when you were fighting Athena."

"I didn't know you studied the martial arts, and I wasn't fighting Athena. We were practicing," I replied.

"You kicked her ass, and I don't know any kung fu stuff." Acid took a sip of her coffee. "I watch a lot of movies. So?"

"So? I fight one style, me style." I grinned. "But I did study anything I could learn to get there."

"Like what?" Acid asked.

I smiled as I remembered my training. "Like everything. I'm not going to give you a list of styles. I just studied everything I could get people to teach me. I know some obscure stuff; I know some mainstream stuff. I don't know everything though. But I studied as much as I could."

"Why?" Acid asked.

It was a fair question, but one I didn't feel like answering. I shrugged. "I don't know. It was something to do at the time."

"Oh hell!" Acid complained.

"What is it?" I asked, concerned something was wrong.

"Bitch is out of creamer," Acid complained.

"So drink it black."

"It's not the same." Acid moped.

I laughed. "Shit, it's nothing. Tell you what, I'll go to the convenience store and get some creamer."

"You don't have to," Acid replied.

"Nah, I can use a walk. I'll be right back."

Acid looked at me with concern. "Just don't…"

"I won't get tanked tonight," I promised. "I don't even have my flask with me."

Acid seemed relieved. "Good."

I stepped outside into the night air. It was late. The streets were empty and quiet. I made my way down the seven blocks to the nearest open convenience store.

Somewhere around the forth block, some unfamiliar arms pulled me into am alley. It was two men, with large builds and they were both packing guns.

"We have a message from Manta," one said.

"Let me guess. It's not a party invitation."

One guy turned to the other. "This one thinks she's funny." The other one laughed and then stayed quiet.

"No," the guy said. "He says he's not that stupid. He found out who you are, and now you will die."

Both men pointed their guns at me ready to fire. I slammed one guy into the other, knocking both their guns away. I wouldn't kill them; I would just disable them and escape. I reminded myself that all life was precious.

Out of nowhere, a gunshot grazed my shoulder. They had a fucking sniper. I went for the knock-out again, when a bullet struck my thigh. It wasn't severe, but I was bleeding. Blood flowed from my leg down to the ground; I saw it forming a puddle. The men recovered their guns and were about to shoot. My heart raced; time slowed; I heard the voice of the Demon inside my head demanding release. I fought it, but something in me snapped. Then it all went black.

***

I woke up the next day in my bed. My clothes from the night before were missing. My shoulder and leg hurt. I checked the wounds. I had performed first aid on them, but I had no memory of doing it.

I made myself some coffee, and watched the news. Two mob hit men were found dead in an alley. There were no witnesses. It looked like the work of a professional. The pictures on the screen showed two men, sliced to pieces, one completely decapitated.

I spent forty minutes going back and forth to the bathroom vomiting. The rest of the day was spent in meditation. The sun was setting before I was able to face reality again. I was about to reach for the bottle on my nightstand when I saw my phone.

There were six messages on my phone from Acid looking for her creamer.

I wanted a drink so bad, but I had just promised Acid. I decided to rough it out.

Then I read the seventh and final text message. It was from an unknown source.

Watch your back, your enemy is closer than you think.

This was starting to feel like old times.

I called Marissa and stayed home the next day. I needed some recovery time.

Not only could I not remember the previous night after being pulled into an alley, but I could not shake the feeling that something else was wrong. It wasn't just what I had done; it was definitely something else. I could almost feel something happening to the universe around me. It was like an itch that evaded scratching.

I got online and did a loose search on that feeling and anything that might be universe impacting. I knew I was reaching, but I had to try something. Most of the stuff I got was stupid occult stuff and pharmaceutical crap for anxiety. I tried using a myriad of word combinations. Finally on one search, tucked away toward the end of my search results, was a reference to a small scientific publication from Poland that looked promising. I ran it through a translation engine. It referred to a man named Amborzy Dudek. He was found dead in his home several months ago. The cause of death was unknown. It looked like someone had crushed every bone and internal organ in his body at once. I was not at all surprised to read that he was a particle physicist.

According to the article, he had been working on a project related to loop space. This was basically a concept which described the existence of pocket universes tucked inside our own. It was all very theoretical because there was no way to test it. In fact, the times some experiments were about to be attempted to explore the theory, they were shut down because of the possibility of accidentally destroying the universe itself. And this was on a scale much smaller even than microscopic. To do anything larger would require crazy amounts of energy we didn't possess.

After finishing the article, I had to know more. I read up on Dudek and learned a couple of relevant facts. The first was he quit the project claiming it was insanely dangerous and he would have no part of it. The second fact was he was good friends with Bianchi.

There was no doubt about a connection. Somebody was trying to do something extremely dangerous and was willing to kill people to keep it quiet. What I couldn't figure out was who. Was it a government, a terrorist group, or maybe a supervillain? None of our villains were that kind of bad. In fact, most of the big names were barely bad at all; well at least not in my view of things. The only bastard sick and evil enough to be behind this was Pain, but he had absolutely no interest in science. He only cared about perpetuating misery and satisfying his own desires. This couldn't hold any kind of interest for him.

I saved all my findings from this research and Bianchi's info onto a flash drive and erased any trace of it off of my PC.

Chapter Twenty-nine

"Good thoughts will produce good actions and bad thoughts will produce bad actions. Hatred does not cease by hatred at any time; hatred ceases by love."

Buddha

I sat in a corner booth of the coffee shop. Athena was getting ready to close for the night. She kept casting suspicious glances at me. I was monitoring the police bands, keeping an eye on air traffic control and plugging into the larger alarm monitoring stations in the area. I also had a chat window opened with Deprave and we were flirting shamelessly.

D: So what you wearing?

Computer: I'm with the team, what do you think that I'm wearing?

D: Tell me anyway.

Computer: Pants, a shirt, underwear.

D: What color underwear?

Computer: Light blue.

D: Ooooh. Innocent with a touch of mischief. I want to pull them off with my teeth.

Computer: Behave yourself tonight and you can.

D: Well?

Computer: Well what?

D: Aren't you going to ask?

Computer: Okay fine. What are you wearing?

D: A sock. Wanna see where?

Computer: I'm in public, no.

D: Come on, checkout the cam.

Computer: I can't. People will see.

"What are you smiling like that about?" Athena was looking over my shoulder.

"Nothin'." I tried not to blush.

"Are you flirting with your boyfriend?"

"I plead the Fifth," I informed Athena.

"Hmm. Just don't lose track of what you're doing here."

"I won't," I promised.

I was spending more of my free time with the team than ever. The operations of my business were now run by Marissa, so my days were a whole lot easier. I was still getting weekly reports from her, but it was just a formality. She was running the company far better than I was ever able to. Somehow, anonymous donations were dramatically up. Many more organizations were getting the help they needed, especially children's charities.

Sometimes I would just go hang out with Athena during the day. I still didn't trust her, but it was better to keep her nearby. Superficially, she was like a friend. I would even fill in for her staff if she was short-handed. We danced around a lot of conversations. It drove her crazy that she couldn't pin down who I was, or where I had been. She kept trying to see if she could get me to slip up, but I was always on guard with her.

We only had two taboo subjects between us. The first was our pasts, the second was my relationship. Even so, Athena would sometimes tease me about going to see my boyfriend. At first I wondered if she knew the relationship was between me and Deprave, but she didn't seem to even care. She was more irritated with the fact I could kick her ass and she had no idea why. It also irked her that I wasted my time behind the computer instead of being out on the front line with the team. She resigned herself to the fact I was more valuable doing what I did, but she still would make an occasional comment about it.

"Mighty is still dating that girl, Freesia." Athena smirked. "I wonder if she's given him the key to paradise yet."

Caught by surprise, I laughed and tea came out of my nose. "Geez, you did that on purpose."

Athena just laughed.

DJ walked in and looked at his watch. "Should I close shop?" he asked.

"Might as well," Athena replied. "There's nobody here but us chickens."

DJ flipped the sign to 'closed' and took a seat next to me. "What's up?"

"Same shit, different day." Athena laughed.

"Speak for yourself," I interjected. "My life is all good."

DJ laughed. "Mine is pretty decent too."

"What's decent? Certainly not your fashion sense." Acid stepped inside ready for verbal combat.

"Life in general," Athena filled Acid in.

Mighty walked in.

"Wow, everyone's on time," Acid remarked.

"Not everyone," Athena corrected her. "Mind and Blue aren't here."

"Everyone who counts," I added. Everyone but Athena laughed.

"Actually, I had a scare today," Acid confessed. "I blanked out trying to answer my cell phone last night and it's been bothering me all day."

"Why?" I asked.

"I know it's crazy. I was just really tired." Acid took a seat in the booth across from where we sat at the counter. "I remembered what it used to be like, before."

"Before?" DJ asked. "You mean before the drug?"

"Yeah," Acid answered. "I was severely epileptic. I wasn't able to do anything. Now I can do more than I expected. What about you, dude? What's your story?"

"Me?" DJ spun himself in her stool. "I was the party man! I also learned that taking E, K, and twelve Red Bull and vodkas nightly could cause severe brain damage after a while. My parents found me in a coma in my room when I was seventeen. I stayed in the coma for a couple of years until the drug was out. I was lucky."

"You don't drink or anything anymore?" Acid asked, casting a glance in my direction. "Do you?"

"No way," DJ replied cheerfully. "I know I'm a drug addict. I go to meetings every week. I will have some Red Bull once in a while though."

"Ah," Athena piped in. "Thursday nights."

"Yep! Everyone's invited to come along any time," DJ replied.

More eyes glanced over my way. I pretended not to notice.

"How about you, Athena? Why did you have to fix your brain?"

Athena smiled. "Nerve agent. I was in the wrong place at the wrong time when I was in the army. Got a near lethal dose of something nasty. They hit me with the drug and gave me a medical."

"Sick!" DJ cringed. "We were both victims of chemistry. How 'bout you Mighty?"

Mighty looked a little embarrassed. "Moderate Asperger's. My family thought it was worth the risk because they wanted me to be happy."

"What's Asperger's?" Acid asked.

"It's similar to autism, but usually less severe," Athena explained. "Was it hard to adjust?"

"Yeah." Mighty nodded. "Sometimes I still see that special ed kid staring back at me from the mirror."

"Mighty, you're the man," I declared. "Even with Asperger's, I bet you were still the man. People just didn't get it."

Mighty smiled and blushed.

"What about you, Miss Sidestep The Question?" Athena inquired. "What happened to you?"

"Who me?" I looked around and saw everyone waiting for my answer. "Severe depression." I didn't mention my real severe mental illnesses.

"Wait." Acid put up her hand. "I thought the drug doesn't cure that."

"No," I replied. "I took it before they knew that."

"So wait." Athena was the first to catch on. "You're still sick."

I shrugged. If only they knew. "Yeah. Guess I am. I just tweak my diet and exercise a lot. It helps some."

"Wait." Acid looked confused. "You're depressed right now?"

"Well yeah technically, especially talking about it," I answered.

"You live like that all the time?" Acid was still trying to fathom the concept. "No wonder you..." She stopped herself.

"Drink? Listen, it's no big deal," I explained. "A lot of people have it. Some much worse than me. I have good days. I have bad days, but I have to learn to live with it. And honestly, it has been a lot better since I've been part of the team. I guess it helps to fit in somewhere."

The room fell silent for a moment until DJ spoke. "Cool! So it's our job to keep you cheerful."

"Guess so." I laughed.

Mighty got a call on his cell. He shot over to Athena and whispered something in her ear. She nodded and told him to calm down. "But we got to do something," Mighty implored.

"We will," Athena concurred. "Just relax until we get all the facts."

"Facts about what?" I asked.

"Dead Beat. Mighty found out he's hitting a lab tonight."

"Nothing's been hit yet," I assured them both. "I'm hooked into the monitoring stations now. Why a lab?"

Athena ignored my question and addressed Mighty instead. "See, it's still okay."

"Yeah," Mighty replied. "But he's in town."

"Crap," Athena and I both cursed in unison.

Meanwhile my chat window was filling up.

D: You there?

D: You there?

D: You there?

D: Come on look at my sock.

Computer: We have a situation here.

D: Not me. I'm at home wearing a sock.

I couldn't help but laugh despite the situation.

"Hey!" Athena yelled. "Focus."

"Yeah, yeah," I replied.

"You'll have plenty of time for your boyfriend after we clean up this mess."

"Oooooh," DJ piped in. "Computer still has her mystery boyfriend. Is he plug-and-play compliant?"

"You betcha." I high-fived DJ and Athena rolled her eyes.

My computer beeped at me. An alarm was going off at the bank a few blocks away. At least it was close. "I got an alarm. Look." I pointed at the map on my laptop so everyone could see.

"Okay, everyone!" Athena started issuing orders. "Let's keep this peaceful. There are apartment buildings there. We don't want any casualties."

"Aye-aye, Captain!" DJ saluted Athena and faded out.

Acid just waved and took off down the street. Mighty paused. "You okay, my man?" I asked.

"Yeah," he replied. "I just have a bad feeling about this."

"Yeah me too," I agreed. "Let's just do what we can."

Mighty took off with Athena and I started the monitoring.

Dead Beat took out the sound so nobody could communicate. Luckily I had them on GPS and they had text messaging units I could send messages through. It took a huge effort to get into the security system. I wasn't sure if I was losing my edge. Either these systems were getting better, or something was up with this lab.

Dead Beat was cracking a safe when Acid caught up to him. Everyone showed up seconds later. Dead Beat, knowing he was outnumbered, dropped everything but an envelope and took off running.

Everyone was fine with letting him go. DJ smacked a tracer on his back as he passed by. The plan was to wait until he got someplace less populated and then we'd get the drop on him. That wasn't Blue Shift's plan though.

From outside the bank there was a loud thud, the sound of gunshots and a crash. The sound came back up.

"What's the sitrep?" I asked the team.

"Don't know," Acid replied. "I'm checking."

A moment later, Athena jumped onto the com. "Dead Beat is down; I don't-"

There was a loud thud and a lot of shouting. I could hear Acid screaming.

"He's already down! Stop!" The sound of more crashing and exploding ripped through the channel, then silence.

The police band went crazy. EMS and fire and rescue rushed to the scene. Outside the window, I could see smoke and the glow of fire in the distance.

Reports were coming in. A two-building explosion, hundreds assumed dead. The team filed in, Mind Master was with them.

"Why didn't you stop him?" Mighty screamed at Mind.

"I tried!" he yelled back as he cast a sideways glance at Athena.

Mighty sat down and buried his face in his hands. "This is not what I signed up for."

DJ and Acid just sat in a corner looking shocked.

My chat window flashed again.

D: What the hell is happening over there?

Computer: I think something bad, hold on.

I looked around at the distraught faces and formed the only logical conclusion. "Blue…"

"Yeah," Athena confirmed. "Blue."

Within minutes the media was on it, trying to make sense of what just happened. And as always there was Blue Shift doing his PR.

It was about ten minutes before the complete interviews made it to the air. Blue Shift was shown in front of one of the destroyed buildings addressing the viewing public. "It was a tragedy that happened here," he explained to the press. "Deprave was testing his latest superweapon on the civilians here. I think he was trying to make some kind of point. But I say this: he will never be able to hold us hostage with his threats. We will never bow down to his demands. I will personally take him out."

"What a fucking liar!" I jumped up out of my chair. "Can you people believe the audacity?"

Everyone looked away or at the floor.

"Aren't any of you going to say anything?" I couldn't believe what I was seeing. "Is this okay with you?"

"No it's not okay," Mighty replied. "But what are we going to do about it?"

"Kick him off the team, would be my first suggestion. Kick his fucking ass would be the next."

My chat window was flashing again.

D: That bastard. You know that wasn't me.

D: I was here wearing my sock.

D: You know that, right?

Blue meandered in like he owned the world.

"What the fuck was that?" I asked.

Blue spun around to face me and stepped forward. "Who told it, it can talk?"

"You know you just killed a lot of people just now?" I wondered what the hell he was thinking. "You just killed them with no remorse."

Blue clutched his temples. "I did not." He blinked and shook his head. "It was Deprave. Are you siding with criminals now? Are you some kind of spy?"

"Come on, Blue." I was stunned. "What game are you playing?"

"You're the one playing games," Blue replied. "You're spying for Deprave and trying to blame the team for his crap."

Before I could do or say anything, Athena grabbed me, and dragged me into the ladies' room.

"You need to calm the fuck down," she scolded me.

"You have got to be shitting me. He believes the crap he's talking? He's psycho. You see he's a fucking bomb waiting to go off. How much longer do you wait? How many more people have to die? We need to cut him loose."

"Yes," Athena agreed. "He's all that and more, but he owns the team."

"Okay," I acknowledged. "So we all quit and we'll make our own team."

"He owns the coffee shop, my coffee shop. He gave me the money to buy it. I owe him."

"Bullshit." I knew Athena was lying. "Crap, I'll get the money. Pay the asshole back and be free."

"Where from?" Athena inquired. "The money you stole? Or maybe your boyfriend's dirty money? Don't look surprised, I know what's going on. I know about the clandestine motel room sex, the chats, and the phone calls. I'm not an idiot. And if I know, eventually Blue will find out."

"Fuck Blue. I didn't do anything wrong. I didn't kill anyone," I lied.

Athena eyed me suspiciously. "Yeah. Sure."

"What?" It seemed that Athena had her theories about me, but wasn't going to show her hand yet.

"Listen, you're already treading on dangerous ground; do you really want to antagonize Blue? He will retaliate through the press. Do you really want that? My suggestion is to shut the hell up, go home and do whatever you do for fun. Let this go. It will take care of itself." Athena was hell-bent on keeping me quiet.

I agreed out of exhaustion more than anything. I was tired of the fight. "Fine. I'll go, but I'm not happy about it."

"Neither is any of us, but we have to deal. Now let me get you out the back before you and Blue get into it again."

She led me out the back and I went home. But that night I made it a point to post in every discussion forum online I could find.

My chat window popped open and flashed.

D: It's a waste of time.

Computer: I know. Blue will just cover it up.

D: It's not Blue. Athena is in charge.

Computer: I know that. Blue is just the face man.

D: I don't think you really understand. Things are not what they seem.

Computer: How so?

D: Just don't waste your time on this small stuff.

Computer: What was in that lab?

D: Be careful. Don't ask questions. Just observe.

Computer: I think I'm worried.

D: I know I am. But it will be okay.

Computer: Easy for you to say.

D: Go to sleep.

Computer: There's too much to do, more to find out.

D: You can't do it in one night. Besides, I tried and everything is locked down.

Computer: I'm better at this than you.

D: Yeah, but they will expect you now. I was detected.

Computer: You dumbass. Now it's going to be harder.

D: Hey!

Computer: Sorry, but it is going to be a bitch to get into anything now.

D: That's why I am telling you to hold off for a little while.

Computer: Great.

D: Just relax and get some sleep. We can deal with this tomorrow.

Computer: Okay, fine. You are a pain in the ass.

D: Sleep well.

Computer: Yeah, yeah. Good night.

I sat up half the night trying to make sense of the conversation. I finally fell asleep despite myself.

I woke up the next day sore, like I had a hard workout the day before. I dragged myself out of bed and made my way to the bathroom, still semiconscious. I was startled awake by the discovery of dried blood in the sink. On closer inspection I notice a nasty gash on my hand. It had been sewn up, and it was clean. I really hoped I didn't do anything stupid the night before. Nothing indicated I did in the news. But now I really was starting to worry.

Chapter Thirty

"A good friend who points out mistakes and imperfections and rebukes evil is to be respected as if he reveals a secret of hidden treasure."
Buddha

The tapping on the car window by the security officer only confirmed that I was lousy at surveillance. I rolled down the window of the generic rental car and tried to look as innocent as possible.

"Ma'am." He flashed the flashlight in my face. I squinted. "You have been parked here all day. Is there something I can help you with?"

"No. Not unless you want to stop the Russians."

"Excuse me, ma'am? Did you say Russians?"

"Yeah, they want you to think we are allies, but they never stopped hating us after the Cold War. And that war is just getting colder with every moment that passes. They will get us if we aren't vigilant."

"Ma'am?"

"You said that already."

"You are parked outside A&Z Electronics. We make components for appliances. We have nothing to do with Russians. I don't even know any Russians."

"Not that you know of." I scratched my head, trying not to mess up the placement of the platinum blonde wig I was wearing. It was killing me. "Roger Jones, now that's a Russian spy."

"Who?"

"My no-good ex-husband. That bastard slept with my sister, then left me with three children and now he claims he has no job or money to pay child support." I help up my cheap decoy camera. "I'm gonna catch that bastard in the act."

"What's your name, ma'am?"

"Tanya. The ex-wife of that no-good Russian spy bastard who needs to pay his child support."

"Tanya Jones. Can I see some ID?"

I pulled out a fake ID I made earlier. I had no idea if it was any good, but to me it looked like the real thing. "Here."

He took the ID. "Hold on one moment, ma'am." The security guard stepped to the side and spoke into his radio-like device. He didn't appear to care that I could hear him. "Joe, can you look up Roger Jones?" There was a pause. "I have some woman claiming to be his ex-wife Tanya Jones, out here." Then there was another pause. "I understand. Yeah, I'll wait." There was a long silence, then he spoke again. "Okay, understood." He re-joined our conversation. "Ma'am, Mr. Jones left the company three weeks ago." He gave me the ID back.

"Where did he go?"

"I don't know, ma'am, and if I knew, I couldn't tell you." Over security guy's shoulder, I could see an unmarked, nondescript, white semi pulling into one of the loading docks.

"That's because you are working with him. You're probably a Russian too!" I pushed the button on the remote I had disguised as a bracelet. It triggered the tiny camera I had hidden in the Crapmart antenna ball. I pulled out my decoy camera. "I'm going to take your picture and see what comes up. I bet you're a Russian spy too!" I started snapping pictures of the guy, with the truck behind him. "You want to take food out of my children's mouths too."

"Ma'am. I am not a spy, and I am going to have to ask you to leave. This is private property."

"No, it's the street."

"Ma'am, you are surveilling a private corporation. I can and will call local law enforcement to have you removed. Or you can just avoid the trouble and leave now." I could see some activity by the unmarked truck. They were being very careful. I could have sworn the workers were wearing radiation badges. My antenna camera should have captured it for me to double-check later.

"Fine! But you tell that bastard this isn't over."

"Yes, ma'am."

I pulled away when the getting was good. I knew I was lucky.

I returned the car and took a cab to a bus stop. I took the bus across town, and hopped buses back and forth across town until I made my way home. I stepped inside and my cell rang, no caller ID.

"Good evening."

"Russians?" It was Deprave.

"Huh? Hold on while I secure this call." I ran my security protocols, and when satisfied it was safe, returned to the call. "We're clear."

"Who told you that you were a private detective?"

"What? Have you been watching me?"

"No, but maybe I should. I was looking around their network at the time you tried to play private dick."

"You had to find a way to throw dick into this conversation. So, how did you find them?"

"I followed the money. How did you?" Deprave asked.

"Hmm. Still seems suspicious. Sure you're not following me?"

"Maybe I'm a Russian."

"Funny."

"We haven't had any disputes with the Russians in decades. What was that about?"

"Don't harass me, boy. I was going with what I used to know."

"Lucky you didn't start going on about Nazis."

"I'm not that old."

"I don't know. I saw a documentary last week that presented cave drawings of you."

"You could be replaced with a battery-powered device."

"Really?"

"No."

"Good. I did like the Roger Smith thing. Nice touch. Hack the HR database?"

"Just found some random sap who left the company recently."

"They were going to call the cops on you."

"But they didn't."

"Yes, they did. I just intercepted the call. I told them to send you away and I'd intercept you down the road."

"You're lying."

"No, you suck at field work. Admit it."

"Screw you."

"Promise?" Deprave's tone changed.

"We're talking business."

"I know." I could hear the perverted grin in his voice.

"Stop."

"Okay, but just for now. What did you find?"

"Plain white trucks making mystery deliveries to grunts wearing radiation badges."

"Interesting."

"Very."

"Wanna meet later and talk business?"

"You don't sound like you want to talk about anything."

"Is that a yes?"

"Yes."

"Excellent. Want me to bring anything?"

"Surprise me."

Chapter Thirty-one

"Holding on to anger is like grasping a hot coal with the intent of throwing it at someone else; you are the one getting burned."
Buddha

It was early evening and the last rays of the sun shone through the front window of the coffee shop. The customers had left a while ago and I sat sipping some tea and moping. Mighty sat down next to me.

"Still peeved about the Blue Shift thing?" he asked.

"He's a waste of life," I replied, looking down at my tea, wishing it was something stronger. "It's all pointless."

"What's pointless?" Mighty kicked me under the table and smiled at me.

I sighed. "All of it. Do we really make any difference? It seems that all we do is monitor ourselves. It's not like we do anything important. We don't cure diseases. We don't improve technology. We don't better humanity in any way. There are people out there who educate, strive to improve the quality of life for millions, explore science, and all we do is make sure some dumbass who shoots static electricity at people doesn't kill anyone. What's the fucking point?"

Mighty sat in silence for a moment, as if pondering the question. "I guess the real question is, do you feel like you are living up to your full potential? Do you, Computer? Lately, it feels like your mind is somewhere else."

"How should I feel? It's not like our great leader even wants me here. I feel useless." I leaned back and stared out the window. I was beginning to wonder where I ended and 'Computer' began. The last thing I needed was another identity. "I mean is this all I'm good for? Am I doomed to be a scapegoat for a bully forever?"

On queue Blue Shift stormed in. "Where is she?" he demanded.

"Who?" Mighty asked.

"Athena, the bitch who isn't keeping the geek on a leash." He stepped up to the table and pointed down at me. "I know what you're up to."

"Good for you."

"It won't be good for you. I will make your life hell."

"Too late."

Before Blue could respond, Athena came out from the back. "Hey, Blue, what's going on?"

"I'll tell you what's going on. You're not doing your job. You had strict orders to keep the useless piece of crap in line and you let it squawk all over the Internet with its lies." He looked like he was about to take a swing at Athena.

I got out of the booth and tried to look as unconcerned as possible. I leaned up against the back of the booth's seat.

"What did she say on the Internet?" Athena asked. "I haven't seen anything."

"You know very well what the cunt has been saying. Spreading her bullshit all over the place. It's taken a lot of work to clean it all up."

"It's only bullshit if it isn't true," I corrected Blue Shift.

He spun around and got up in my face. He was much larger than me so it was more like his chest got into my face. "What did you say?"

"I said," I stood my ground, "it's only bullshit if it's untrue."

"You little geek cunt bitch."

"Oh, your extensive vocabulary so intimidates me." I paused for effect. "Static Boy."

I could almost hear everyone's jaw hit the ground when I said that, and to be honest, I am really not sure what I was expecting as a response. Whatever I was expecting, it certainly was not the right hook to my face that I received. Despite the surprise attack, I still could have dodged it. I could have fed Blue his teeth and used his body as a punching bag. But I had Athena looking on. She was waiting to see if I could lay Blue out. I so badly wanted to. I wanted to beat the crap out of him and use his limp body to beat Athena down too. But I knew he was a pawn, and right now, somebody else was pulling the strings. Before I took him out, I needed to find out who his master was. I already gave Athena the message that I was no wimp, so I wasn't going to give her a show. Instead of giving her the satisfaction, I stood there and took it.

He knocked me the hell out with the one punch. I hadn't realized how strong he actually was. I flew across the room and landed back first on a table. It took a good fifteen minutes for me to regain consciousness. Now I finally knew what my opponents had gone through. When I was able to stand again, Blue Shift was gone. Everyone helped me up. Athena read me the riot act, something about stirring up a hornet's nest, but it was all very hazy. I just made my way home. I didn't cry until nobody could see me. I actually felt powerless for the first time that I could remember.

I reached for the bottle the minute I got home. My face was already swollen and I felt like a complete loser. Although I knew better, I felt like I lost a fight. I must have drunk and sobbed for a good hour before passing out. I would have slept well into the afternoon of the next day, if the text messaging on my cell hadn't gone off at nine a.m.

D: Where are you?

D: Want to see my plans for Jupiter?

D: Hello?

D: Okay, I was kidding about Jupiter.

D: Come on, answer me.

D: Answer me.

D: Answer me, or I'll crash the international banking system.

D: You know I'll do it.

D: I'm about to push the button.

D: 10

D: 9

D: 8

D: 7

Computer: Leave me alone.

D: Okay, what did I do?

Computer: Nothing, just leave me alone.

D: What happened?

Computer: Nothing, just let me rot here.

D: Are you still in bed?

D: Don't ignore me.

D: Are you still in bed?

Computer: Just forget about me and find someone who's not a loser like me.

D: Are you drinking?

Computer: Just let me die.

D: I see. I'll be right over.

Computer: Bullshit, you don't know where I live.

Computer: Fuck it, I'm going back to sleep.

I flung the phone across the room and located a fifth of vodka. I drank until I passed out again. A few hours later, I woke to someone sitting on the bed.

"Come on." Deprave's unmistakable voice was comforting.

From underneath the covers, I asked, "How did you find me?"

"You're not the only supergenius in this relationship." He rubbed my back through the covers. "I have your cell number."

"Uhhh," I moaned then immediately regretted it. My face hurt pretty badly. "How did you get in?"

"Your back door was unlocked."

"No it wasn't."

"Okay, I picked the lock, but nobody saw."

"I have a security system."

"Had. You may want to fix that later."

"You'll have to show me how to pick modern locks."

"That's not very heroic of you."

"Maybe I don't want to be a hero anymore."

"Okay, enough of this. Time to get you out of bed." He pulled the covers off of me; I covered my face.

"What the fuck is that?"

"Nothing."

He pulled my hands off of my face. He was wearing a black hoodie and a matching pair of sweats. Even incognito, he had an air of power. "That's a hell of a fucking nothing."

He stormed off out of the room. I heard noise from the kitchen and he came back with an ice pack. "This isn't going to feel good," he warned me. He put the ice on my face. I winced and tears of pain flowed down my face.

He did his best to console me, but he was too angry to remain calm. "Who did this?"

"It's no big deal. I just said the wrong thing at the wrong time. You know how I get."

"I want a name," he insisted. "Who?"

"Do you really need to ask? Blue. He found out I was telling on him online and then I called him Static Boy and he..."

Deprave didn't seem to know if he should laugh or go ballistic. "You called him Static Boy to his face?" He was unable to hold back his laughter. "That's...you're my hero."

He adjusted the ice pack on my face and I whimpered again. "I feel like a wuss. Each day I'm getting weaker." I reached under the bed and pulled out another vodka bottle.

"No," Deprave disagreed. "You stood up to the bastard. You are braver than your whole team."

"I've stood up to far worse. No, I should have dodged him. Fuck that bitch. I feel so stupid; I didn't accomplish anything." I cracked open the bottle and started drinking.

"Yes you did," Deprave explained. "You got under his skin."

I smiled, but it hurt.

"You know he's going to pay for this," Deprave stated. "I can't let this go."

"What? You're going to declare war on him?" It hurt to laugh.

"He's not worth the time." Deprave took my hand. "But you are."

"No, I'm shit."

"You need to stop drinking." He took the bottle from my hand. "You need to stop hating yourself."

"What the fuck do you know?"

"More than you think. I may not know what has you so angry, but I know how it feels."

"Fuck. You know nothing. You should stay the hell away from me before you get sucked into my hell."

"What hell?" he asked.

"I'm having blackouts again."

"Well stop fucking drinking."

"It's not the liquor," I replied. "It's the other thing."

"What other thing?" Deprave asked. "Are you doing drugs too?"

"No! Shit. Never mind. Forget I said anything."

"No, talk to me. Tell me about the blackouts." He was being very patient.

"I…" I reclaimed the bottle and took a swig. "Bad things happen when they start. Horrible bad things."

"Like what?"

"Like people getting hurt. Like pain and suffering. If it happens, you need to stay the hell away from me."

"How would I know? How could I possibly see if you were having a blackout?"

"Oh, you would know. Trust me." I hit the bottle again.

"Okay, I'll do my best, but I really can't promise because I don't understand." Deprave sighed and looked away, seeming apprehensive about something.

"What is it?" I asked. I figured he finally got sick of me and would be out of my life soon.

"There's something else..." he looked down at the floor, "something big that you need to know. But I'm afraid it will change things, change you. Plus you're in this state now. There's some strange stuff happening."

"I don't understand. What? Let me guess, it has to do with physics. Hmmm. All that shit with Bianchi still? Or is it the shit with Dudek?"

I thought Deprave was going to faint. "Where did you hear that name?"

I shrugged. "Research, investigation, curiosity. Someone killed him because of his research. I suspect he found a way to tap into loop space. Since it would take so much power to do, he must have figured it didn't matter how far he went. But then Bianchi found the way to generate the power, and the rules of the game changed. He must have quit and threatened to go public. What he was speculating could do some serious damage if actually attempted. He would have known this and tried to stop it. But who the hell would be motivated to pursue it with no regard to the fate of the universe?"

Deprave looked at me with that same expression he did when I first encountered him. His jaw hung open and he stared at me in amazement.

"It's okay, one day you may be as clever as me, grasshopper." I smiled and patted his cheek.

"Your life is in danger." He seemed a little panicked. "You need to watch your ass."

"I thought that was your job." I grinned, then took a gulp of vodka.

"I'm not joking now." Deprave cradled my head with his hands and looked directly into my eyes. "Swear to me that you will stop prying into this for a while. Please, just lay low and be careful. It's really dangerous now."

"Danger used to be my business." I laughed, but saw that Deprave was not even smiling. "Okay, I promise, but I really don't need protecting. I'm a danger to myself and others."

"I know you are some kind of master fighter, but this is serious. And Athena is not your friend. There's a reason why Bianchi calls her the devil. Please tell me that you didn't tell her anything. Do not tell anyone but me anything." He continued to look intently into my eyes. "Promise me."

"I have a good idea what Athena is. But don't worry, I never told anyone but you. I promise not to tell anyone else. But…"

"Yes?"

"Well, I just have to ask. What are you actually up to? This isn't proper villainy."

Deprave smirked nervously. "I know."

"You're not going to tell me." I could tell I wasn't going to get a straight answer from him. "Okay, fine. I won't push it now, but I'm on to you."

"Good." He seemed a little relieved.

"There's something else. I think Blue was trying to kill Dead Beat."

Deprave nodded. "Dead Beat knows too much, knew too much. Shit. I don't even know if he made it or not." The stress returned to his face. "I can't stay too long. You don't want people noticing me here." He seemed suddenly extremely paranoid.

I shook my head in acknowledgment.

He helped me out of bed, into the shower, and once I was clean, he helped me get dressed. Too soon, it was time for him to go.

"I want you to take it easy. Watch yourself." He kissed me on the forehead. "Promise me again."

"Yeah. I promise."

"And stay away from that asshole for a couple of days. Okay?"

I nodded. "Okay."

He pulled the hood over his head and left through the back door. I felt a small pang of emptiness when he left. I missed him already.

I got out of the house and went to the mall. It was hard, because everyone kept staring at my swollen face. I didn't like being in public to begin with, but now more than ever, I needed to reconnect to humanity a little. I got a bunch of small stuff and played in the video arcade. I ate some sushi for dinner and went to a silly movie. By the time I started home, I felt a lot better.

That is until I actually got home. As I turned the corner to my house, I noticed a nondescript car parked across the street, down a few houses. People were in it, not even bothering to conceal they were watching my house. It looked like they'd be there all night.

Once inside my place, I pulled out my swords from the closet I stored them in. I examined each one and remembered how beautiful they were. They were unique. The blades and hilt were deep red, almost black in color, and they were balanced specifically for me. In the correct light, it almost looked like they were flaming or glowing hot. I almost felt a longing for the old days when I held them.

After some meditation, I placed my arsenal around my bedroom. I remained sober, knowing I was now on alert. My sleep took on the feel of the old days; I slept lightly, prepared for an attack. I was surprised how easily I could switch back to that mode of existence. It was unsettling. The Demon inside me stirred, and told me it was ready.

Chapter Thirty-two

"Three things cannot be long hidden: the sun, the moon, and the truth."
Buddha

A few days later I took the risk and went to the coffee shop. My face was still a rainbow of bruises and a little swollen. I had been icing it a lot so it wasn't as bad as it could be.

Acid greeted me as I walked in. "Hey! If it isn't my favorite rebel." She pointed at my face. "Doesn't look as bad as it could."

I shrugged. "It hurts like a bitch."

DJ was cracking up in the corner. I must have given him a strange look because he explained, "Dude, do you have a brother or something?"

"Uh, no. Why?"

Acid gestured DJ to shut up as Athena walked in the room.

"Your boyfriend was here." Athena stepped up, stopping mere inches from my face.

"My...what?"

DJ was still laughing. "Dude came in all dressed in black sweats, didn't say shit. He just Kung Fu'd the shit out of Blue and left."

My jaw just hung open.

"Yup." Athena glowered at me. "Somehow he found this place."

"I didn't tell anyone anything."

"Are you sure about that?"

"Absolutely." I wasn't going to tell her about the impromptu visit.

"Still, he knew what happened."

I shrugged. "So what? It's no secret that Blue and I don't get along."

"So you promise you had nothing to do with this visit?"

"I swear." I held up my hand. "I didn't send anyone over here. I did not know anyone was coming here, and I didn't tell anyone where here is. I just cried like a bitch because my eye was swollen shut and I couldn't eat." I added the last part to invoke some sympathy.

It worked. "Blue is an ass," Athena muttered. "Keep your boyfriend away from here. I don't like the fact he found this place. So, what the hell happened to your hand?"

I had completely forgotten about it. It was still stitched up. "I cut myself in the kitchen."

Athena grabbed my hand and looked at the wound. "It's pretty long and deep for a kitchen knife, unless you were cutting tomatoes with a *katana*."

"Uh, no." I had no good answer for her. "Just spastic I guess."

Athena didn't even try to disguise her disbelief. "Been practicing?"

"Cutting tomatoes?" I grinned.

"What are you?" Athena released my hand.

"I'm a drunk who shouldn't be allowed in the kitchen with sharp objects."

Athena sighed. "You know I'll find out eventually." She shook her head and went back to what she was doing.

Acid pulled me aside. "I was by the door when it happened with Blue," she said in a hushed tone. "I saw his face. I know who it was. He smiled at me."

"What did Athena do?" I asked.

"Nothing." Acid shook her head. "She muttered something about it not being unexpected and walked away. Blue wasn't happy that nobody came to his defense."

I nodded. "Okay. Don't worry. Nothing weird, correction, nothing sinister is going on, well, no, not that. I'm not double-crossing the team or anything."

Acid nodded. "Just be careful. You're mixed up in some heavy crap. Things could get very ugly."

"How so?" I wondered what she knew.

"Don't ask. When you ask, they get mean. Just watch. I've been here a while. That's why I stand back and let the politics alone." Acid looked deadly serious. "Really, stay out of it. Something else is going on here. I don't know what."

"I'll do my best. But you know I can't stop myself from starting shit." I was amazed at how many people seemed to want to protect me lately.

"Just stay quiet for a while," Acid pleaded. "I don't want to see anymore ugliness."

"Okay." I smiled. "Did he really beat the crap out of Blue?"

Acid laughed. "Oh my God, it was hysterical. Blue had no chance to do anything. He just got destroyed and it only took a minute."

"Wow. I never had anyone defend my honor before."

Acid looked around, and then pulled me outside by the arm. "Come on." She was laughing.

"What?" I asked.

Once we were well out of view from the coffee shop, Acid spoke. "Okay, spill it. You're really doing him, aren't you?"

"I don't know what you mean." Sometimes I was terrible at playing dumb.

"Yeah." Acid wasn't buying it. "So what's he like? Apparently you keep him busy, because he hasn't been up to much since the moon."

"You know nothing. This conversation is only happening because I trust you." I knew Acid could keep her mouth shut, but it didn't really matter since Athena already knew. Hell, Mighty already knew. I might as well have put up a billboard by now.

"Well spill it."

"Okay. He is a sweet lay."

Acid exploded with laughter. "No way. I must have details. Does he live up to his name?"

"Yes, he does." I felt myself blush a little. "He has a body that could stop traffic, and he knows how to use it."

"Your crime-fighting methods rock. And they sound like a lot more fun than anything I have to do."

"Well, you know I got it like that." Acid and I both burst into laughter.

"Hey, want to go grab some pizza?" Acid asked.

"Yeah." It sounded like an excellent idea. We blew off the coffee shop and went down the street to the local pizzeria.

I ordered us a pie, and we took a booth in the back of the restaurant. I sat with my back against the wall and stretched my legs out over the booth. I took a moment to enjoy the stress free moment.

"So does he talk like that in bed?" Acid prodded me for more of my 'crime-fighting techniques'.

"No, yes, not really." She succeeded in making me blush again as the pizza arrived at our table, steaming and gooey, fresh from the oven.

"Mmm." The aroma of pizza delighted my senses. "It's been so long since I've eaten junk food."

"You're an alcoholic."

"No, I'm a drunk. I don't go to meetings. But I still eat right and exercise. Imagine how messed up I'd be if I didn't."

"Kinda makes sense." Acid shrugged. "Hey look..." Acid pointed at the door where Mind Master was walking in. "Should I call him over?"

"Why the hell not?" I had no real beef with Mind.

Acid waved Mind over. He approached cheerfully, that is until he realized I was there too.

"Come on." I patted the seat next to me. "Sit with us. We have yummy pizza."

Mind looked uncomfortable. He looked around and grabbed a chair from one of the tables and sat at the edge of our table, instead of sitting in the booth with us.

"She doesn't have cooties," Acid said.

"No offense, but I can't sit near her; we have a problem."

"Since when?" I was surprised by this new fact. "I thought we were cool with each other."

"We are," Mind replied, "but not me and it."

"It?" Acid asked. "It what? What are you talking about?"

"Acid," my eyes didn't leave Mind, "can you get us some sodas?"

"Yeah," she agreed. "I'm going to the bathroom too, but I don't like this."

Acid and I exchanged glances. I didn't want her to feel like I was blowing her off. I hoped she would understand. Acid sighed and walked off.

"You're overreacting," I explained to Mind. "It's not what you think; it's just a nickname for my insanity. Where did you hear about it anyway?"

"You're not insane. Nobody told me anything. I see it inside of you. This is what I do. This is why I don't go on many missions. When everyone's fighting the bad guy, it doesn't help anyone to have me advise them that the universe is sick."

"Is the universe sick?"

"You tell me," Mind countered. "Or should I ask it? Maybe you'd like a moment to confer."

"It doesn't work like that. I have no direct contact with that part of me. In fact, I spend most of my energy trying to keep it from surfacing."

"You don't control it. It controls you. It lets you do what you want only when it suits its purposes. Don't ever forget that."

"Oh, okay." He was pissing me off now. "You know me so fucking well. Prove it."

"Okay, Computer. Tell me, what is your first childhood memory?"

"What?" Bare feet running through the woods; the sound of dogs barking in the distance; the fear of being captured: all were my first memories at the age of sixteen. It was very hazy and so long ago.

"What's the first thing you remember?" he asked again.

I looked at him, unable to respond. I knew what he was getting at. I had no childhood that I could recall.

"I hope I took long enough." Acid approached with a tray of drinks.

"Perfect timing." I forced a smile.

"You were saved by the bell," Mind added.

"Nah," I said. "I never needed to be saved by the bell."

"You did this time." Mind cracked a smile and took his drink from Acid's tray.

"You know, I bear you no ill will."

"I know. But if anything happens, remember that I will always take the side of light."

"Light, dark, who the hell cares!" Acid threw up her arms in mock frustration. "Are we gonna eat pizza or what?"

"We're going to eat pizza," I replied.

"Most certainly," Mind said.

"Good." Acid put the tray on the table and slid into the booth.

For a few hours, the three of us ate pizza and felt like normal people for a change. Mind even seemed to have a good time.

Chapter Thirty-three

"You can search throughout the entire universe for someone who is more deserving of your love and affection than you are yourself, and that person is not to be found anywhere. You yourself, as much as anybody in the entire universe deserve your love and affection."
Buddha

It was a beautiful Saturday afternoon, so I took a long run. I hooked on my music player and just went. I was feeling good despite the Blue Bastard dramas. My face healed up okay. Blue didn't have to worry anyway, because nobody paid any attention to anything I said online. I guess it was easier for the world to live in denial, than to come to terms with the fact that their biggest hero was a fraud, and even worse, a criminal himself.

We all seemed to bounce back from these incidents, no matter how bad Blue's deeds were. Athena said it was because we were resilient. I disagreed and said we were all just chicken; we were all just too scared to deal with it, so we folded it up neatly into a package within our minds and buried it. Athena and I agreed to disagree, but even that didn't solve the real problem.

I made it a few miles from my house when I got the feeling I was being watched. I didn't see anyone, but there was something. I considered calling in, making sure DJ wasn't up to some prank, but this didn't seem like DJ's style, and I didn't want to make this team business yet.

I turned as my attacker jumped out at me. Instinctively, I prepared for battle. I centered myself and struck. I watched how he responded and stepped back. Another person stepped up behind me to join the party. I got a glimpse of the second person and realized they were in uniforms.

"Fucking henchmen! Why can't I just go for a run without somebody's minions fucking with me?" The sound of a weapon discharging resonated from within the bushes. I avoided a dart as it was launched at me, but a second and then a third followed. The third one struck me in the leg; before I could pull it out, I was overcome by dizziness. I slumped to the ground and passed out.

***

I awoke in a strange bed, in a strange room. I sat up and did a mental assessment. I didn't have a headache or any other physical discomfort, and I didn't appear to be missing any body parts.

I got out of the bed and shivered as my feet hit the cool tile floor. The floor itself was beautiful, ornately patterned and flawless. Orange light from the setting sun filled the room with a warm glow. I pulled aside the sheer curtains to look outside, but the glass was frosted.

I glanced into the mirror on the wall and noticed that my clothes were gone. Instead of my exercise clothes, I was now clad in a black leather bustier and a weird pair of matching crotchless panties. There was a pair of black leather stiletto-heeled boots by the door, but I chose to remain barefoot. This way I could kick ass more effectively. Somebody was going to pay.

I tried the door and found it unlocked. I stepped out into a long, dimly lit hallway, which was also tiled, but in a different pattern than the room. Since there were no windows, there was no ambient light. Small, dim sconces lined the walls, several yards apart from each other.

There were doors to other rooms throughout the hall. I tried them, but they were all locked. At the end of the hall, there was one final door. It wasn't like the others. It was solid and heavy, and when I tried it, it opened.

I stepped in, and there sat Deprave, barely clad in a robe.

"Hello, beautiful," he greeted me.

"Oh man, I should kick your ass."

"That's an odd way to say hello."

"You could have just invited me. I would have come voluntarily."

"I know. But I decided to skip all the formalities. So how do you like the lab in person?"

I looked around and took it in. "Impressive. It's even more incredible in person."

Deprave grinned. "I know."

"So, what's with this tacky outfit you put me in?" I asked.

"I see you didn't put on the boots."

"Well I didn't want to risk breaking my ankle in them while beating my kidnapper. So what's the deal with these weird crotchless panties? You know the hole is off in them?"

"No it's not." Deprave leered and pulled out a respectable-sized dildo. "The hole is to hold this in place."

My cheeks got hot from embarrassment. "That's, um, pretty kinky."

"Come on, my sweet, stop being a prude. You said you were going to bend me over. Don't tell me that you're all talk and no action."

"You honestly want me to...?"

"Why not? You have unresolved control issues. Here's your chance to deal with them." He sauntered over to me, and slipped the dildo in my pants so it stuck out of the hole in the front. "It vibrates." He reached into my underwear and flipped a switch. He didn't pull his hand back out, instead he stoked me, until I was physically aroused. "You won't feel the vibration until you thrust. I did careful research to find the one that will give you the best thrill." He pulled his hand away, leaving me hungry for more. "Come on, Computer, take me." He undid the tie on his robe and let it fall to the floor. "Come on, take what's yours."

I hesitated, feeling awkward and inhibited. He had obviously put a great deal of effort into planning this, but I was unable to get my nerve up.

"If you're not going to take care of me, I'm going to have to take care of myself." He started playing with himself. "Maybe you just like to watch."

Watching him touch himself only increased my level of excitement. I was breathing heavily and my heart felt like it would beat out of my chest.

"Don't let fear stop you from taking what you want. One of the things that attracted me to you is your defiance. You do what you want, even in the face of disapproval. This is between you and me; the world can go to hell. Take me; give me what I want. Empower yourself."

Something in his words made sense. I never felt I had empowerment issues, but my aggression could be better channeled. It wasn't like I was hurting anyone, since he was consenting. I took a deep breath and went for it. I stepped forward and grabbed him by his hair and slammed him face first into the lab's control console. I took the belt from his robe and tied his hands behind his back.

"Yes," he panted.

The embarrassment and self-consciousness faded as I started to have my way with him. "Should I stop?"

"No!" he pleaded.

"What will you do for me?"

"Anything. Please give it to me."

I stopped for a moment just to tease him. "Like what? Tell me what you'll give me."

"The moon. You can have the moon."

"That's not enough."

"I'll give you the world. I'll take the planet and give it to you."

"Still not enough. Give me more."

"The solar system. No, the galaxy."

"The galaxy, yes!" I let myself go, completely overwhelmed by the experience. "Keep begging or I'll stop."

"The galaxy is yours to command. Oh God, please don't stop!" He gasped and writhed in rhythm with me. "Don't..." His body stiffened and trembled. He screamed unrestrained and in absolute ecstasy.

That drove me over the edge. My knees buckled; the fire within me exploded into an intense and utter state of rapture. The feeling was so intense that tears ran down my face and my body convulsed uncontrollably.

"Oh my fucking God!" The sensation was overpowering. "Oh my God."

The feeling gradually subsided and I slumped over him, trying to catch my breath.

"There's nothing like that rush of power, is there?" Deprave asked breathlessly.

"I never felt anything... Wow, and nobody died." I felt weak and drained, but very satisfied. I peeled myself off of him and sat in his chair.

"The best thing is that we can do it again." He pulled himself off of the console and knelt in front of me.

"Yeah. I guess we could. Wanna switch next time?"

"Switch, really?" he asked with hesitation in his voice. "You mean really switch?"

"Yes." I smirked. "I'll let you do me up the ass."

His face lit up with a huge grin. "Well in that case, I'm getting the galaxy back."

Chapter Thirty-four

"When we feel happy and peaceful, our happiness and peace radiates around us, and others can enjoy it as well. This is called 'the enjoyment of others of our body of bliss'."
Buddha

I opened my eyes to find myself floating down a river in a boat. The current gently pushed me down through a cavern, the walls of which bled what appeared to be human blood. I was clad in a white robe and a pair of sandals and armed for battle. I held my large sword by my side. It took a moment for my eyes to adjust, but I could see the outline of figures in my peripheral vision ducking in and out of view.

I felt very cold. I could see my breath. There was no sound but that of the water against the boat. My heartbeat pounded audibly and then suddenly stopped.

I was on my way to hell.

I didn't remember dying. I wondered if Deprave killed me in my sleep, or maybe someone else snuck in and took me out. Either way, it was time for me to pay the check.

Moans of my victims echoed from downstream. They cried out for vengeance; they begged to be put to rest. As their cries reached my ears, I could feel their pain. I felt every wound I inflicted, every death I caused. I could do nothing but feel the agony, knowing I would feel it forever. I slumped down to my knees, using my sword to hold me up, fighting to keep from falling out of the boat.

The boat drifted ashore, ready to deposit me to the eternal damnation that waited. I stumbled out of the boat; the anguish built up until I was completely overcome by it. I screamed, but there was no one to hear me. Just as I was about to give up and let the pain steal away the remainder of my insignificant soul, Deprave stood before me.

He was dressed in black, and stared down at me intently, yet he still smiled. He took my sword and examined it for a moment. He looked at me and cocked his head; then he raised the sword and brought it down on me.

It was a forceful blow, splitting me down the front of my body. I looked down at the wound, but there was no blood, no guts; instead a golden light emanated from inside and wrapped me in its warm glow.

I woke up in Deprave's bed. I opened my eyes to catch him staring down at me smiling. The sun shone in from a window behind him and illuminated his face. He looked like an angel.

"What are you doing?" I asked.

"Watching you sleep."

"Sounds very exciting. Want to go watch some paint dry?"

"As exciting as that sounds, I was thinking of breakfast first." He stroked my shoulder.

I gazed at his beauty and wondered what I had done to deserve it.

"What is it?" he asked.

"I dreamt about you."

"What did I do? I hope it was good."

I smiled. "You rescued me."

"Yeah, from what?"

"From hell."

"Ah, but it was just a dream; you wouldn't be in hell."

I shook my head. "No, if there is a hell, I am going to it. There is no doubt."

"Well, then I'll come rescue you." He put his arms around me and kissed my neck.

"I really believe you would."

"Of course I would. Want to eat breakfast on the balcony?"

"Sure."

He got up and helped me out of bed. I grabbed a robe from the chair next to the bed and followed him out of the room and up a set of stairs just outside in the hall. He opened the door and sunlight rushed in; we stepped outside into a tropical paradise. The air was hot, but tempered by a gentle breeze. The fragrance of flora of various types nearly overpowered my senses. Everything was bright, colorful and full of life. I stopped dead in my tracks. It was absolutely breath-taking.

"You like it?" He pulled out a chair for me by the table.

I sat. "It's incredible."

A young woman came out through another door with a tray of fruit and coffee. She left it on the table and scurried off.

"I thought you sent everyone away."

Deprave poured a cup of coffee and handed it to me. "I sent the henchmen away. I need the staff to keep the house running."

"You know we were really loud last night." I sipped at my coffee.

"They're paid not to hear us."

"No. They're paid not to tell anyone that they heard us. But they definitely heard us. Geez, all that stuff we said."

Deprave sighed. "I still owe you the galaxy."

"Yup, but I did swear allegiance to you and to lead your robot army into battle."

He laughed and gazed at me for a moment. "You could stay, you know. You don't have to leave."

"Wow." I put down my coffee. "I wasn't expecting that. I…"

"I didn't mean to make you uncomfortable." Deprave took my hand. "But I really would like it if you stayed here, with me."

"I want to…"

"But?"

"My team, and…" I really couldn't think of any other reason not to move in. "I just owe the team not to take off."

"Do you really want to work with that buffoon your entire life?"

I shook my head. "No. It's not him I am thinking about." I sighed. "Listen, I'm not saying no. I'm saying let me tie up the loose ends first. You do make me…" I paused and considered the implication of what I was about to say.

"Yes?"

"You make me happy."

"You make me happy too." He squeezed my hand. "I'll fly you home tonight. You take whatever time you need. Okay?"

"On what?"

"My chopper."

"How the hell can you navigate a chopper through all that crap?"

"I'm a supergenius, remember?"

I nodded, not in the mood for a scientific debate. "Are you going to knock me out again?"

"Nah. Once you let a woman sodomize you in your lab, it's probably okay to let her know where you live."

We both laughed.

Deprave's cell rang, he looked at it. "I have to get this. Hold on." He stepped away a few feet, but I could hear a few words.

"She's here," he said into the phone. There was more jumbled conversation. "…yes, please not..." The conversation went on for a while before he hung up.

He sat next to me and took my hand. "I'm sorry for what I am about to do."

"Are you going to try to kill me or something?" I asked, half joking.

"No, I'm going to rescind my request that you stay out of trouble." He sighed.

"Why does that bother you?"

He looked away. "I'm putting you in danger. I am asking you to risk your life."

"Nobody else has been able to get into this stuff, have they?"

"No." A tear ran down Deprave's cheek. "I'm afraid to fill you in on much more, because I don't want anything to happen to you. If it were up to me, I'd keep you here and surround you with bodyguards. I know that's selfish, but I don't want to lose you."

"You won't lose me." I wiped away the tear. "I'm not what you think I am. I've been in trouble long before you were even born. I think I had this coming to me somehow, on a karmic level."

He shook his head. "I know there's something you're not telling me. Is it why you drink so much?"

"I've slowed that down recently," I replied. "I guess you're a good influence on me."

Deprave laughed. "I'm a supervillain."

"No," I corrected him. "You are not. I used to be a villain. I was once a horrible, evil monster. You're just bored and stirring up a little trouble."

"I don't believe it. What did you do?" he asked.

"I…" I paused. "I'm not ready to talk about it." I started shaking and instinctively reached for something to drink. There was nothing nearby.

Deprave grabbed my hand. "Shh. We don't have to talk about it."

"I'm sorry. I don't know how you can stand me."

"You are as twisted and messed up as me." Deprave smiled.

I shook my head. "You just don't know."

"I'm not stupid. I'm aware you're no angel. I know more about you than you think. Like I know you were kicked out of pro fighting for being too violent. I know you never go anywhere unarmed. You also made mention of a handler that time. But on the other hand, I know you visit a little old lady in the nursing home regularly." Deprave paused for a moment, laughed and then added, "Almost forgot, I know you sleepwalk carrying your weapons, and practice in front of a mirror with a creepy smile on your face."

"When?" This revelation frightened me. The stuff moved around my house; the cut on my hand; it all made sense now.

"A few times at the hotels. But you never leave the room, and you barely pay any attention to me."

"Oh, God." He had no idea what he had witnessed. "I'm so sorry. I didn't mean to put you in that danger."

"Danger? I don't think so. You couldn't hurt me."

"You don't understand. That's not me. That thing…" I was shaking again.

Deprave stoked my cheek softly. "It's okay. Whatever it is, you or a thing, it knows I'm no threat."

"How the hell can you know that?" I was considering all of the ramifications of this new discovery.

"You, it told me."

"The freaking Demon spoke to you?"

"Demon?" Deprave grinned. "Okay, that's weird. But yes, you, uh, it spoke."

"Well?"

"Oh. It said 'You' and pointed a sword at me. Then it said, 'You live.' I just thought you were having bad dreams."

I shook my head. "I have something like a multiple personality. I thought it was gone. It started like this the last time. Blackouts, for a while, then I started to have an idea what was happening. I wouldn't be able to do anything about it. I'd just be there for the ride. Shit. I was sure it was gone, but it's starting just like before. I can't remember everything that happens during the blackouts, until it all comes back in my dreams. Sometimes, that takes a while. It's bad."

"So you really are crazy." Deprave was beaming. "I like having a psycho girlfriend; it's good for the image."

"This is serious. I could hurt someone."

"So what's with the swords? Guns are easier."

"Never mind about the swords. It's trouble. I'm putting you in danger."

"So what? Who cares?" He put his arm around me and started stroking my neck. "Whatever it is, we'll deal with it. Now, it's a perfect day, let's not ruin it by worrying about what could happen. There will be plenty of time for drama later. Today, let's have fun."

"Okay," I forced a smile. His touch made all the anxiety fade away. "But no more jello, it took forever to get that out of my hair."

"Okay, but only if I get to wear the chicken suit."

Chapter Thirty-five

"I am always at the beginning."
Buddha

After the visit to the lair, Deprave and I started seeing each other more frequently. We would meet in remote hotels two or three times a week. I found the more I saw him, the more I wanted to see him. I regretted my decision not to stay with him that day.

Today Deprave arrived first and got the room before my arrival. He sent me a text message with the room number and I met him there. As I opened the door, I was assaulted by the stench of alcohol. The place smelled like a barroom at the end of a Saturday night. I saw Deprave sitting up on the bed, swigging at a bottle of tequila. There was already an empty on the floor beside the bed.

"Are you okay?" I asked, cautiously approaching the bed.

Deprave laughed and took a swig. "Why wouldn't I be?" he slurred.

"Um, well, I don't know. You're kind of hammered there. That's normally my job."

He started laughing again. "Hammered, yeah, you don't even know."

"Do you want to talk about it?" I sat on the bed next to him and reached out to hold his hand.

He pushed my hand away. "No." He took another gulp out of the bottle.

"Did I do something wrong?"

"Why do you keep asking me that? Just shut up and leave me alone."

"Keep?" I thought back to the last time we had this kind of exchange. It had been a long time, a year... "Oh crap. It's that time of year."

"Shut up," Deprave muttered and finished off the bottle.

"I don't think you should drink like that. You'll hurt yourself."

Defiantly he reached over and grabbed another bottle and broke the seal. "Too late."

"Okay." This was becoming painful to watch. "Why don't you tell me about it?"

"No."

"Why not?" My voice betrayed my growing frustration. "What could be so bad that you can't tell me? Shit, I've bent you over your console and did you with a dil-"

Before I could finish my sentence, Deprave threw the bottle at the wall. It smashed, splashing everything near it with glass and tequila. "Shut up!"

"Okay, I said the wrong thing." I reached over Deprave and grabbed a bottle of cheap whiskey from the case of assorted booze he had acquired. I cracked the seal and swigged. It felt good.

"You shouldn't drink that," Deprave advised me.

"Fuck it. Let's do this self-destruction thing together." I took another swig.

Deprave didn't reply, and we sat in silence for a good fifteen minutes. "Kiet," he finally said.

"What?"

"My name," he explained. "My real name is Kiet."

"Nice to meet you, Kiet. I'm Becca."

"Becca." He took a pull from the bottle. "I like it. It's sweet. It will make it feel even more dirty when I violate you."

"Violate me? Jesus! What is it with you?" Now I was really hitting the bottle. "Give it a fuckin' rest already."

"What do you expect? I am as I was made." He laughed sardonically. "You knew what I was when we started fucking."

"Yeah, well you promised there was more to us than that." I stared off into space feeling like an ass, knowing it was just his pain talking.

There was another long awkward silence. I started feeling the effects of the alcohol.

Kiet muttered to himself in Thai again and continued drinking. "I'm a piece of human garbage."

"You are not." The self-loathing was far less surprising to me than it should have been. "Where is that coming from?"

He started laughing and drinking again. "This is coming from the retard; didn't you know that's what I am?"

I sighed and looked directly at him. "Listen, I know you were mentally challenged, but…"

"Challenged?" He laughed again and spilled some tequila on the bed. "Oops. That was challenged of me." He took another gulp and finished off this bottle. According to my count, that made two and change. "No, not challenged, my sweet, re-tard-ded. Say it with me." He kept laughing, and reached for another bottle. When he wasn't immediately able to grab one, he gave up and continued speaking. "It's funny, even when you're so bad that they can't even fucking toilet train you, you can still remember everything." He clutched his head and whimpered. "Why won't it go away?"

"Shhh." I caressed his back.

He pulled away, apparently repulsed by his moment of weakness and grabbed for another bottle.

"I think that you've had enough." I reached for the bottle, but he pulled away.

"No." He cracked it opened but didn't drink. "This will make me forget."

"For how long?" I asked. "A few hours? And then what? It doesn't last. I know."

"It doesn't matter!" He poured a shot down his throat. "It kills the pain."

"What pain?" I demanded. "What holds this kind of power over you?"

"The people who owned me, the fucking *farang*, shit everyone." He paused and took another drink. "I come from a shithole. The kind of place you see in those commercials to save children for pennies a day. You know the ones." He turned his head and looked at me. When I nodded, he turned back, staring into space. "My family was shit. I was one of a whole litter of children that my mother just kept spitting out." He took a swig. "The others were useful. They could earn money. Everything was about money. But I..." He hit the bottle again. "Well, it became clear I wouldn't be of any use. I'd never work in a factory, or in the fields. I couldn't even beg properly. All I could do was shit and piss myself and eat. So one day, my parents put me into a car and sent me away. I can only assume they got paid something. Even retards have a value; they are flesh and flesh sells."

The reality of his last statement hit me and I felt the anger inside me burn. I took another gulp from the bottle and stared speechlessly as he continued.

"I made good enough money for them for a while. The white men liked me because I didn't complain and since I didn't look like a retard, they took it to mean that I enjoyed it. I was treated okay, considering. They fed me, gave me a place to sleep. I just had to take it up..." He broke down for a second but caught himself. "Anyway, after I hit puberty and stopped being cute, they kicked me out on the street. I wasn't there for too long when the drug company picked me up to run tests on me. They treated me okay, too. I got food, and a bed. All I had to do was get shots and endure some pain. After months of testing, I got smart. I saw what happened to the others who showed any signs of intelligence and decided I wanted to live a little longer than they did. So I pretended to still be stupid, ended up back on the street, and well, the rest is history."

I couldn't find any words. I watched him drink, trying to find the right thing to say. Finally I just grabbed him and pulled him close. I expected a fight, but instead he slumped into my arms, buried his face in my shoulder and started sobbing. "I never told anyone." He wrapped his arms around me and held tight.

"You want to hear my secret?" I asked.

"Mmmm."

"I'm in love with you."

He didn't say another word; he just clung to me and sobbed himself to sleep.

Chapter Thirty-six

"Of all footprints, that of the elephant is supreme. Similarly, of all mindfulness meditations, that on death is supreme."
Buddha

"Don't you have a company to run, Slaughter?" Lila's voice was weak, but her words still echoed her defiant spirit.

"I quit. I have better things to do now."

Lila smiled. "That man keeping you busy, huh?"

"He asked me to move in with him." I sat in a chair next to Lila's hospital bed. They had her on dialysis. Her kidneys had failed, and the rest of her was only hours behind.

"What did you say?"

"I told him that I had to wrap up some loose ends first." I held her hand. I could feel her life slowly slipping away.

"Don't let me stop you."

I shook my head. "You know there's more to it than that."

"I miss Mo," Lila lamented.

"I know." I felt my insides twisting when I thought about it. "He was your boyfriend."

"Yeah," Lila agreed. "I guess he was. He always got me a muffin every morning. He would come barging into my room and harass me until I got up. He used to say that if we were twenty years younger, he'd do me right there. I'd tell him we'd need a case of male enhancement drugs and a gallon of lube. He'd help me to my chair and we would just be together. You know, no expectations, no plans, we'd just go about our days, but we had each other. I miss him so much." A tear ran down her cheek, but I didn't wipe it. I knew she wanted it there. She wanted to feel his loss; in that way, he was somehow still with her.

She smiled at me. A melancholy feeling filled the room. We both knew this was the last time we'd see each other.

"I want you to be happy, Becca."

"I will," I lied. My throat tightened; I found it difficult to speak. "I'll miss you."

"It's okay. You'll be here someday, and it will be okay too. Just take advantage of the gift you've been given. Let yourself feel. Even pain can be good. It gives you something to compare the joy with."

"Okay." My voice was barely a whisper.

"Tell me the truth." Lila locked eyes with me. "Why are you punishing yourself, really?"

"I…" I forced in a breath. "I killed a lot of people."

This actually surprised Lila. "Really? You said you were joking."

"I didn't want you to stop being my friend." I shrugged. "I was a horrible, horrible person."

"Tell me," Lila requested. "I won't stop being your friend. I promise."

I looked away from her in shame. She was too kind to be soiled by my presence, yet she invited me anyway. "I, um, was never a very good person.

Even before I lost my soul, I had a sick bloodlust I could never satisfy. I was about to lose my job. The rumors were true. What I didn't tell you was that I knew I was being brutal; I enjoyed it. I hurt too many people too badly in the ring. I ran out of people to fight, since nobody wanted to get near me, so I was useless to any promoters. I met Nelson in a bar after my last fight. He took me back to his room and we screwed. God, it wasn't even any good. The relationship was really bland, but I was so naïve. I had no idea what I was doing, and who I was doing it with." A lump started forming in my throat.

"It's okay, Becca," Lila tried to comfort me.

I shook my head. "No it's not." I grabbed a tissue in preparation for the tears. "You see, I had a natural aptitude for killing, and Nelson was good at spotting raw talent. He sought me out, made it look like a chance meeting. He found a way to channel my darkness in a way I wasn't even conscious of. He fractured my mind. Oh my God." The tears started. The pain I had buried for all the decades flowed out through my words. "He was my personal guide to my decent into hell. It only took one small step and I spiraled into an abyss I remained in for years. I killed so many people. First I did it for Nelson, then for my country. Soon I did it for money, and it wasn't too long until I did it because I liked it. When people talk about bloodlust, they don't understand. I really got off on killing people. I don't mean figuratively. I would wake up places, sweaty and spent like I had been screwing all night."

"Wow, so the pain and death of others made you hot. No wonder you were afraid to date again."

Lila was good at seeing the humor in anything. "So were you a sniper or something like that?"

"No, I was a martial artist; I killed up close and personal. I had a thing for bladed weapons; I even had a sword just for decapitations. People knew when I had done a job. I left corpses that were practically diced up. Only I made sure they would be recognized so my employers would know the job had been done. I was very good at what I did. People paid handsomely for my services. And when I struck, everyone knew 'The Fat Lady' had done someone."

Lila coughed in an attempt to laugh. "Did you have a weight problem or something?"

"No, silly. When you saw me, you knew it was over."

"Ah." Lila smiled warmly. "But that's who you were. Not who you are now."

"No, there's more, something even more horrible than that." I clutched the memory stick around my neck. I could almost feel the ghosts of the dead call me from inside it. "I was in Chechnya, right before the asteroids and the bomb accident. I was sent in to kill the guy who detonated it. They stashed him away, knowing the US didn't sanction the plan. NATO already had troops in the area poised at all known launch facilities. Everyone told them launching nukes was a bad idea. It was supposed to be a near miss. The Russians were so sure." I paused to wipe my eyes. "I didn't know any of the politics at the time. Nobody told me why I was killing this guy, just that he was some kind of renegade terrorist. Nobody ever told me why I was killing anyone. I didn't care. I had no idea about the nuke or any of it. I just knew I was paid a lot to take out this guy. I was even looking forward to it. It had been a while since I got some killing in. I got there and had to take out eleven people just to get to the bastard. I found him in a room upstairs; it was like he was expecting me. He just sat there and let me kill him; he put up no fight at all. After I landed the final blow, all he did was tell me that I was too late; the launch sequence had started, and the world was saved."

I paused to catch my breath. I was shaking again, and I was having trouble breathing. "I felt something that day for the first time since I started down that path. I felt fear. All I knew for sure was that a nuke was involved and I didn't want to be anywhere near it. I didn't try to stop the bomb. I had no idea what they planned. I didn't call anyone. I only cared about my own ass. I ran out of that place and stole a motorcycle. I sped over to the airport, dropped ten thousand dollars on the counter and told them to get me a flight out. I didn't care who they had to bump. They didn't even flinch, they just took the money and put me on a plane. I..." I stopped, unable to continue. I clung to the edge of the bed sobbing. I was about to tell Lila the words I was really afraid to say out loud for fifteen years. I was about to confess my biggest sin.

"They kicked off a little girl. I saw them walk her off the plane. She..." I struggled again to breathe, my guilt bearing down on me, reminding me what I was. "She couldn't have been more than four. They traded my life for hers, me a soulless demon walking the Earth killing, in exchange for the life of an innocent child."

I stopped speaking again. The words burned like the sin itself. Lila said nothing; she just patted my hand gently. After several minutes, I continued. "We were in the air for a couple of hours, when the bomb exploded. That's when the realization of what I had done hit me. I tried to convince myself that she got on another plane, but I knew better. We landed somewhere in eastern Asia. I don't even remember which airport. I got off the plane, grabbed my crap and just walked. Until I got off the plane, I hadn't even realized I was still in the same clothes I wore during the assignation. I was still covered in blood. I literally looked like I came straight out of hell. Anyone who saw me just ran away. I walked for days. I walked day and night. I ate nothing. I was exhausted but I didn't care. I just kept going, with no thought what I was going to do. I think maybe I was waiting to die. Finally, I collapsed. I have no idea where, or when. I just dropped. I don't know how long I was out, but they found me, and took me in, knowing what I was."

Lila smiled. "The fortune cookie talk. You were saved by Buddhist monks, weren't you?"

I nodded. "They were the only ones who weren't afraid. They saw something in me worth saving."

"How long?" she asked.

"It took me over twenty years just to learn how to feel again. Then they told me I had my soul back and to go out into the world to find my way and do good."

"You are doing good."

"Not enough. I don't get it most of the time. I'm a drunk and I'm morally ambiguous. The dark part of me is like a separate entity, and I just found out it's back. I'm a danger to everyone around me. No matter what I do, it will never be enough. I know I am going to hell."

"No." Lila squeezed my hand. "You haven't hurt any of your friends. And you do try to help others. You try to redeem yourself every day. And most importantly, you've learned to love. You've already been saved. Just don't lose that love. Promise."

"I promise." Maybe she was right. Maybe I could be saved.

"Well, I guess I'm getting into heaven. You really helped the grading curve for the rest of us." Lila laughed, and so did I.

"Well, even without my help, I think you are a shoo-in. God loves whores," I replied. "You provide a valuable service to your community."

"Yeah, and we leave less of a mess then your kind."

"I guess used condoms are easier to sweep up than corpses." I couldn't believe we were laughing about this, about death.

"I don't know; I've had to clean up after quite a few corpses in my day." That broke me. I laughed until I cried, and then I laughed some more.

I spent the night with her. We talked and laughed until she couldn't anymore, and when that happened, she drifted off to sleep. She slept peacefully, with a smile on her face. By morning, she was gone.

Chapter Thirty-seven

"Let us rise up and be thankful, for if we didn't learn a lot today, at least we learned a little, and if we didn't learn a little, at least we didn't get sick, and if we got sick, at least we didn't die; so, let us all be thankful."
Buddha

With the loss of Lila, I focused on information gathering. I needed to distract myself from my grief, and keep my mind occupied. Besides, the whole thing kept gnawing at me. Bianchi, Dudek, the murder. Who was behind it? Someone took over those projects, but who? I decided the best way to find anything is to follow its trail. And the trail for research projects is money.

I hit the banking systems, the creditors, schools, charities, everything was a dead end. The money had to come from somewhere. But maybe I was doing this backwards. Maybe I needed to figure out who had the money and power to back all of this.

I considered that it could be our government, but it was too far-reaching, even for them. No, it had to be something else. But who could wield that kind of power? I knew the supervillains; none of them were capable of this.

I didn't know Pain. He was the only wild card in the equation. Nobody interfered with him, even our government. The fact he was dangerous really was no reason to stop trying to erode his powerbase.

It seemed more likely that the governments of the world were in bed with him, than afraid of him. I couldn't imagine an entire world afraid of just one man.

I was going for the big game. I decided to hack Pain and see what he was up to. I shut myself into the house and went to town. It was extremely difficult, but I managed to get by his firewall and into his accounts payable computer. It was isolated from the rest of his network, presumably because it had to interface with the rest of the world, and he wanted to keep the potential damage down.

I found a bunch of payments going to a pair of people. They were Dr. Adams and Mr. Zachary. It was the very foundation my company was funding-the Adams Zachary Foundation.

I tried to track down any network these people were a part of: nothing. I tried to find other references to the names anywhere: still not a damned thing. They simply didn't exist. I had to warn Marissa, get her to cut off funding to the foundation, but how could I without making Marissa a target and alert the wrong people that we were onto them?

I tried to infiltrate Pain's main servers around two am, by five I still hadn't hacked in. Deciding to try a new approach, I hacked into the Adams Zachary human resources systems. I was not too surprised by what I found. A large number of the scientists who were unemployed by the science funding crisis, were now employed by various Adams Zachary subsidiaries. They were gainfully employed and making much more than they did in the scholastic sector. The benefits package alone was more than most professors' salaries. This part was odd, because there was no reason to pay them so well. These people needed the work; they would have taken anything. Someone wanted them happy and quiet.

After I gathered everything I could from Adams Zachary, I pulled up Athena's records. I hadn't gone on a deep fact-finding mission about her yet. Part of the reason was out of respect, but also because I didn't want to dig into the places I suspected her information would reside in. At this point, neither reason was a strong enough argument to dissuade me any longer.

As I suspected, most of her records were classified. She had been some kind of operative. She was no longer in the employ of the government, officially. She was either rogue or deep undercover, either way, she was going to be a pain in the ass.

She had been to many hotspots right around the times of major political and economic change. She showed up; someone died; change happened. She picked up my job where I left off. It looked like the bitch even imitated some of my techniques. She wasn't just shooting people, she was also cutting them up. She called herself 'Sanitizer'. She wanted to be the Demon.

At five thirty a.m., my network connection went down. Oops. I must have spent too much time in the wrong places.

It was hours before my connection was back up, but I got the message loud and clear. Out of sheer paranoia, I went to a computer show and got a whole new setup. I stashed my old one away, afraid that it now contained some kind of tracking software or other pesky souvenir.

I wondered what I was getting myself into.

Chapter Thirty-eight

"The tongue like a sharp knife... Kills without drawing blood."
Buddha

"You need to stop funding the Adams Zachary Foundation." I sat across the desk from Marissa, who occupied my old desk. It was an odd feeling.

"You're kidding." Marissa had an odd presence about her. She had changed. Her demeanor was more professional. It was something intangible. She seemed more confident.

"No."

"Why would we possibly stop doing that?"

"Because they're a front for something else."

"And how would you know that?"

I didn't answer right away. I just looked away, trying to come up with a response that would both satisfy her curiosity and my need for secrecy. After several moments, I still had nothing.

"Well?" Marissa asked impatiently.

"I've been investigating stuff."

"Okay, why?"

"Why?" I sighed and fell back into my chair. "Why? Okay, the Adams Zachary Foundation is a front for supervillains. Don't ask me how I know. I just do."

"I knew you couldn't stay out of it." Marissa grinned. The familiar glow returned to her face. "Which one are you?"

"Oh, geez. Seriously, I considered letting it go because I didn't want you to become a target, but I think this is something too big to risk."

Marissa shrugged. "It's too late."

"Huh?"

"The funds were moved somewhere else. We were hacked last week."

"What?"

"Yeah. Some hacker redirected all of our funds."

"To what exactly?"

"Children's charities of all things. We reported it to the authorities, but decided to leave the money alone. We had an emergency company meeting and took a vote. The staff decided if someone felt that strongly about helping children, we should just let it go. Besides, we stopped getting reports from the AZ people months ago. We were thinking about dropping them anyway."

"I just can't believe someone hacked the network. I thought it was locked down."

"It was. We even had security and forensic experts check it. Whoever hacked us was some kind of genius."

"That bitch." I laughed. I could only think of one viable suspect.

"You know who it was?"

"I think I have a good idea."

"You think it was Computer?"

That jolted me into an unanticipated state of anxiety. Lost in the moment, I forgot I was with a civilian. "No. I don't think it was Computer."

"Why not?"

"Because I'm sure Computer has better things to do than hack a small not-for-profit company. I think it was someone else."

"You actually know Computer?"

"Yeah, kind of. I know a bunch of them, as well as you can know someone who has a secret identity."

Marissa grinned. "You never told me which one you were."

"No, I didn't."

"You are one of the good guys though, right?"

"Why the doubt?" I asked.

"I did what you suggested and looked up your bio. You were violent, greedy and aggressive. You weren't a very good person when you were young."

I grinned. "That's an understatement. No, I wasn't a good person at all. At least now the body count is much lower."

Surprisingly, Marissa didn't even flinch at the body count comment. "Well, whoever you are now, I hope you know what you're doing."

"I'm just winging it."

"That's not what I wanted to hear. My faith is running thin."

"Don't lose hope. Things will be okay."

"Promise?"

"I can't promise that. I can only try my best."

"Promise. I need to know that it really will be okay. First they cancel research, than we lose the moon, what's next?"

"Oh, the moon. I wouldn't worry about that too much. That is resolving itself."

"Really? How can you know that?"

"I just know. The moon is in good hands."

"Oh, God. Whose side are you on?"
"The right side. I promise."
"Just promise me it will all be okay."
"Okay, fine. I promise. Everything will be okay."
"Good," Marisa said. "I'll hold you to it."
"You always do."

Chapter Thirty-nine

"If a viper lives in your room and you wish to have a peaceful sleep, you must first chase it out."
Buddha

It was a slow night when I arrived at the coffee shop. The streets were silent; it was a good night for television, as crime was down. I enjoyed the calmness of the air outside. It was still and less polluted than normal. It was almost difficult for me to go in from outside. I wanted to find a field somewhere and gaze up at the stars. My mind drifted to Kiet. I wondered what he was doing and considered how beautiful the night must have been on his island paradise. It took a moment, but I pulled myself back from my daydreaming and stepped inside. The whole crew minus Blue and Mind were inside the coffee shop and the room was filled with an air of levity.

"Okay," DJ said to Acid. "Why Acid? You don't spray acid; you don't do anything acid like."

"What do you think I should be?" she replied. "Fire Girl? Flamethrower? I didn't want something stupid and obvious. Acid does burn."

"Okay," DJ acknowledged. "But I still think you could have tried harder."

"Yeah, like DJ Ghost is so slick," Mighty piped in. "You're not a DJ. You're supposed to be a superhero."

"Yeah." DJ glowered. "Okay, Mighty, where did you get your name? Your mother?"

"No, my niece." Mighty grinned. "And I am proud to use it."

I laughed; it was good to see Mighty show pride in his wholesomeness. My laughter drew DJ's attention. "What about you? There is nothing original about being named 'Computer'."

I shrugged. "I don't know anyone else using the name. Besides, I didn't name myself. Athena, Imp and Deprave named me. It stuck. It's better than my old names."

"Yeah, like what?" DJ asked.

"Slaughter," I replied.

"Slaughter is a supervillain name," DJ remarked.

I shrugged. "It's better than say 'The Sanitizer'." I cast a sideways glance at Athena, and watched her squirm. "Slaughter, it was my professional name, back in the day."

"Oh my God," Mighty muttered. "I remember you…"

The others, aside from Athena, looked puzzled. She looked perturbed.

"I used to be a cage fighter," I explained. "When I was young, the first time."

"Ah!" Acid interjected. "That's why you know all that kung fu stuff. Were you good?"

"She wasn't good, she was the best! She had a flawless record," Mighty answered for me. "Slaughter Sanderson was the first woman to be put in the ring with a man, and she kicked butt."

"I didn't know you followed fighting, Mighty."

Athena rolled her eyes at me.

"Yeah," Mighty replied. "I used to want to be a fighter, when I was a kid, before I wanted to be a superhero."

"Slaughter." Athena finally spoke. "Weren't you banned for being out of control?"

"Yeah," I admitted. "I broke too many bones. But then I found work where my skills were put to better use." I smiled. "Like you."

Athena snarled at me and clenched her fists. This was the first time I made her completely blow her cool. I almost wanted her to take a swing at me.

"So," DJ continued his inquisition, not noticing Athena's current level of agitation. "How did you get your name Ath-"

Mind barged into the coffee shop. "Don't kill him." He was talking to me. "I tried to stop him, but you know how he gets."

"What did Blue do?" Athena demanded.

Before he could answer, Athena turned on the news. "...our main story this evening. There is evidence that a member of Team Power has been responsible for most of the recent crime in this city. The team member was kidnapped, brutally tortured, and sexually assaulted by ruthless supervillain Deprave."

The glass of tea I was holding exploded into hundreds of pieces, making a mess and cutting my hand.

The news continued. "Blue Shift and authorities were able to confirm the validity of explicit footage sent to Blue Shift by Deprave. The film, too graphic for television, details Deprave carrying team member Computer into his lair unconscious. He then filmed himself raping and sodomizing her until she swore her loyalty to him."

Everybody was looking at me. My phone was vibrating like crazy with text messages. I felt like a sideshow freak on exhibit. "It's not true," I muttered.

The TV continued to pile on the humiliation. "Blue Shift has declared war on Deprave and he has assured the public that he will eliminate this threat. He also promises Computer will get the best psychological treatment available to overcome this tragedy.

"Turn it off," I demanded. Everyone just kept starting at me. "I said to *fucking turn it off*!"

Athena shut off the TV. She looked like she was enjoying this. "It's going to be okay, C. Just..."

"Fuck you, Sanitizer. You lame ass wannabe piece of shit." I really shouldn't have said that. I should have just shut my mouth and walked out. Instead I went off on her. "You act like you have no idea what Blue is doing. You talk like you're acting in our best interests. Who are you handling us for? You fucking liar."

Athena raised her eyebrow. "Yeah. I saw the detailed pictures of the assassins you dispatched. You employed some familiar techniques. Maybe you're the wannabe, or could you be the real thing? Or maybe you're just drunk again, Slaughter?"

"Fuck you." I wished I was drunk. "You know, I don't fucking care what you do to a piece of shit like me, but the others don't deserve to be dragged down into your stinking armpit of a lifestyle. They are not your pawns. I'll take you out before I let you twist Mighty the way you twisted Blue."

The rest of the team watched in silence. They had to be piecing this all together by now.

"I didn't twist Blue," Athena refuted. "It was Deprave and Gloom."

"You fucking lie." I got up in her face, but spoke loud enough so everyone could hear. "I know evil. I lived it, like you did. Deprave and Gloom and their whole fucking group never killed anyone. They never hurt anyone. They just stole money, and mostly from bastards. You, me, Blue, we fucking killed people. We're the evil bastards. Don't fucking lie about who did what. I swear, if you do anything to harm anyone on the team, I will personally take you to hell myself." I heard Mind gasp and step back. I grinned; he was still buying into the demon possession thing.

Athena said nothing. I grabbed my stuff and headed for the door. I figured she wouldn't do anything aggressive in front of the others; I was wrong.

She had a tranquilizer gun. She waited for me to start stepping through the door before she hit me with it. I could hear her saying how she was going to get me help. I barely made it a few steps before I felt everything go rubbery. My limbs were paralyzed. All my stuff landed in a pile on the sidewalk. I couldn't grab it. I couldn't stand. I just sat, slumped against the building, feeling slightly dizzy and very vulnerable.

I heard Mighty objecting and Athena telling him to back off. I hoped he would stay out of this. I didn't want him to become a target for Athena. Lucky for Mighty, moments later a van pulled up and some generic men threw me into the back. I was too drugged to make head or tails of where we were going. When we did stop, it was at a generic-looking medical building. Two goons dragged me to my feet and into the elevator. We went up to the top floor to a private office. One of the generics rang the intercom.

"Who is it?" a voice inquired through the speaker.

"Delivery for Doctor Green."

"Ah, the troublesome one." He buzzed the door. "Bring her in."

They dragged me through a waiting room and into the office. The place looked like any generic therapist's office. It was decorated in standard muted colors. The walls were covered with beiges and pale yellows. The carpet was one of those multicolored patterns you could only find in a business setting. The pictures that hung on the walls were reprints of Matisse, Picasso and a few generic watercolors. The artwork didn't really match. It was as if it were all thrown up as an afterthought, just to cover the walls. The place had a strong odor of disinfectant. My nose was assaulted with the smell of pine and ammonia. Somebody had recently put a lot of work into cleaning this place.

An older man sat in one of the chairs of the office itself. He bore the likeness of any psychiatrist. He was dressed in a light brown suit, and smoked a pipe. As I was dragged into the office, the smell of chocolate and tobacco tempered the smell of the cleaner. "Drop her in that seat." He motioned to the seat across from him.

The two men put me in the chair and waited.

"That is all," the man, Doctor Green dismissed the goons. They left and shut the door behind them. I didn't want to be alone with this guy, but I didn't have any choice.

The doctor spoke, his tone and dry and unemotional. "Have you ever been interrogated before?"

"My parents on prom night." I went for sarcasm, hoping to ride this out with minimal grief. I wasn't feeling very hopeful about it though.

Doctor Green laughed, but his laugh was empty, there was no real feeling behind it. "I heard you could be amusing. I also hear you can be very irritating. Are you going to irritate me?"

"Not me, but you may want to check your laundry detergent."

He smiled. "Don't be afraid. This should be easy, if you cooperate. I have no desire to harm you; you still have some use to us."

"That's nice to know." I was feeling even more impaired, the drug wasn't wearing off. My body felt extremely heavy. I tried to move my arm, but could barely raise it.

"Don't bother trying to move. You've been hit with a drug with induces temporary paralysis. Rest assured, it is temporary, and you can still feel everything." The last part of his statement set off all my internal alarms. I remembered men like Green from my younger days. I was in deep shit. Now I knew what Kiet had been so worried about.

"You are an interesting case," Doctor Green continued. "Normally recruits come through me before joining the team. Most of the time we are able to indoctrinate them into the group with minimal adjustment. Of course, there are exceptions."

"Blue." They must have destroyed him. "You fucked him up."

"No." Doctor Green grinned. This really amused him. "Supervillains got him. Didn't you hear? It was a terrible tragedy, all that horror he went through. I heard he used to be a much different man before those nasty bad men got him."

"You're a sick fuck," I responded. "You twisted him into a monster. That poor bastard. You fucking programmed him to be evil. Why?" Despite the drugs and my wishes, my heart was pounding. I was unarmed, unable to move and for the first time in my life, I could not think my way out of trouble.

Green didn't even dignify my question with a response. He continued with his train of thought. "Athena wanted you to be a loose cannon. She knew you would be able to ascertain who knew what. She just didn't realize how deep you would get. She underestimated your intellect, and your other talents. She also neglected to study her history. You've had her and all of us completely fooled." Green grinned an unholy smile. "Lucky for me that you lost your edge, or I suppose I would be dead by now. You can't imagine how thrilled I am to have such a celebrity in my presence."

"Want my autograph? Just give me something with a blade."

Green was ecstatic. "Unfortunately, there's no time for fun. It's now up to me to fix this problem. So, do we have a problem, Becca?"

"Yeah, global warming," I replied. "Pollution, war, bigotry."

"Yes. The world is going to hell." He paused as if to wait for me to say something. When I didn't, he began speaking again. "I meant, do we have a problem with you?"

"Everybody has a problem with me these days," I grumbled. "I'm used to it."

"Were you assaulted?" The question was direct enough.

"No," I replied. "I just got caught on film getting laid. Is that a crime?"

"Your choice of partner might be." Doctor Green leaned back in his chair. "Tell me, was it worth it? Did it feel as good as killing?" He must have read my psych profile. He knew exactly what I was.

"Better. Shit yeah, he's an excellent lay. I don't even need to draw any blood to have a good time." I was telling the truth. "He does things to me, I do things to him, and we both get off and leave a huge mess. You have some of the footage."

Doctor Green was laughing. "We have all of the footage. Why didn't you move in with him?"

"How did you know?" He didn't have to answer. I finally accepted that they knew everything; then I realized it was what they wanted me to think. They wouldn't need to interrogate me if they knew everything. "Because I didn't like his choice of decor."

"Maybe it was because you wanted to continue spying for him."

He used the 'S' word. Now I was sure where this was going. It wouldn't matter how cooperative I was, or how repentant I appeared. This man was going to hurt me. The only thing I could do was try to maintain some shred of dignity. "I was spying for your mother."

He didn't flinch at the mother comment. Not that I suspected he would. "Who do you work for, Becca?"

"I work for aliens. They need women."

The doctor made some notes, still smiling. "Tell me, where is Deprave's lair?"

"Fuck you."

The doctor smiled at my crude response. "Do you actually love him?" He seemed disgusted with the idea.

"Fuck you."

"You see, I'm going to put this very simply. Given your current condition, your intellect may be impaired." He looked up from his notepad. "We are going to hurt him. Kiet will suffer more than he ever did in his young joy boy days. We are going to make you watch us do it, too."

I still had the sense to know this was a trick. "Kinky. I like to watch."

Green studied me for a minute, no doubt looking for a weakness to exploit. "You don't care what we do to him?"

I laughed. "I only care about who I get to kill next. I'm also imagining how your blood would taste right now."

"So predictable. What do you think we should do with you?" he asked. "You aren't being very cooperative."

"I'm going to hell anyway." I had to find a way out. "It doesn't matter what the fuck you do."

"Of course it matters," Doctor Green disagreed. "What about your other abilities?"

"I can suck a golf ball through a hose."

"What about the hit men you killed? Tell me about that." Again he sat silently and waited for me to speak.

"They were tasty."

He didn't acknowledge my statement at all. "How did you stop those bullets, Computer?"

"Your mother took them up the ass." I had no idea what he was even looking for.

"You can't lie; we will find out." The doctor pressed on. "How did you stop the bullets?"

"I used my superbreath and blew them away." I laughed again.

The sound of a door opening and closing occurred behind me. "Where's the lab?"

"Up your ass!" I tried to get up knowing my legs were too weak. "Screw you!"

"Tell me about Adams and Zachary."

"They fucked your mother too." I heard a door open behind me.

"What do you know?"

"Fuck you!" I slurred.

"Tell me what you know about the plan," he demanded.

"Fuck your mother."

"What did Bianchi say to you?"

That question was unexpected, but I answered along the current theme. "He said to fuck your mother up the ass."

"Interesting." Doctor Green scribbled madly. "You are very problematic."

"Screw you; screw Athena; screw your mother; screw you all."

The doctor leaned back in his chair and tapped on the armrest with his index finger. He made a few more notes and cleared his throat.

A voice said from behind me, "Looks like we do it the hard way."

Behind me, I heard the sounds of some kind of preparation. The man spoke again. "I brought my own electrical cord this time."

"Good," Doctor Green replied. "I'm tired of losing lamps."

The new man grabbed me from behind while Green tore my clothes off. I briefly feared they were going to get their cheap thrills off of my body, but they had other things in mind. When I finally got a look at the new man, I could see he was like every stereotype of a torturer rolled up into one. He was in black. He was scarred and extremely unattractive. He had cases of devices that looked very menacing. Although he was wearing leather gloves, he threw on latex ones over them.

"Put some gloves on, Green," he said. "She's sleeping with that degenerate, who knows what diseases she has?"

They threw me up onto a metal bedframe, and tied me into place with ropes and zip ties. They seemed overly concerned in keeping me secure. Maybe they feared the drug would wear off before they were done with me. They already knew what I was capable of. Although I had never been tortured myself, I had witnessed it before. I knew exactly where this was going. This was going to get really ugly, really fast. I just had to get through the pain. Nothing I would say could stop this; nothing I could do would change what was about to come.

The torture guy punched me in the face. He hit me in the mouth and my lip split open and blood dripped down my chin. He then held a pair of pliers in front of my face. "We are about to give you a new life experience, my dear."

In one quick movement, he took the pliers and ripped out my fingernail. I screamed. I used to think I knew what pain was, but I was wrong. Tears streamed down my face. They pulled out another one and they laughed. This went on for a few fingers and toes.

"Look, Anguish, she's not so scary now." Green laughed. "I'm going to enjoy this."

"Ready to cooperate?" Anguish asked.

I tried to disconnect my mind from the pain. My years of meditation had given me an advantage, but I was never formally trained about surviving interrogation. I always avoided being in a position where this might happen. This was a brand new life experience alright, one I could have lived without. I just had to keep reminding myself that I was getting what I deserved. The Demon was slowly waking.

When he didn't get an answer, Anguish asked again, "Are you going to cooperate now, Computer?"

"Fuck you," I whimpered. The Demon was repulsed by my show of weakness.

I had no idea who the hell Anguish was, but I knew his name was accurate. He took a bucket of water and splashed me with it. He then produced a long extension cord from one of his cases. One end of it was cut off, and each of the two wires was attached to a metal rod. He plugged the other end into an electric socket and approached me. He electrified the bedframe, and me. I convulsed as every cell in my body burned and tightened. He stopped and stepped back.

"We have some people for you to take out," Anguish stated. "Swear your allegiance to us and this will stop."

The Demon didn't like receiving orders; I didn't either. The Demon would never let me become beholden to these people, or any like them. I felt my consciousness start to drift away as the Demon spoke. "No," it hissed.

"Maybe if we power up the Computer, we can get the data." Doctor Green was taking great pleasure in my misery.

"Let's plug her in." Anguish dunked each rod into what I could only assume was some kind of conductive gel. "Guess where these go, Computer." Anguish continued to approach me. He and Green both laughed.

The Demon laughed too, but not for the same reason. "I will send you to hell," it warned. I blacked out as the Demon took control and prepared for the worst, knowing its vengeance wouldn't be too far off.

Chapter Forty

"*If you don't find God in the next person you meet, it is a waste of time to look any further.*"
Buddha

After what must have been hours of humiliation and pain, I woke up naked in a gray, empty alley. I had no idea how long the torture had lasted, and how much damage I had received. I felt like every part of my body was charbroiled. I didn't have the strength to get up. I didn't even have the strength to cry. Rain poured down from the sky, like it was crying for me.

I lay there for a few minutes and the sound of footsteps approached. "Computer!" a voice cried out. It was Mighty. "Oh my God." He looked at me in horror. "What did they do to you?"

"Nothing," I slurred. My mouth was swollen. "And you saw nothing."

Mighty took off his raincoat and wrapped me in it. "Let me get you to a hospital."

"No," I objected. "Just get me home."

Mighty was about to object, but before he did, I explained, "If they know you found me, you will be hurt. If I go public, a lot of people will be hurt. We have to pretend this never happened. Do you understand?"

Mighty nodded. He picked me up and put me inside the backseat of his car. I lay down out of sight. I needed to go somewhere, but I couldn't go home. "Just drop me at a hotel." I realized I had no wallet, no credit cards, no phone.

"Okay, but you'll need this." He handed me a bag with all my stuff in it.

"How?" I asked.

"I picked it up outside the shop. I also followed them. I'm sorry, I should have rescued you, but I had no way to get in and…"

"No, you did the right thing by waiting. They didn't see you, right?" I didn't want him dragged into this.

"No. I was careful." He looked worried.

"You have to go back and pretend like none of this happened. Athena can have no idea what you know. She's only dangerous if she thinks you aren't buying her crap. You need to make sure the others stay quiet too."

"I will. Acid is already in that mindset. She told me that she warned you to stay quiet."

"She did," I replied. "And look what happened when I opened my mouth."

We pulled up to a motel. It was one of the places where Kiet and I met regularly. I threw on Mighty's coat and stepped into the pouring rain; it washed the remaining blood off of my face. I flipped the collar of the coat up to try to hide the swelling.

"Wait here. I'll be right out."

I stepped inside the rental office. It was oppressively drab, but clean. The fluorescent lighting gave the sensation of stepping into an alternative existence, one outside the reality of night-time. It was artificial, plastic day. No matter when you entered, time remained the same. The people changed, but the environment was constant.

The girl behind the Plexiglas enclosure jumped to her feet, startled by the sound of the door opening. "Oh, it's you," she said. As sad as it was to be a regular at a seedy motel, it was extremely convenient tonight. She made no inquiries to why I looked as I did.

"Yeah, it's me," I responded. "I need a room for a couple of nights." I slid my credit card through the opening on the counter. She took the card, swiped it and slid it back with a set of keys and a receipt to sign. I signed and slid back her copy.

"Have a good evening." She smiled.

"Thanks, you too." I waved and exited the office. I made my way through the never-ending pouring rain to Mighty's car.

"Wanna come in for a minute?" I asked him. "Have a quick beer."

"Yeah," he answered. "I really need one."

I popped into the passenger seat and we parked the car a few rooms down from the one I rented. When we got inside the room, I grabbed some towels and started drying myself off. The one good thing about this particular motel was that they were generous with their towels. The room had the same otherworldly feel as the office; the light just wasn't quite right and the room was dreary.

"Computer..." Mighty sat on the edge of the bed, the bed almost sank to the ground under his weight. It wasn't just that he was that heavy, he was over three hundred pounds of solid muscle. But the beds here were just that old.

"You want to know what I was talking about with Athena."

Mighty nodded.

"I can't give you much, because of what we talked about before." I grabbed a beer from the mini-fridge and handed it to him. "Let's just say that Athena is a cheap knock-off of what I used to be when I was younger. She's just not as cool."

Mighty took the beer, popped it opened and took a long gulp. "So you were what?"

"Evil."

"Evil." Disbelief appeared in Mighty's eyes.

I opened my beer and sat next to Mighty. The bed barely registered my weight. "I did shit for money that most people don't have the stomach for. Nobody with any humanity could have done the fucked-up shit I did. Even worse, I was the best. I try to do the right thing now. But it seems like no matter how hard I try to get away from evil, it just follows me like a shadow."

"Like what did you do before?" Mighty asked.

I grabbed the full stock from the mini-bar and cracked one open at random.

"I killed people. A lot of them." I chugged down the tiny bottle.

Mighty sighed. "I figured it was something like that. Was it for the government?"

"Yeah at first." I moved on to the second bottle.

"It must have been really bad to make you drink like that every time it comes up. So, you have flashbacks?"

"Yeah." I put the bottles on the bed next to me. "All the time. The messed up thing is that I don't remember any of it most of the time when I'm awake. I switched into another mode when I was on the job. I kind of disconnected. I wouldn't remember any of it, but it leaks through at the worst moments. Sometimes I'll see the news and remember something horrible. A lot of times, I just dream about it. Drinking seems to silence it, but I know it's no cure. I've tried meditation, psychotherapy, even a few years in a monastery studying Buddhism. I still have this monster inside me. I can't kill it."

"Maybe you need to stop trying to use violence against it. You say you want to kill it. Maybe you should just learn to live with it. Stop picking a fight with that part of yourself."

"Wow." I was impressed with Mighty's insight. "I'm scared to do that. What if I lose control?"

"And being drunk leaves you in control?" Mighty countered. "I'm less than half your age and even I know you are handling this like a moron."

"Gee thanks."

"You need to stop drinking," Mighty explained. "You need to stop punishing yourself and get on with your life. You were a shitty person in the past, but you need to realize that this is now."

"Yeah, people tell me that, but how can I be happy in good conscience when I ended so many people's happiness?"

"Listen," Mighty replied. "If someone killed you and then tried to reform, would you wish them to be miserable forever, or would you rather see them happy and doing good? You can't do good if you feel bad."

"How did you get so wise at such an early age?" He amazed me.

"I'm not as young as I look." He smiled.

"Well join the club."

"So what are you going to do?" he asked.

"Not much yet. First I have to figure out what the hell is going on and how to fix it, before anyone kills me."

"Despite what I just said, I think I'm starting to really hate this world," he lamented.

"It will get better," I assured him. "I promise, and I am always good for my promises."

Chapter Forty-one

"Believe nothing.
"No matter where you read it,
"Or who said it,
"Even if I have said it,
"Unless it agrees with your own reason
"And your own common sense."
Buddha

Mighty spent a couple of hours with me before leaving. He wanted to stay longer and keep an eye on me, but I kicked him out with the understanding it was for his own good.

I spent the following day trying to hide my injuries and finding a way to get some privacy. Getting clothing was the first challenge. I had to pay the maid to go buy me some clothes at the thrift store on her lunch break.

I didn't seem to be permanently damaged, which shocked me. Parts of me were singed, but I wasn't broken. These guys were complete pros, and it was apparent they really weren't ready to dispose of me. They must have been acting under somebody's orders. I didn't know what they found out, but knowing the Demon, it wasn't much.

There was something else, something extremely dangerous. Ever since the attack from Blue, I felt myself losing control. The balance inside me was being tipped, and all my meditation and focus had barely kept it in check. I feared the worst. The Demon, who slept for so long, now had a reason to wake. It continually whispered in my ear, urging me to set it free. It was angry, and it wanted to taste blood again. It took hours to calm it enough just so I could go out in public.

I finally left the hotel to get some food. Since I used my own credit cards, I was found with no trouble. Everywhere I went, everything I did, no matter what, there was a car stationed nearby with two people pretending not to watch me.

Finally, Kiet sent me a text message with a safe place to meet. It was the cellar of a building in the projects. This was like something out of a thriller. A person, who I had never met before, was our lookout as we sat in a corner on some lawn chairs and talked.

"Are you alright? You know your life is in danger?" Kiet asked.

I smiled. "I'm not dead yet." I still hurt though. The Demon laughed, hoping for any excuse to be unleashed.

"Are you okay?" Kiet's concern was unmistakable. "You don't look right. Are you hiding injuries?"

I should have known I couldn't fool him.

"I was given a warning." I tried to downplay it.

"What happened?" His voice was shaky. "Take off your clothes."

"This isn't the place for that." I tried to make a joke, but instead of laughing, I started crying. All the frustration and rage of the week poured out through my tears. The Demon scoffed in disgust and went back to sleep.

Kiet held me and let me cry for a while. After some time, I pulled myself back together. "I was trying to keep you away from the ugliness." He wiped the tears from my face. "Tell me what happened."

"You don't know ugliness." I sobbed. I took a breath and tried to compose myself. "I was tortured. I'm not sure what they know, but I'm sure you are safe."

"They tortured you? What the hell did they do?"

"They drugged me. They questioned me. I didn't answer." I held up my hand. "They ripped out some nails. They hit me. They tied me to a metal bedframe and electrocuted me. I think they raped and sodomized me with a live extension cord. Electricity is not my friend." I was trying to play it cool, but it was impossible to hide how traumatized I really was.

Kiet stared at me in shock. "Oh God, I'm sorry. It's my fault."

"Not really. I deserved it for all those years of being a bastard anyway." I managed to smile again. "I did everything without being coerced. You tried to warn me many times. I have absolutely no regrets."

Kiet smiled and took my hand. "None at all?"

"Besides not moving in with you, none at all. Oh yeah. They have sex videos of us. How the hell did they get those? You promised it was safe."

"The maid was an undercover agent," Kiet admitted. "It was very sloppy of me. I figured it out when she left without notice."

"It won't be long before they're on the Internet." Normally we would have laughed, but now even our own jokes weren't funny. "Well, I guess it's okay to discuss the forbidden topic, at least for the moment." I looked down at the floor.

Kiet nodded. "What did you find?"

I shook my head. "A ton of scary stuff. They plan to poke a hole into a pocket dimension. The plan is to use it to circumvent the need for space travel. It's a completely irrational idea. I have no idea why they would even try this, but I have an idea who is behind it."

"Go on." Kiet was literally on the edge of his seat.

"I tracked the money trail to Pain. He's in bed with a bunch of governments and global corporations. He's funding the Adams Zachary Foundation. I tried to get into Pain's servers all night, but couldn't; he shut me down after hours of hacking. I should have stopped a lot sooner, but I just couldn't let it go."

"I love your tenacity." Kiet smiled. "What did you piece together?"

"Well, I knew about the foundation. They are supposed to be a charitable organization, preserving pure scientific research to advance mankind. But I already had the strange feeling that they aren't really altruistic at all. They appeared all too conveniently when the other projects were halted. Something didn't feel right."

"No," Kiet replied. "They're not altruistic at all. We found the other half of this. It's more twisted then you think."

Now I was on the edge of my seat. "Well?"

Kiet continued. "Yes, they're telling everyone they are developing dimensional travel to get around the problem we have with the asteroid belt. Their claims are that we can use other dimensions to travel through space by cutting in and out of our universe."

"Crazy. That would take more energy than cleaning up the mess in the sky. Crap, you got drones to the moon. If you can do it, it proves we can set up a platform on the moon. It's just difficult. Dimensional travel just makes no sense."

"It's not just that they are planning dimensional travel. It's to what end they are doing it. It has nothing to do with traveling to other worlds, or bettering humanity. They're selling tickets to the world's elite to sit back and watch the end of the world from a pocket dimension."

"Wait, say that again." I was having trouble believing what I was hearing.

"They want to send the rich and powerful to a pocket dimension to witness the end of the universe."

"No. That is too lame."

"No, really, that's the plan. They're going to pop into the pocket dimension where time runs differently from here. Leave a biological agent with a short half-life behind. Wait for everyone to become extinct in a couple of generations and come back to reclaim the planet. They want to get rid of all the riff-raff and have the planet to themselves."

"Oh geez, Adams and Zachary. A and Z, Alpha and Omega. It's a project name. A really stupid one too."

"The name?" Kiet asked.

"No the project," I explained. "It can't work."

"Well now I know who's behind it. Maybe it's his plan to take all the money from the rich."

"No. He really plans to punch a hole in the universe. That fact is certain from the evidence we found. Even with his resources, he still needs the funding and backing of the world's rich and powerful. But he's playing them about reclaiming the world. It just makes no sense."

"Maybe he's going to do a demo and then get more money to do something else," Kiet offered.

"No, it's a one-shot deal. Gravity waves," I said.

"What?"

"They're going to destroy the local star cluster doing it." I ran it through my head again, and still came up with the same result.

"They produced numbers that prove it's safe."

"No. They may have produced numbers, but not accurate ones. It's not possible. Show me their numbers, and I can guarantee they are bullshit. It can't be done. The gravity waves alone will fuck everything up. It would tear the planet and everything within a half-dozen light years to pieces. And that's not even considering the gamma radiation. It's insane."

"'The way to madness is through holes in your pocket,'" Kiet quoted.

"He knew. He tried to stop Zeus when he figured out what they were planning to do with it." It was hurting my head. "I have no idea how to stop it. I don't know where they are building this thing, or exactly what it is. I don't even know why someone would want to do this. It's insane."

"Why would somebody do something like that?" Kiet asked.

"Maybe they were really fucking bored or miserable," I answered.

"Which one is it? Kiet asked.

"Doesn't Pain claim to be basically immortal and megapowerful?" Now I was glad I studied.

"What? He plans on surviving and taking the planet for himself?"

"It's just too crazy," I explained. "It would kill him, and he would have no place to actually be once the solar system is gone. I don't get what he's trying to pull off. I'm missing something."

"You would think that of all people in the world, we would be able to figure this out," Kiet lamented.

"We need a bigger boat."

Kiet smirked. "Know any other smart people?"

I sighed. "Not really. This is going to be problematic." I pondered the problem for a moment. "There's another thing that's been bugging me. Why do you and Bianchi refer to Athena as the Devil?"

"Ah," Kiet replied. "She's evil. Really, nobody has any idea who she really works for. She says it's the government, but who's? You're right, she used to be an undercover agent for the U.S., and she was ruthless. You know the nuke that went off in the Middle East?"

I shuddered, visibly. "I barely escaped the blast," I muttered.

Kiet raised an eyebrow. "You are just full of surprises."

"Told you." I shrugged. "I was a horrible monster. You don't believe me."

"You're right. I don't believe it. Besides, you're not a monster now."

"I'm not sure about that either. Time will tell." I just didn't want to focus on that. "How was Athena involved?"

"They say she was one of the people out to stop the Russians. They say she did so knowing the asteroids were definitely on a collision course with the planet. She was guaranteed a space in a hardened bunker somewhere, so she had nothing to lose. The word is she sabotaged the nuke that misfired. She caused the nuclear destruction of Chechnya. The only reason she didn't get the rest was that she ran out of time. Another operative was sent in by the other side to make sure the launch codes weren't compromised."

"Another operative." The realization impacted me like the nuke itself.

"Yeah, the Russians hired some badass through an intermediary."

"Who?"

Kiet shrugged. "No, idea. Whoever it was, was killed in the blast."

"Crap." I took a deep breath and a moment to regroup my thoughts. "So Athena is a self-serving bitch. God, that is so pathetic. You don't fight to save your ass. You fight knowing you are going to die. What, did she go rogue?"

Kiet raised an eyebrow and looked into my eyes. Surprisingly, he stuck with the topic of Athena. "Worse than that. She was still an operative for the Americans. They figured out the asteroids wouldn't hit the U.S. directly and planned on using that to their advantage. They were going to move troops in a 'peacekeeping capacity' after the disaster. Then they never planned on leaving. They planned on annexing entire sections of the planet during the resulting chaos and aftermath. Athena knew the entire plan. She will do anything she is ordered to do. She has no conscience. She doesn't care who she hurts. She would kill a baby in front of its own mother if that's what it took to complete her mission. She destroyed millions of lives, without any hesitation, without any thought. That's what makes her the Devil."

"She's not the Devil. She just sold her soul to him." I wondered what Kiet would think of me. "Damn." I shook my head. "Poor bitch."

Kiet seemed surprised by my reaction. "You really have been through hell, haven't you?"

"Yeah." I nodded. "I have. And they call you the villain. How the hell did that happen?"

"Well when they made me public enemy number one, I decided it was easier to go with the image then to try to fight it. Gloom and I started working for Pain at first. We were angry at the world. It seemed like a good idea to get some kind of vengeance on the people who tried to destroy us, but it wasn't too long before we realized we weren't really cut out for serving up evil. We kept the act up for a while. Luckily Pain got bored with us before he took notice of our change of heart. I'm sure he knows where we stand now. He just doesn't consider us as any kind of threat. Gloom and I enjoyed the act so much, we kept it up. We know it's over the top, but it's too much fun."

"Ah." I smiled as the picture became clear to me. "So, that's why you've been stealing from Pain himself."

"You tracked that down. I just hope he didn't."

"Nah. You covered it really well. So what were you doing all this time?"

"We were taking out the financial backing to the projects. Dead Beat wanted to take a more direct approach, so we let him do the fieldwork. He wasn't very good at not getting caught though."

"No," I agreed. "He pretty much sucked at it. At least Bianchi managed to do some damage."

We sat in silence for a moment as it all sank into my brain. "Wow." I sighed. "It all makes sense now. Pain has the government serving as his personal dancing monkey. They never bothered with Manta because he wasn't worth the time and he makes a great diversion. Team Power is a joke used to manipulate the media and keep some pressure on the real good guys. Damn, I can't believe I was being used, again."

Kiet took my hand and smiled. "Well screw it, shit happens. Don't focus on that. Even if this is it and the planet goes, at least we had fun."

"I can't believe I am saying this, but I'm not ready to go yet." I grinned. "Besides I promised two people everything was going to be okay. We have to stop this. Somehow."

Chapter Forty-two

"May all that have life be delivered from suffering."
Buddha

The first thing I needed to do was get help. The problem was, getting people I could trust and who would be willing to help. The next problem was not being caught.

I called Mighty and Acid. I trusted them without question. DJ was still Athena's errand boy. He didn't know he was doing anything wrong, but I had no time to deprogram him.

I told them to meet me at a private reggae club across town from the coffee shop. It was close enough not to arouse suspicion about their travel, but it was Athena-proof. The club was owned by one of Ganjasaurus' men. I had guaranteed safety in his territory.

We met during the day. There was no band playing yet, but music played in the background. The place was very organic. It was all light-colored wood. The tables had splashes of color from fruit baskets and flower arrangements placed on them. The people inside smiled and exuded a sense of well-being. It didn't hurt that the place was filled with smoke of the intoxicating kind. One couldn't help but get a contact high just by sitting there for a few minutes.

I was seated in the corner with a good view of the door. After ten minutes, Mighty and Acid shuffled inside and I waved them over.

"This is an 'otherside place,'" Acid muttered as she sat, futilely trying to fan the smoke away from her face.

"It's a safe place," I explained. "And it's DJ proof."

"Ah, the smoke," Mighty observed.

"Yeah," I replied. "Athena sends him to watch us. He doesn't suspect her of being duplicitous, so he just does what she orders."

"Duplicitous?" Mighty asked.

"Two-faced," I replied. "You both know she is working for someone else and technically you are working for her. The whole Blue Shift thing is a device to keep you all in line."

Mighty frowned. "Athena just classified you a renegade. You're not one of us anymore."

"Figures." I looked at the two of them and knew my chances of recruiting help from them were nil. I would have to do this alone.

"We both know there is a lot more to this," Mighty added. "They tortured you; I can't even guess what they are up to that would cause them to torture you. The problem is that Athena is watching us all the time now."

I was now certain I couldn't recruit them. I remembered the torture and knew I could not put them at risk. I remembered how Kiet wanted to protect me, and now I wanted to protect them.

"It's okay," I said. "You guys can't help with this one. I guess I just wanted to say goodbye. I don't think I will be able to see you for a while."

"Were you really a killer?" Acid blurted out from nowhere.

"Yeah. Where did you hear that?" I wasn't going to lie to her.

"I heard Athena talking to someone on her cell. She didn't know I was there. She seemed, scared."

I smiled. I couldn't hide it. "She should be." I saw Acid and Mighty looking uneasy. "You don't need to worry. My gripe is with her and the other bad guys, not you and the good guys."

"What's going to happen?" Acid asked. "I'm scared. I have no idea what's going on, just that it's big."

"Someone Athena works for is planning a science experiment that would break the universe and I'm going to figure how to stop it from happening so we can all be happy again." I thought that summed it up well enough.

It must have been a good answer because Acid smiled. "That's why you're working with Deprave. Because he's trying to stop it too."

"Yeah," I replied. "That and I like to work with him naked."

Mighty laughed despite himself. "Is he good to you?" he asked.

I smiled. "Yes, he really is. He makes me very happy. He's not at all what you think, but then again, neither was I."

Mighty nodded. Acid smiled.

"I'm getting hungry," Mighty stated.

"Must be the contact high you're getting. Let me order some snacks."

I signaled the waitress and she brought over a fresh fruit basket. We all started snacking on it.

"So what happens now?" Acid asked as she shoved a grape in her mouth.

"We have lunch." I shrugged. "You two maintain the status quo until I come up with something. Until then, we can't talk or meet anymore. It's not safe for you."

Acid looked away. "I'll miss you."

"I'll miss you," I responded. "And I'll miss you, Mighty, and DJ. But this isn't forever."

"Okay," Acid agreed.

Mighty ordered a round of beers and we enjoyed a long lunch together. I really was going to miss them all.

Once we finished eating and drinking, we said our goodbyes and they walked over to the door, waved and walked out. I no longer belonged. I was completely on my own.

Chapter Forty-three

"It is our very search for perfection outside ourselves that causes our suffering."
Buddha

Things were a bit difficult between Kiet and me. Besides the ill effects from my newly acquired post-traumatic stress disorder, we were having trouble meeting. He was public enemy number one and couldn't show his face anywhere. I was being watched all the time. They didn't even try to hide it anymore.

I knew Pain wasn't ready to make his move yet. I monitored him from public networks. I never checked from the same place twice. I learned my lesson about being careless. He was still several weeks away from completion. Though it sounded like a long time, it would fly really fast. It was going to take more resources than I had available to take him down. I needed so much more help than I could obtain now.

The only thing I did have to look forward to was Gloom and Alicia's upcoming second wedding anniversary party extravaganza. This year it was supposed to be all-out. I wasn't going to miss it. I would be able to mingle and possibly recruit for our cause. Not only that, but it was also the anniversary of Kiet's and my first night together.

I could have gone with the black dress thing again, but I realized I wanted to make a better impression this year. So I decided on something more practical-body-hugging, personal armor. The design was straight out of a science fiction novel. The armor was black and transparent, giving the appearance of cut-out regions. It fit like a spandex suit, but it was obviously hardened armor. I even added low-power beam weapons to make it completely functional. It was completely over the top. I loved it.

I arrived at the hotel and took the elevator up. When I reached the top floor, I realized I didn't have an invitation. This could be a really short night for me. I stepped up to the maître d'.

"May I have your name?" he asked, not even fazed by the full body armor.

"Computer," I answered proudly, hoping I was on the invite list.

"Please, go on in." He waved me inside.

I walked in and my name was announced over the thumping of the music. Then the music simply stopped. Manta turned ready to leap. I leveled my arm and pointed it at him, a red dot from the laser target glowed between his eyes. He backed down.

I started forward toward the table where Gloom and Alicia sat, overlooking the party. Deprave was there at Gloom's side, apparently laughing at my interchange with Manta. My entrance couldn't have been better if I'd tried.

I reached the table, and addressed the guests of honor. "Congratulations on another year of happiness. I wish you an eternity of happy anniversaries." Alicia smiled and thanked me.

Gloom turned to Deprave and nudged him. "You're still tapping that? Nice job." Alicia smacked him. Deprave laughed.

By the time I stepped away from the table, the music was going again and everyone was either dancing or engaged in conversation. I grabbed a glass of champagne and went out to the balcony where it all had started.

This time the balcony was occupied with various people chatting and smoking. The weather was much warmer this year. I sipped my champagne and enjoyed the outside air.

It was only a moment before Kiet stepped out to meet me.

"Wow," he remarked. "What an entrance!" He smiled. "I love the outfit, and the laser target on Manta was a sweet touch."

"Thanks, Muppet Head had it coming," I replied. "Besides, I learned to be diabolical from the best."

He closed the distance between us, and pulled me up against him. "I've missed you."

"Ditto," I said.

"Ditto? That's very noncommittal."

I laughed and gazed into his eyes. "I'm no good without you."

"That's better." He smirked and took a step back. "I have something I need to ask you."

"I'm not pressing any rape charges." I grinned.

"God." He shook his head. "I missed your sense of humor." He reached into his pocket and pulled something out.

"What's that?" I asked.

"Open it and see." He handed me the box. I opened it to find the most amazing ring I had ever seen. It looked like a miniature model of the Milky Way galaxy. It was made up of what must have been hundreds of small gemstones. The stones in the center were varying shades of yellow, orange and red, with one small black diamond in the middle. Spiraling off from the center, diamonds made the arms of the galaxy. It was breath-taking.

"I promised you the galaxy," he said. "So will you?"

"Huh, will I?" It took a second to register what he was asking. "Oh... Yes!"

He grinned and put the ring on my finger. "I love you," he said and then he kissed me.

I could feel the love inside, just like Lila said. Finally, I found joy.

Chapter Forty-four

"A dog is not considered a good dog because he is a good barker. A man is not considered a good man because he is a good talker."

Buddha

After the night of the party, I initiated procedures to move in with Kiet. I started packing, and spoke to a realtor about possibly renting out my home. A lot was happening, and I was still feeling very unsettled.

That night I went to bed reflecting on my anxiety. Lila was gone. She wouldn't get to meet Kiet or see us get married. My friends were ordered to stay away from me by someone I just discovered was a soulless murderer, and I had to solve a problem that was beyond me. The only thing I had was Kiet. I made sure to thank the universe for that. He was a gift I appreciated beyond what words could express.

I drifted off to sleep. I dreamt of Lila's peaceful day. I was dressed in white flowing silk; my hair was loose and fell down my back. I walked through a field of green grass without any shoes on my feet. The ground felt cool and soothing. A gentle breeze caressed my face. The sun felt warm on my skin. I looked over and saw Kiet sitting under a tree meditating. He was dressed like me, only in black. The symbolism was so blatant that even in my state of dreaming, I understood.

I sat down next to him. He looked so calm, I dared not disturb him. A moment later, he opened his eyes and gazed on me expressionlessly.

"It's time for you to wake up." He pointed at a door that stood in the middle of the field. It hadn't been there before.

I didn't want to wake up. Here, I was free of the pressures of life. I didn't have to save the world.

I knew I had no choice, however. So I stood up and walked over to the door. As I approached, it opened. I saw a bright light emanating from inside; I stepped through.

I was in my bed again. It was still dark. I got up and went to the kitchen to get a drink. As I stepped into the hallway, the door appeared again. A bright light burst out from behind it, escaping through the cracks around the frame.

"It's almost done," Bianchi's words echoed in my head. I reached for the handle and the door opened. Again I stepped through.

I stood in a dark room. I was still in the same outfit as before. My feet felt cold stone beneath them. The room suddenly lit up. It was empty, except for the torches that illuminated it. There were no doors, no windows. There was only a stone room, with a stone floor and featureless ceiling. I waited.

I waited some more. Impatiently I searched the room, but still there was nothing else. What was I missing? Why was I stuck in this room? Frustrated, I sat. Something jingled in my pocket. I reached in and pulled out the key to the coffee shop. I examined it for a moment, and then looked back up.

I was inside the shop now, seated at the counter. Nobody saw me. I watched as the patrons left. Then I saw everyone file in, one by one. I even saw myself talking and smiling with the others. I saw Blue gazing in the window from outside. Mind stood in the doorway, noncommittal to being inside or out.

Athena wasn't there. I looked around. I didn't see her. I stood up and looked around; she was no place to be found. I decided to check the back. I had only been through there once, to get out the rear door. I never spent any significant time in the back. But Athena did. She always seemed to pop out of there. Nobody ever questioned it. Why would they?

I decided to take a peek. I was sure I'd find her there. Just as I was about to step through it, the door was engulfed in blinding light. Nobody else noticed. I reached out and touched the light. It dimmed until it was no longer light; it dimmed to the point of nothing and into complete darkness. It was the darkest blackness I had ever seen. It was like a black hole without the event horizon.

It grabbed my hand where I had touched it and started to pull me in. I struggled to get free, but it was useless. Then it was a hand holding my wrist and it was attached to Athena, who was unmistakably dressed as the Devil. She smiled wickedly as she twisted my arm.

"Give it up, old lady," she said. "You lived your life, now let the world die."

"No." I continued to struggle.

"You've wanted to die since you were thirteen, why stop now?"

I tried to pull away, but she was stronger than me. The more I tried to escape, the tighter her grip. Finally exhausted, I let her pull me in.

I was floating in space. The universe moved around me. In the distance, I saw Earth floating gracefully in the cosmos. Without any warning, a huge wave of gravity rippled out from the planet, destroying itself, annihilating the solar system, devastating the neighboring stars, and continuing forth obliterating everything in its path. In a corner of the universe, sitting on a small asteroid, Athena sat clad in human skin. She held a remote control with a single big red button. Her finger was pushing it.

I woke up in a pool of sweat. "That wasn't blatant enough," I muttered.

I got dressed, and prepared for combat. It was a sweet rush, just like the old days, only this time I was the good guy. Before I stepped out the door, I texted Kiet. *I'm going to save the world now, remember that I love you.*

Chapter Forty-five

"An insincere and evil friend is more to be feared than a wild beast; a wild beast may wound your body, but an evil friend will wound your mind."
Buddha

I got a few stares as I walked through the streets. I was dressed in my infamous white silk gi-like killing outfit. It was the first time I wore anything like it in over twenty years. It was no more comfortable than sweats or a regular gi. I chose it for no other practical reason than to scare the living hell out of Athena. There was no question that she'd recognize me now. I also wore two of my swords and a staff across my back. I didn't intend on killing anyone, but if she got in my way, Athena was going down.

Arriving at the coffee shop just before closing, there were still a few patrons inside, along with the crew, minus Blue and Mind as usual. I slammed open the door and made my entrance.

Everything stopped.

I addressed the patrons politely. "Please leave now. Violence is imminent." I didn't have to say it twice. They scurried off in seconds, leaving me face-to-face with Mighty, DJ and Acid.

They stood frozen, their eyes affixed on me. I stepped by them and behind the counter. None of them moved. "What the hell is going on out..."

Athena came out from the back. She looked at me and smirked. "Nice outfit. I always imagined you a little bigger."

"No, just deadlier."

"Does this mean it's over for me?" I read real fear in Athena's voice.

"No, you don't get off that easy." Out of nowhere, Athena pulled a weapon. She had what looked like a traditional Japanese samurai sword. She unsheathed it and stepped forward. I also got a glimpse of a gun on her hip. She was expecting me.

"You're out of practice," she warned. "I'll go down fighting."

"Nah." Before she could do or say anything else, I closed the distance and drove both my fists into her shoulder joints, dislocating them and leaving her arms unusable. I followed it with a punch to her head. She slumped down, and I caught her. "I don't have time for your shit," I muttered as I pulled her out from behind the counter. Behind me the team still stood in shock.

I dragged Athena into the broom closet, tied her up, removed all her belongings and locked her in. When I was done, I threw her things in a bag, and left them on a nearby table. I addressed the team, "I am going to save the world now. Can you please warn me if the bad people arrive?"

Mighty was the first to respond. "Maybe I should come with you."

"No," I replied. "I have to do this on my own. It may not be safe for you to be near me; I can get really ugly. I just need all of you to be Computer tonight."

"Okay," Acid responded uneasily. "But we don't have any equipment."

I grabbed Athena's comm unit from the bag. "This is all I need. Call me if *anyone* comes in here."

They all nodded.

I headed into the back. Mighty watched from the entrance. The room was filled with supplies, a few refrigerators, and not much else. There were two doors. One I knew led outside; the other went elsewhere. I tried the door. It was locked, so I kicked it in. It was a staircase to the basement. I started down.

"Are you sure?" Mighty asked again.

"Yes. I'll call if I need help."

I made my way down the stairs. The basement was sparsely scattered with cleaning supplies, a few pieces of furniture and some spare coffee machine parts. There were some boxes piled in the corner labeled napkins and plastic ware. I opened one just to be sure and found electronic parts. In another, I found high-end scientific equipment. In fact, none of the boxes contained anything coffee shop related. Athena was moving supplies for Pain. But how?

I felt like a moron checking for secret doors, but I had to look. I spent a few minutes checking and came up empty. Then I noticed the small roll-top desk in the corner. All the other furniture was piled together in a different corner. The desk was set apart from the rest, and it looked like it was used regularly. I opened the top and was greeted by a colorful array of blinking lights. The underside of the top itself was an LCD.

I smiled. "There you are."

I studied the lights and switches. Athena had the whole shop under surveillance, but there was more. I soon realized this was a decoy too, when I noticed a weird latch under the desk. I opened the latch and the surface of the desk flipped up. Underneath was a small array of buttons. They were labeled 'open', 'close', 'send', 'call' and 'talk'. I pushed 'open' and the wall faded out of existence. It was a holographic force field.

Before me was a tunnel with a track running through it. I pushed the 'call' button, and a small gust of wind started blowing. Within moments, a small empty monorail car stopped and opened its doors.

I reported into the team. "Mighty."

"Yo."

"There's a freakin' train down here. I'm going to see where it goes."

"I'll secure the basement," he replied. "Be careful."

"Check. Have someone watch the bitch. Make sure she doesn't get out."

"Acid is already on it," Mighty explained. "DJ is with me guarding the doors."

"Leave him on the back door. Have Acid watch the closet and the front door. You secure down here, but *do not* follow me. Understand?"

"Roger. DJ at the back, Acid at the front and me in the basement, do not follow."

"Okay." I stepped into the train. "I'm out."

I pushed the green button on the control panel, the doors closed and the train lurched forward.

Chapter Forty-six

"Endurance is one of the most difficult disciplines, but it is to the one who endures that the final victory comes."
Buddha

The tunnel appeared to be very dated. It must have existed already, and whoever owned this monorail just put it back into use. The trip took some time. It was twenty minutes before I even saw light ahead. There were several other platforms along the route. No doubt there were many others involved in this bizarre plot.

The train started to slow. Up ahead, I saw movement. I considered ducking behind a seat, but I wasn't going for stealth. This would be a direct head-on attack. I was tired of games.

Two guards stood at the platform. They were armed, but even so, henchmen got my stick. I readied my weapon and leapt out at them as the door opened. They didn't even have a chance to draw their weapons, before I knocked them unconscious.

I threw their guns onto the tracks and took their radios and IDs. Now I could hear them, thus increasing my advantage.

In front of me was a large steel door, with a card reader next to it. I swiped one of the cards and the door opened. I stepped inside to find myself staring at a huge laboratory. Having been in Kiet's lab, I had seen some serious shit, but this was like nothing I had ever even imagined. The ceiling went up forever; catwalks wrapped around and crisscrossed throughout the lab. Workers moved about, laboring on various panels, and work stations. There were people soldering wires, typing in data, adjusting mechanical parts, and carrying clipboards around. So far, none of them had noticed me; that was about to change.

This was because I quickly figured out what I was staring at. Before me a huge spherical device rose up over six stories. Beyond it was a tunnel that ran for what I could only assume was miles. I was staring at the doomsday machine.

I gasped, attracting the attention of one of the workers. He saw me and pulled an alarm. The place erupted into several straight minutes of complete chaos, as workers locked down their stations and evacuated the area. And just like that, everything fell silent except the alarm wailing in the background.

The silence was broken by the sound of approaching boots. The minions had been rallied. I was sure I wouldn't be able to defeat an entire army, but I could do as much damage as possible to the machine.

I drew my swords and stepped forward. Every breath of air I inhaled filled me with power. Every step I took brought me closer to victory. I raised one of my swords, walked around to the back of the sphere and jumped onto it. I climbed a few feet and plunged the sword in up to the hilt. A jolt of energy threw me back, and the whole sphere cracked, buzzed and popped. The sphere was Bianchi's design. He told me not to wave a stick. Smashing it would not work. Puncturing it, on the other hand, would fuck it up. It also helped to have read his plans, thereby giving me the advantage of knowing its weak spots.

I got up, drew my second sword and plunged it into the other weak point at the base of the device. Sparks flew, lights flickered, and alarms buzzed. Now I was down to just my stick. I decided to help things along by smashing a few key computer systems. I went from station to station, destroying and smashing. It all happened very quickly.

By the time I had smashed the fifth computer station, the troops had me surrounded. They stood with their weapons leveled at me. Bianchi's machine smoked and buzzed. The sphere's pressure increased and shot my swords back out. One was behind me, the other landed on the floor at the door to the monorail. It was going to be a glorious explosion.

Nobody moved. The minions had no idea what to do. They were awaiting instruction. I had to escape the way I came. To do this, I would need to spill some blood. I returned my stick to its place on my back, and dove for the sword behind me. One of the minions fired, unloading a round of bullets into the lab. Shots ricocheted off the floor; one struck me in my side, and the rest of them hit various pieces of equipment. Once the gunfire ceased, I grabbed my sword and took off running toward the exit.

As I engaged the first group, the rush of bloodlust started to rear its ugly head. I gave them no chance to draw their guns, and since they surrounded me, the rest of the guards really couldn't fire at us. There were nine of them in this group. One pulled out a pair of nunchucks; another pulled out a chain. The others fumbled for their weapons. I kept them on my radar, but did not need to engage them yet. I raised my sword and paused, giving them a chance to rethink their attack.

The first guard came at me with the chain. He swung wildly, but showed some degree of skill. It just wasn't enough. He was so busy swinging at me, he left his entire torso and lower body unprotected. I didn't want to kill him. So instead, I sliced him lightly across the chest. I gave him a wound that would sting and bleed a little, but not damage him significantly. He stepped back and the guard with the nunchucks stepped up to the plate.

I checked the rest; now they each held a melee weapon of some kind. They had at least minimal training. It would be a fair fight, and would not be easy. The nunchuck guy tried to intimidate me by swinging around the chucks and showing me his prowess. He swung at me and I stepped out of the way. He wasn't too pleased with this result and swung and missed again. He lost his temper and started swinging blindly.

Now the guy with the chain decided he didn't get enough of a lesson the first time, so he stepped back in. This prompted the rest of the nine to get up the nerve to attack; I swung at the closest one, slicing his arm badly. Blood spurted from the wound, spraying hot and sticky all over me and the other combatants. My heart pounded harder, and I grinned. My victim dropped to the ground, screaming, trying to stop the flow of blood. The rest stepped back in fear and considered their attacks. I took a breath and tried to focus. Although I didn't want to kill anyone, I knew I had no choice. I lamented the fact I would have to kill today, but I could feel my conscience slipping away with every heartbeat. With every second that passed, my love of all living things faded into a hunger for destruction. I laughed as I breathed in the sweetness of death and battle; my Demon burned inside me. I was barely in control; it took more effort not to lose myself than to do the fighting itself.

I waited until my opponents engaged me again before taking them all out. My initial assessment was wrong, there was no effort involved, it was easy. They were sloppy, and I could taste their fear. Each one stepped forward and attacked. Each one received a first-hand view of his own blood. I hacked off limbs, sliced open chests, and ran my sword through torsos; the screams and misery only intensified my hunger. It was just moments before I found myself standing in a circle of human pieces, drenched in blood, and smiling in ecstasy.

I took a moment to recover my wits. I stepped up to the monorail door and tried to get it open. Setting off the alarm must have locked it down. I was stuck. I had no time to hack it due to the army ready to destroy me. I was bleeding moderately, but I was too hopped up on adrenaline to let it distract me. My comm went off. Mighty was trying to reach me, but I had no chance to respond.

A loud inhuman scream echoed through the lab. Pain levitated down from whatever place he had been in. He looked at the sphere, and then back at me.

I stood there, bleeding, covered in human blood, holding the two swords that not only took out a handful of his men, but utterly destroyed his weapon. I laughed defiantly, and gazed into his eyes. "What?" I hissed.

He went ballistic. I felt my throat closing, and realized it was him doing it. I dropped to my knees. Rage filled my thoughts. Meanwhile, my comm continued to go off. There was a sound behind me, the door opened, Pain yelled something and the pressure ceased. An arm reached in and pulled me out of the lab. It was the team. No, it was the team plus one. Kiet smiled as he helped me to my feet. The others eyed me with concern.

"Is that your own blood or theirs?" Acid asked.

"Yes." I coughed.

Acid stepped back uneasily and went to work on the monorail.

Kiet managed to close the door and destroyed the controls. I regained my breath as he led me to the monorail. "There are guns on the tracks," I wheezed. Mighty grabbed them and threw one to Kiet.

"The train won't go," Acid reported.

"Must be the alarm," I panted. "Run."

We took off running. Acid fell; I caught her and pushed her along. Unfortunately, I dropped one of my swords in the process. I tried to turn back and grab it, but Kiet grabbed my arm and dragged me forward. The sounds of pounding and grinding came from behind the door.

"We have to get to the first platform and take our chances." My airways were opening back up.

"Agreed," Kiet replied, but just as he said it, a new problem presented itself.

As we approached the first platform, a platoon of Pain's forces exploded out of it. We were surrounded.

"Tell me, Computer," Mighty inquired. "Tell me you had a plan to get out of this."

"Uh, no," I replied. "I told you not to follow me. I was prepared for a one-way trip."

Kiet put his hand on my shoulder. "Well, we go down together."

DJ and Acid stood silently as they also realized the gravity of our situation. Smoke started to fill the tunnel. The explosion was imminent.

"I'm useless," DJ muttered. "The smoke."

Mighty nodded. "We'll all do what we can."

Pain calmly walked down the tunnel. His troops stepped aside, clearing a path for him. He stopped and picked up my sword. "This is what you used to destroy years of work."

I didn't answer. None of us did. Pain continued to walk toward us. He looked at Kiet and shook his head.

"Deprave. Very disappointing. You had such potential."

Kiet smiled and shrugged. "A man needs his priorities. You know me, live by the sword…"

Pain grinned menacingly. "Die by the sword." Before anyone could react, he flung my sword, sending it plunging it through Kiet's chest.

Kiet fell to the ground. Everything stopped.

"No." I fell to my knees next to him. "No, no, no, no, no."

He looked up at me and smiled. "Becca." He reached up and touched my cheek.

I held his hand to my face. "Kiet, stay with me." Panic started to set in.

He winced in pain, but his smile didn't fade. "Nobody ever loved me before." His body shuddered and the life left his eyes.

"No." I shook him. "No, Kiet, no." I screamed in agony as I felt every molecule of joy being ripped from my soul.

Everything went black.

Chapter Forty-seven

"This existence of ours is as transient as autumn clouds.

"To watch the birth and death of beings is like looking at the movements of a dance.

"A lifetime is like a flash of lightning in the sky.

"Rushing by, like a torrent down a steep mountain."

Buddha

The next thing I could remember was sitting in an alley. The sun was high in the sky. I checked the time. It was twelve twenty-three p.m., three days later. I looked down at myself. I was still in my bloodied gi, and I had my stick and one of my swords. My body hurt. It felt like I had been in combat for days. There were parts of me stitched up, obviously by me. My throat felt like it was all bruised, my head throbbed intensely, and I was extremely hungry. I must have gotten into some serious shit.

I picked up the phone and tried to call Kiet. I got no answer. I tried to text him, no response. I tried my remote connection to the lair. It was down. I started to panic. Something was definitely wrong. I remembered my dream, going after the machine, then nothing.

I dialed Mighty. He was there. He could tell me what the hell was going on. He answered in a very hushed tone. "Hold on," he said.

A moment later he came back on the line. "Oh my God, where are you?" he asked.

"I'm not sure," I replied. "Some alleyway somewhere. What the hell's happening?"

"Do you remember anything that happened?"

"No. No. What is it?" My voice was hoarse, and my throat hurt. "Something's wrong, isn't it?"

"Hold tight," Mighty advised. "Just poke your head out and tell me what street you're near."

I stuck my head out and looked around. "It looks like Third Street, by the deli."

"Okay, I'll be right there. Stay put."

I sat back down on the ground, and waited. Nobody seemed interested in the alley, which was good for me.

After a short wait, Mighty appeared. Instead of helping me up, he sat down next to me. "I brought you something to eat." He handed me a bag which contained a corned beef sandwich and a bottle of water.

I inhaled the sandwich.

He held up a medicine bottle. "Take one." He opened the bottle and poured out a pill.

"What is it?" I asked.

"Valium, to help with your stress." Mighty handed me the pill. I looked at it. It was yellow with a V in the middle. I cracked open the water and popped the pill.

"How bad?"

Mighty looked down at the ground. "Very bad, Computer."

"Oh God. Did I kill anyone?"

Mighty nodded.

"Ki-" I corrected myself. "Deprave isn't answering."

Mighty just shook his head, and looked away.

"He's not? Oh God."

Mighty grabbed me and held me as the realization hit. "I'm sorry."

"Where's his body?" I sobbed. "I want to see it."

"Missing," Mighty replied.

I struggled to breathe, but the air wouldn't come. Mighty continued to console me.

"Is she ready?" Alicia stepped into the alley.

Mighty nodded. "Computer. You need to go with her." Mighty held my hand. "It's not safe for you yet. You need some time."

"Why? What's happening?" I felt anxiety creeping in again.

"Shh, shh." Mighty tried to calm me. "She'll explain everything. But you really need to go."

"Come on." Alicia motioned me for to follow her. She led me to her limo and into the backseat. It wasn't long before the tranquilizers did their job and I fell asleep.

I was semiconscious when they led me into Gloom and Alicia's fortress. There was a lot of commotion going on around us. I remember a bath and washing myself. I was then taken to a room with a comfortable bed, where I fell asleep.

I woke up in a room with a bed, table, television and a locked door. I tried kicking the door, pounding on it and body slamming it, but I was definitely locked in. After I had given up, Alicia walked in.

"Are you done with your tantrum?" she asked.

"Why am I here?" I asked.

"Because you have no place else to go, since nobody wants you near them," Alicia responded.

A man walked in and put a tray of food down on the table.

"I have no reason to live."

"I am not dealing with this. You eat, or I'll have somebody beat you."

"You're just going to drug me again, aren't you?" She seemed just too intent on me eating for it to be just out of concern for my well-being.

"The food is drugged, but the dosage is lower," Alicia admitted.

"Why?" I asked.

"Food first. Questions later."

I did what Alicia suggested, because I didn't have the strength for a fight, and I really didn't wish to be beaten. She sat and silently watched me eat. Once I finished the meal, she waited another fifteen minutes until I was showing signs of intoxication. I was feeling pretty high.

She got up and turned on the television. She threw in a microdisc and hit play. She sat down across the room and watched me, as I watched television.

It was security footage from the tunnels. Pain must have had the whole place monitored. The screen was split into six perspectives, each a separate camera. She fast-forwarded the part where I had first made my way to the lab. The perspective of the cameras made it impossible to see who was in the monorail. Pain must have been really confident in his other security systems to leave this one so vulnerable. The footage had no sound, but it didn't need it. I saw the monorail leave right after I entered the facility. A few seconds later, the team returned in it. Alicia slowed the video to normal speed.

I could see why Alicia drugged me. I was about to witness the death of my soul mate. I saw us running down the tracks, then as we were surrounded and Pain arrived. I saw Pain throw the sword, Kiet get hit, and drop to the ground.

As I remembered, I was by Kiet's side, screaming in horror. But then I saw something I wasn't expecting. I watched myself stand up. I was still screaming, but I stood, turned and faced Pain. That's when something weird happened; he ran.

Next, I saw him point at me from down the tunnel; a barrage of bullets came at us from all directions. But before they could hit us, they all stopped and fell to the ground. Pain bellowed out orders and continued to point in our direction.

Then his team showed up. Anguish stepped up and pointed at me. He must have thought I would be intimidated by the memory of his torturing me. He had absolutely no idea I had gone bye-bye. Behind him a few other costumed combatants stood, one of which was Blue Streak.

Anguish shot a ray or something from his hand. It deflected off the force field I was apparently generating. It struck the wall and the stone aged and crumbled in a flash.

Blue Streak stepped up and tried his electricity attacks. When that didn't work, Blue and Anguish tried in unison to wear me down. Mighty initiated an attack. He stepped forward and took a swing at Blue Shift. Blue took a punch to the jaw and stumbled backwards. Anguish noticed this and raised his arm to fire his death ray at Mighty. Before he could get the shot off, Acid threw a fireball to stop him, but my shield diminished its power, causing it to dissipate before doing any damage. This caught his attention though and he focused on Acid instead of Mighty. Acid stepped forward, outside of my shield and fired again. Anguish was barely able to duck the attack, but now he had something to worry about.

DJ tried to circle around Blue to launch a surprise attack. Unfortunately, his invisibility was rendered useless by the increasing smoke. Now he was little more than a regular person with minimal combat training. Mighty ordered him back. DJ did as he asked and started guarding the rear.

Mighty took another shot at Blue. Blue was able to avoid the punch this time. Anguish took advantage of Mighty's position outside the shield and hit him with a death ray. Mighty went down.

Acid fired another attack at Anguish. He dodged it and laughed, grinning at Blue Shift. In unison, the pair attacked Acid, both struck, sending her flying back into the wall of the tunnel. Mighty started to get up, but he was still dazed. DJ ran over to Acid and pulled her into the shield. She was moving a little, but definitely out for the count. Mighty crawled into the shield and stood up. He was getting ready to try another attack.

It looked like the team was in dire straits. It wasn't a question of if we would go down, just when. But the Demon hadn't made any moves yet. The Demon watched the events unfold. Nobody had taken it into account. They seemed only to perceive the shield.

Blue and Anguish started going for the shield again. They were trying to take it out so they could finish us off. The Demon looked at Acid and Mighty, and then back at Blue and Anguish. They were trying to kill more members of my family. The Demon seemed to know this. Maybe it knew how I felt about them, or maybe it just realized they were good people who were undeserving of this kind of death. Either way, the Demon was displeased. Its expression charged. It stepped forward, focusing on Blue, the traitor.

Blue immediately picked up on it and stepped back, but it was already too late for him. The Demon was upon him; a flurry of slashes and cuts ripped open his body. Blood gushed out everywhere. I didn't need sound to know I was laughing. My face had taken on that familiar, misshapen expression of evil. After striking the final death blow on Blue, I, the Demon, threw my head back basking in the bliss of his despair. Blue stood there for a few moments, blood pouring out of his wounds, and then he dropped to the ground twitching. Everyone but the Demon looked horrified.

The recording continued. At this point, most of the minions and the other opposing team members backed off. Anguish, however, went for another attack, still not fully comprehending what he was up against. He tried his death ray attack on the Demon and when it failed, he decided to pull a set of kamas on it. By using a sickle weapon, he must have thought he was going with some kind of death theme, but pulling a bladed weapon on the Demon was a very bad idea.

The Demon grinned. It took its sword, licked the blood off of it and returned it to its sheath. Anguish mistook this action for the Demon letting its guard down. He took the opportunity to strike, stepping forward and swinging. In one swift move, the Demon parried his attack and punched him in the arm, causing him to drop one of the kamas. Then the Demon picked up the kama, and used it to slice the other arm. Anguish dropped the second one, and stepped back clutching his wounds.

The Demon was in its element. It inhaled the scent of Anguish's blood off of his kama and grinned in delight. All around, anyone left standing was backing away. At the realization of his plight, fear overtook Anguish. His face twisted in terror, as the Demon stepped forward to finish the job.

The Demon vivisected the man, piece by piece until he was dead. The speed of the attack was incredible. Anguish didn't even have the chance to scream. He just gazed in horror as his body was hacked away bit by bit. Afterward he lay in a pile on the ground, and the rest of Pain's army ran. I, the hideous Demon, stood there, appearing very satisfied. I could see my team off in the distance making a run for it.

Alicia stopped the video.

I turned and looked at Alicia, who was obviously uncomfortable being in the same room with me. I didn't know what to say. I was barely able to live with it myself. Some things were clearer now; the interrogation about my 'other' power; the blackouts; the dead hit men; Athena's reports to the feds. I was still a danger, not to myself, but to everyone else around me. The beast I thought I had banished was only lying in wait for the first opportunity to be released. I was never in complete control.

I made eye contact with Alicia; she didn't turn away. "You should keep me drugged. I understand now."

She agreed. "I'll leave the door unlocked. You can feel free to use the public areas. Your weapons are hidden. Don't try to leave. Don't try to enter any restricted areas. You will need to take your medication every six hours. You can take your meals in the dining area with everyone else; I'll have your pills ready up there."

I nodded and sat on the bed. I was running low on reasons to live.

Chapter Forty-eight

"Hatred does not cease by hatred, but only by love; this is the eternal rule."
Buddha

After a brief five-hour nap, I dragged my sorry ass over to the dining room. The place was packed with what looked like medical staff. They all looked very uneasy, and extremely unhappy. They took little interest in me, chattering amongst themselves about some medical issues they were dealing with.

I sat at the table and a meal appeared in front of me, a small cup holding my medication sat next to the plate. The server waited for me to swallow the pill before leaving me alone. He even made me open my mouth to show him that I swallowed it. I wasn't completely comfortable being in this state of haziness. Between the medical staff and my sedation, I was having flashbacks of the torture and of my past. It took a lot of energy to keep it together.

The place was buzzing with activity. Normally I would have been intrigued and done some investigation, but I was fresh out of motivation. I spent the next two days in a routine of eating, being drugged, sleeping and crapping. I felt like a waste of life. Eventually, in light of my growing state of anxiety and depression, I decided I had to do something, anything, even if it meant being beaten.

On my next dose, I put the pill between my cheek and my gum. When I opened my mouth, it wasn't visible and I was able to avoid the sedation. It took skipping a few doses before my head fully cleared. I had to act sluggish and brain-dead so nobody would catch on, but I noticed there was something significant going on.

The first thing I noticed was a bunch of mail and packages addressed to me. I opened a few and they were all from various villains, most of whom I didn't even know. They contained gifts of varying types and notes, each swearing allegiance to me. Killing Blue must have really made me popular with this crowd. But there were also a few notes from some heroes I knew. My team congratulated me on saving them from Pain.

The next thing I noticed was that the place was indeed fully staffed with doctors and medical researchers. They were all top specialists in their fields. They specialized in transplant surgery, tissue regeneration, pulmonary medicine, cardiology, immunology, vascular surgery, and thoracic surgery. Since I was not an idiot, a picture was forming in my mind. Kiet's body was missing. The place was staffed with doctors. He was here somewhere. It was a small chance, but there was some hope.

I observed the chaos for a while. I would just have to grab a disguise and slip in. Alicia had cleverly clad me in black, so I would stand out. I just had to get to the laundry, which was not off limits to me. I slowly crept my way down to the basement, being sure to look as inebriated as possible. Once in, the staff was too concerned about getting their tasks done to even notice me. I grabbed a nurse's uniform, ducked in a supply closet and changed.

Once upstairs, all I had to do was follow the rest of the medical staff into the restricted zone. I carried a bunch of sheets to cover part of my face as I walked in. I faced no resistance at all. The area was a small wing of the house converted into medical facilities. One room was closely monitored from an outside nursing station. Surveillance cameras were mounted at almost every conceivable angle throughout the area. I managed to get a good look at security monitors without being detected myself. I was right. Kiet lay in a bed with tubes sticking out of his body. He was conscious and talking to Gloom who sat in a chair next to the bed.

I should have taken a deep breath and calmly approached the situation. I should have been logical and not blown my cover. But I should have done a lot of things in my life. I took off running out of the nurses' station, into the room, and up to the bed. I pulled off the nurse's hat and stood over the bed grinning.

"Hell no!" Gloom jumped up, grabbed me with one arm, swung me out of the room, and slammed me into a wall in the hallway. He shouted into an intercom on the wall next to me. "Dammit, Alicia, get your ass down here. You said you had her under control."

I struggled to escape. "No," Gloom growled. "We just put a new heart in him. We have him on at least four drugs to keep his heart rate and blood pressure down. We all know what will happen the minute you get near him."

"Is he going to be okay?"

"If you don't kill him first," Gloom replied.

"How?" I asked.

"After we started losing people, Kiet had biomonitors implanted in all of us. If the signal was lost, the heart stopped, or respiration increased significantly, we could dispatch a rescue party." He grinned. "I knew about the two of you the moment it happened. I almost kicked in the door to the hotel suite because I thought you were killing him. Lucky for you that you're both loud."

Before I even had a chance to be embarrassed, a real nurse came running out of the room. "I'm sorry, sir, but he says he wants to talk to her."

Gloom grabbed me by the back of my dress and lifted me into the room. "No, Kiet, she'll kill you."

Kiet laughed. "I have some self-control. Besides, all these drugs kill any chance of me getting it up. Leave her here and wait outside."

Gloom skulked off, waiting outside the door.

"Love the nurse's look." Kiet grinned. "We'll have to explore that possibility when I get out of this."

"I promised not to kill you, so stop thinking about that." I took his hand and sat next to the bed. "I thought you were dead. I was so worried."

He squeezed my hand weakly. "They were trying to protect me. I didn't know they were keeping you in the dark." He grinned. "Look, I'm going to have a couple of wicked scars."

"Yeah, from my own sword." I frowned.

Deprave smirked. "You never told me why you have swords anyway. Why don't you carry guns like normal people?"

I shrugged. I knew he was just messing with me, but I wasn't in a joking mood.

"This was definitely not the first time you've spilt blood," Deprave continued, still smirking.

I still didn't answer.

"I'll let you off again, but you will talk." He laughed and squeezed my hand again. "I love you."

"Nobody ever loved me before either. I thought you were gone. I thought my life was over." Tears welled up in my eyes.

"Not over, just beginning. After I'm up, we'll run away and get married already." He smiled.

"About that."

"Did you change your mind about marrying me?" There was a hint of panic in Kiet's voice.

"No, but you will." I pulled the memory stick off of my neck. It contained the pictures of each of my victims, my various profiles from different agencies, and the only picture of me in action that existed. It was taken with a security camera, and it showed me in mid-attack, covered in my victim's blood and holding a decapitated head. If it wasn't real, it would have been a cool image. But it was real, and it captured the essence of me at my worst. I handed it over to him. "This is everything. Read it all and decide."

"What is it?"

"It's the truth." I got up and walked out of the room.

It took little time for me to find the liquor cabinet and start drinking.

Chapter Forty-nine

"Work out your own salvation. Do not depend on others."
Buddha

I was well into a bottle of tequila when I was located and summoned back into Kiet's room. I walked in, still holding the bottle and threw myself into the seat next to the bed.

"I have to ask you something."

"I'm over twenty-one," I replied, holding up the bottle.

He laughed and then coughed. "Stop before they kick you out." He recovered and then motioned me closer. "You really killed over six hundred people?"

I nodded. "Much, much more than six hundred."

"Holy crap, Becca. When you said Demon, I thought it was some kind of expression or exaggeration, I figured maybe you even killed a few people. Even after the videos where you sliced and diced, I never suspected you were a soulless demon roaming the Earth." He smiled and shook his head. "And I'm quoting the CIA profile. They call you a fucking demon. You were a scary bitch. Getting off on killing people is pretty sick, even sicker than me."

"I understand if you want me to leave," I said. "I will never be able to make up for all the damage I've done."

Kiet shook his head. "No, I just want to understand. I'm in no position to judge. What happened?"

"I made big mistakes and lost my soul. I became a monster. I was given another chance and then you saved me."

Kiet reached up and stroked my cheek. "I rescued you from hell."

"Maybe, but the Demon isn't gone like I hoped. It's still inside. You saw it," I lamented. "And I doubt I'll ever be able to completely control it. I'll never be able to atone for all that evil."

"Maybe not, but you try. You certainly made a dent with Pain." Kiet smiled. "Come on, you've seen the news footage, right?"

"I saw the security footage where I killed Blue and that guy Anguish who tortured me." The mental image of that was almost more horrific than the one of me being tortured.

"You didn't see the rest?" Kiet seemed surprised. He hit the button to call the nurse. She popped in.

"Can you please send Ed in here?"

The nurse agreed and popped back out of the room.

"Ed?" I laughed. It never dawned on me that Gloom had a real name too.

Ed arrived within seconds. He was by the nurses' station standing vigil in case I had to be dragged out of the room to spare Kiet's heart.

"You wanted me?" Ed announced as he entered. "I am not filming any amateur sex videos."

"Yeah. Speaking of videos." Kiet was not laughing. "Why didn't you show her the whole thing?"

Ed looked at me and then back at Kiet. "She was stressed out enough. We didn't think she needed to have everything dumped on her at once."

"Just bring it," Kiet demanded.

"Just bring it," Ed mocked Kiet as he walked out of the room. Moments later he returned with a microdisc and put it in the player. "If she goes ballistic, you're paying to fix everything."

Kiet waved him off and hit *play*. I watched the scene unravel just like before, but the recording didn't stop in the tunnel this time. The scene changed to a news report. I was standing on a pile of rubble looking very menacing. Smoke rose from the debris around me; the area was in ruins. This must have been the spot where the lab used to stand.

"This is my favorite part," Kiet announced gleefully.

A helicopter landed nearby and a cloaked figure stepped out. It was Pain. A bunch of troop carriers landed around the area. There was a lot of grandstanding and gesturing. Finally the audio came up. It was poor, but the station had added subtitles.

"I will just try again," Pain decreed. "The world will be destroyed. My misery and boredom will end."

"I will stop you again and keep stopping you until I am defeated," I replied.

Pain did not like my response. He signaled and a platoon of his men charged me. They fired, but my force field stopped the bullets. It also stopped Pain from using his powers on me. They dropped their guns and came at me with cold weapons. They presented no challenge and in seconds all lay on the ground twitching and bleeding.

"You will die."

"Then I will go back to hell and burn until I am again freed. But I will never stop hunting you." It was the Demon speaking. This was the first time I had ever heard it speak. The Demon walked toward him; Pain summoned another platoon of troops with a wave of his hand. The Demon still had the force field, so no weapons fire could get through. They attacked with melee weapons. Wave after wave of platoon was sent to attack me, and each one was dispatched by the Demon. Pain was relentless; he allowed barely two minutes between attacks. It went on for almost forty-five minutes; we had to fast forward through it all. It was bloody, gory and ugly.

"I won't allow you to harm the innocent!" the Demon yelled, as it fought. "I will protect them, no matter how many men you send after me!"

The Demon took out the last soldier and stumbled. It looked visibly exhausted, and my body was bleeding from several injuries, including the bullet wound from earlier. The Demon and I had pushed myself beyond the point my body could handle. I wouldn't be able to take much more of a pounding.

"Why would you bother to fight for this world full of misery?" Pain asked.

"Because this soul I live with still feels love." The Demon continued forward.

Apparently, Pain had an extensive army, because reinforcements arrived on the scene.

Pain responded angrily, "The world is gray and empty. It should end."

The Demon countered, "In the sky, there is no distinction of east and west; people create distinctions in their minds and then believe them to be true."

Pain signaled the next platoon to step forward, but just before they attacked, another army arrived. Not only were my teammates now by my side, but we were being backed up by a company of marines.

Pain signaled his army and retreated.

Kiet sat beside me laughing and coughing as we viewed the battle footage. I couldn't help but smile myself when I saw his reaction.

"No wait. The next part is my favorite." He laughed again. "I just love the whole thing."

The video cut to another news clip which had sound. The anchor person announced that the station received a clip from Pain. It was the first press release he ever made. It played full screen across the television.

Pain declared war on me in front of the entire world.

"Holy crap." I looked at Kiet. "What does this mean? And why are you so happy about it? Shit, I killed a lot of people."

"You killed henchmen who knew they were working for a bad man. Even if you are a bloodthirsty demon, you were protecting the innocent. That proves you are not completely evil. Maybe I'm wrong, but I think it's great. I bet Pain will have recruiting problems now. And the Demon says you love me." Kiet beamed.

"Of course I love you. But seriously, this doesn't bother you?" I asked. "That I am host to a demon that massacred countless people, and enjoyed it."

Deprave shrugged. "Maybe it should, but it doesn't. I suppose that I love every part of you, even the darkest. I wonder what the Demon's like in the sack." Kiet smirked.

"You could lose a limb. Don't try it. Really."

"Okay, but you should know, the idea really turns me on."

"Everything turns you on." I sighed. "So you're really okay with all of this?"

"Well at first I was a little jealous of Pain." Kiet was very amused with himself. "See, I'm supposed to be your nemesis. But then I realized I'm not, since we're getting married and everything. So since we're on the same side now, I had Ed check, just for hell of it, to see the status of Pain's little doomsday machine."

"Okay…"

Kiet grinned, his face lit up. "You destroyed the damned thing. You saved the planet. Bianchi's plans only make sense to Bianchi and you. Pain can't rebuild. Dudek is dead, so no holes in the universe. The project is dead. He has no science knowledge of his own. So now he's devoting all his energy into trying to destroy you."

"Great, the worst parts of me saved the fucking world, and now I'm toast."

I hadn't heard Ed walk in, but he sat in a chair across the room. "It's not like he can kill you, apparently nobody can. You're like the undead or something. Besides, in a weird way, you are Pain's reason for living."

"What?"

"Yeah," Kiet added. "You gave him a purpose. He now has something to work toward. I think he may have paid someone to steal the moon from me, just to get your attention."

"Crap, did you see the mail? They're all pledging their loyalty to me. This is nuts." The whole situation was a bit overwhelming.

"This is why we didn't dump it all on you at once," Ed explained.

Kiet apparently thought the whole thing was hysterical. He laughed and coughed and laughed some more. "You are now the queen of the underworld and protector of the planet. How does it feel?"

"Wrong, just wrong." I sighed. "Does this mean you have to lead my robot army now?"

"No way! I had to give you the galaxy, you lead the army. Oh yeah…"

"Oh yeah, what?" I asked, afraid of the answer.

"I've been borrowing something from you."

"What is that?" Now I was really getting nervous.

"You know that company you have?" Kiet smiled sheepishly. "I've been using it to filter money to some charities."

"I know. You hacked into my company to fund children's charities. I should beat you for that."

"Sorry." Kiet shrugged. "I found it tracking the money trail; I knew it was the perfect vehicle for dispensing dirty money to charitable causes. That's what your company does."

"Yeah, except for the 'dirty' part. But you hacked me."

"I've done more than hack you, my sweet." He smirked. "You never minded me gaining access before."

Ed laughed as he left the room.

"Just get better." I squeezed Kiet's hand.

"Only for you, my dirty little Computer." He coughed again. Ed walked back in with some doctors who poked at Kiet for a while. I stayed with him all night.

Chapter Fifty

"Neither fire nor wind, birth nor death can erase our good deeds."
Buddha

Blue Streak's funeral was a media frenzy, much like his life had been. Even in death, people talked about him like he was actively orchestrating the event. Mighty and I went together. I dressed and carried myself as low key as possible, but even so, I knew there would be a degree of friction due to my presence.

Mighty and I walked toward the church. Blue's immediate family stood at the entrance greeting everyone. My head was throbbing and my stomach ached. I just wanted to pay my respects and leave, but I knew it wouldn't be that simple.

"I'm very sorry," Mighty said to Blue's mother, whose grief was further amplified by her disgust for Team Power and all things superhero. She made no attempt to hide it.

Blue's mother didn't bother to respond to Mighty, instead she addressed me. "You're the monster who killed him." She didn't mince words. "Why are you here?"

"I..." I didn't have an answer. "I didn't want him to die. I wish things were different..."

"So do I," she said. "I wish my son was still alive. But you people had to destroy my beautiful child." She broke down sobbing. A man came over and led her away, consoling her, agreeing as she spoke ill of us.

"That went well," I remarked after she was out of hearing range.

Mighty shook his head. I could see he was having a harder time than I was with this. At one point, Blue had been a hero to him. I was also a bit more comfortable with death than him.

We made our way up the last few steps and to the entrance.

"I wish you wouldn't," a voice said from behind us. It was Mind.

"What now?" I asked.

"You know what. You can go to the graveyard but I'd prefer that you didn't defile the church."

"Oh come on," Mighty objected. "Enough is enough. You know what really happened."

"It's better for all parties concerned," Mind said. "Ask her how she feels."

"Please." I was sick of all of the aggravation myself. "I'm hungover. I just figured it would be a good idea to attend this function, you know, sober."

"I am willing to bet that the minute you leave these grounds, you'll feel just fine."

"This is ridiculous," Mighty complained. "What is your problem?"

"He thinks that I'm not crazy, but really demon possessed," I explained. "He thinks I'm going to somehow desecrate holy ground by walking into that church. Just..." Now my head was really throbbing. "Go on in, and I'll meet you over at the gravesite. I don't need this grief."

Mighty cast a dirty look at Mind. "Fine. This is stupid." They both went inside; I walked over to the graveyard. My headache did fade, but I was certain it was due to my distance from Mind and the drama and not some reaction to holy ground.

I stayed out of the way of the reporters and onlookers. I gazed over the cemetery and reflected on my life and on recent events. I wondered what was to come in the future. I wondered why I wondered about the future. I never before considered it, now I had a reason to keep going.

It wasn't long before Mighty and the rest of the funeral guests came out.

"You didn't miss much," Mighty whispered. He took my hand and smiled. "How are you holding up with everything?"

"Better than I was last week. He's still in critical condition. Everything seems to be okay, but we won't know for sure until he starts moving around."

Mighty nodded. "He'll be fine. You'll make sure he is."

"I know." I grinned. "Wanna be a bridesmaid?"

"I don't do tights. Besides, I think Acid is already making plans."

"Guess she's the maid of honor then. We're probably getting married before the actual wedding. We don't want to wait."

"Why not?" Mighty asked.

"We both have issues. I don't think you want to hear about them."

Mighty nodded.

"Besides," I continued. "someone has to kick his butt into gear. I get the feeling he's going to be a pain in the ass when it's time for him to go into physical therapy."

"Do you have to be married for that?"

"No. But it gives me legal rights to harass him. So it doesn't hurt."

Mighty snickered. "So you're going to move into his evil lair?"

"Yeah. I'll keep the house though. It's closer to everyone, and doesn't involve flight to get anywhere from."

"Hmmm." Mighty was momentarily lost in thought. "Might make a good safe house."

"Yeah," I agreed.

"So."

"Yes?"

"What about the drinking?"

"What about it?" I hated this topic.

"Are you going to at least try to stop?"

"I guess. I'll at least try to cut it down. I need my liver."

"Yes, you do." Mighty stared off into the distance. "We need you."

"I don't frighten you? The team isn't terrified after what they saw?"

"Oh," Mighty answered. "we all think you're scary. We just know whose side you're on. We trust you."

"Even though I'm an insane drunk with a murderous past?" I smiled.

"Even if you are the demon Mind says you are. Besides, you are the queen of the underworld now. We need to stay on your good side."

I had to laugh at his comment. I still found the concept ridiculous. "I really have to deal with this demon thing, though."

"Have you considered therapy?"

I shook my head. "I tried it years ago. Didn't help. They just wanted to medicate me. I couldn't let that happen." I sighed. "No, I'll have to work it out on my own."

"Not on your own." Mighty put his hand on my shoulder. "You'll have help."

I smiled and nodded. "Yeah. You're a good friend, and I'm about to have a great husband too. I have no choice but to get my shit together. I'll try what you said. I'll stop fighting it; maybe have some kind of truce with it. Don't know how though, we don't exactly speak."

"Leave yourself video messages, write notes or have one of us relay conversations between yourselves. We can find a way."

"Yup." I knew this would be a long road ahead. I was just starting to learn what it was like to be human, and it was as painful as it was exhilarating. "So..." I changed the subject. "Why hasn't anyone arrested me or anything yet?"

"I won't lie. They considered it. Even though we all told them what happened, and they had the footage, the police or whatever they are wanted you in jail. The public was on your side though and Athena pleaded on your behalf. She agreed to plead guilty if they let you go."

"Why?" I asked.

"Well. She told me that she was going to jail anyway. There was no use in both of you going. She also told me to warn you not to become complacent. Her words. She said they could try to reacquire you."

"Great. I owe Athena my freedom, and I still have to watch my ass."

Mighty chuckled.

"What?"

"Nothing. It's just that when you said watch your ass, I remembered something."

"What?"

"The videos." Mighty was fighting the laughter and failing.

"What videos? The ones from the fight?"

"No. The other ones. They're out on the net now."

It took a moment to register, but when it did, I could only sigh.

"At least the public knows the truth now." Mighty grinned. "Now it's scandalous, instead of criminal. It's the most downloaded media this year."

"I can't go anywhere in public now."

"Nah, someone blurred your faces before releasing them. You're lucky."

"Lucky, huh? Did you watch it?"

"No. I didn't want to know. No offense, but I heard it was way out there."

"No, it's cool. I'm really glad you didn't. Someone still has to respect me."

"Well, the tabloids love you. The team misses you. So at least you're loved and wanted, even if you're not respected."

"Gee thanks."

"You're very welcome." Mighty replied. We laughed for a moment and then he led me over to the gravesite. We watched the burial unobtrusively and paid our respects. This time nobody tried to stop us.

"Those who are free of resentful thoughts surely find peace."
Buddha

THE END

Lightning Source UK Ltd.
Milton Keynes UK
UKHW042143160820
368333UK00002B/254